MADE *for* YOU

ALSO BY MELISSA MARR

Wicked Lovely
Ink Exchange
Fragile Eternity
Radiant Shadows
Darkest Mercy

Wicked Lovely: Desert Tales
(Art by Xian Nu Studio)
Volume 1: Sanctuary
Volume 2: Challenge
Volume 3: Resolve

Faery Tales & Nightmares

Untamed City: Carnival of Secrets

Graveminder
The Arrivals

Bunny Roo, I Love You

Writing as M. A. Marr, Coauthored with K. L. Armstrong
Loki's Wolves
Odin's Ravens

melissa marr

MADE
FOR
YOU

HARPER
An Imprint of HarperCollinsPublishers

Library of Congress Cataloging-in-Publication Data

Marr, Melissa.

Made for you / Melissa Marr. — First edition.

    pages cm

Summary: "Southern small-town darling Eva Tilling wakes up in
the hospital with the frightening ability to see through the eyes of the
victims of a serial killer, and realizes that she, too, is a target of the
depraved stalker"— Provided by publisher.

ISBN 978-0-06-201120-6

[1. Serial murderers—Fiction. 2. Visions—Fiction.] I. Title.

PZ7.M34788Mad 2014   2013047951

[Fic]—dc23   CIP

                                                                      AC

Typography by Joel Tippie

15 16 17 18 19   PC/RRDH   10 9 8 7 6 5 4 3 2 1

❖

First paperback edition, 2015

For the nurses, techs, and doctors in NICU, CCN, and Pediatrics at Eastern Maine Medical Center in Bangor, Maine. There aren't words enough to tell you how much I appreciate your care, support, and love this past year.

DAY 0: "THE PARTY"

Eva

"Did you see her?" Piper whispers, lifting the same plastic cup of wine she's been holding the past two hours as if it hides her. It's a prop. She's sober. She always is. She's also hopelessly prone to melodrama.

I nod, face carefully blank. Of *course* I saw her. I've seen every single girl that flirts with Nate at these parties.

I'd rather not be a witness to it, but that's one of the downsides to being me: I'm expected to be at every party. Like Piper and the rest of our crowd, I am here because it's who I am and what I do. Nate isn't one of us, hasn't been for a couple years, so he doesn't always attend, but when he does, he inevitably goes upstairs or down a darkened hallway with some girl. I pretend not to care. My act works on everyone but Piper and Grace, who sit on either side of me.

"She's not even that pretty," Piper lies.

Grace says nothing.

The girl is no prettier than us, but she's not *less* attractive either.

Nate is a lot more than good-looking. Tall and lean without being gangly, short dark hair that's cut in an almost military style, and muscles that make it hard not to find an excuse to touch his arms. Even though he has no social standing, he has to use exactly zero effort to convince girls to wander off into the dark with him.

We used to be friends. He used to be my best friend. Then his parents got divorced, and he became someone I didn't know. I still watch him, but I never speak to him. I haven't since the start of sophomore year. Every time I see him glance my way as he walks past with a girl, I think of the last time I tried to talk to him.

It's the first party of the year, and my parents are away again. I'm sitting with Grace, a new girl who moved from Philadelphia to tiny little Jessup, North Carolina.

"Who's he?" Grace asks.

"Nathaniel Bouchet." I look at him, standing in the doorway surveying the room like a hunter. He doesn't look like my Nate anymore. He's always been wiry, but now he looks like he works at his physique. I swallow, realizing that I'm staring and that he can tell.

"Excuse me a minute," I say.

Robert and Reid are sitting with us, but I excuse myself to walk over to Nate. It's been forever since we spoke. He hasn't called or come to see me in weeks. I never catch him at school either. I miss him. Even after he stopped being around the rest of our friends, he was still my friend. I thought that would never change, but now, I think I might be wrong.

I've had a couple drinks, and it gives me the courage to ignore his dismissive glance and walk up to him.

"*Nate,*" *I start.*

I only want to talk, to go back to the way we were, but he looks right at me, his gaze roaming from my sandals up my jeans and over my blouse and ending on my face. "*Not interested.*"

Then he steps around me like we're strangers. He just walks past me like I'm not there, like he doesn't know me, like we haven't been in one another's lives since we were in preschool. I feel like everyone there is staring at us, but if they are, no one mentions it—not to me, at least. My last name protects me from that, and for a change, I'm glad to be a Cooper-Tilling.

Nate, on the other hand, has just sealed his pariah reputation. It was bad enough that his parents divorced, and he suddenly seemed to forget that there were clothes in colors other than black. Now, he's been rude to me in front of everyone. If he was trying to make the rest of my friends declare him invisible, he just succeeded.

On Monday, I find out that he slept with Piper's cousin, Julie, who was visiting. She's three years older than us, a freshman at Duke. After that, it became a thing to talk about which girl he chose for the night when he turned up at parties. After that, I didn't talk to him—or let him see me watching him—ever again.

Piper is waiting for her cue, for me to tell her what to think. It's how things are in Jessup. She's one of the elite, but I'm the one *she* follows. My parents are the top of the food pyramid here. It's not a situation I cherish, and I pretend not to notice.

I simply play my part, fulfill their expectations and smile. It's the best plan I have.

I know that Piper is hoping for permission to tear Nate down, but I'm not going there. "She's no different than the last three. He'll leave in the morning with her phone number, but he won't use it."

"What are you two whispering about?" Reid asks as he flops down next to Piper and drapes an arm around her shoulders. They're not dating; he simply has no awareness of personal space.

Piper shrugs him off. "Losers."

"I'll protect you," Reid promises.

"Who's to say you weren't the problem we were discussing?" Piper says, but she doesn't mean anything by it. Reid is one of us.

"Yeung." Reid glances at Grace and nods at her, then turns to me. "Eva."

"I have a first name!" Grace snaps.

Before they start bickering Piper quickly redirects the conversation. "Did you guys want to go to Durham for the Bulls game? Daddy has a bunch of tickets that he said we could use."

I tune them out. It's far too easy to do, really. The conversation, the people, the whole party is like most every other

Friday for the past couple years. Sometimes I want to ask them if they're happy, if they enjoy their lives or if they feel like they're just playing roles like me.

Grace tolerates Jessup, but this is only a pit stop for her. Reid is hard to decipher; he never gives a straight answer. On the other hand, my boyfriend, Robert, seems to like being one of the town darlings. He has an entourage everywhere he goes—and likes it. I don't. They're my friends though, so I smile at them before I top off my glass of lukewarm wine from a bottle that has my grandfather's last name on the label.

Politely, I carry the bottle over to Robert where he still stands with Grayson and Jamie. Robert absently kisses the top of my head and holds his cup out toward me. The other boys are drinking beer, but Robert always drinks wine from the Cooper Winery when I'm with him.

I don't glance toward the doorway that leads to the bedrooms. I don't think about Nate kissing some girl who isn't me. No, not at all. Not even a little.

After I fill Robert's cup, I wait. I'm not clingy; I don't interrupt. I simply wait until the boys notice and walk away. Once they're gone, Robert looks at me carefully, studying my face for a moment before asking, "Is everything okay?"

"I'm bored."

He laughs. "All of our friends *and* a bunch of people from school are here, and you're bored?"

"Piper only wants to gossip. Reid is . . . *Reid*. Grace is pouting or maybe arguing with Reid by now. You"—I poke him in the chest—"were over here, so yes, I'm bored."

He grins, sips his wine, and waits. I can't deny that he's one of the best-looking boys I've ever seen. He's certainly one of the best-looking in Jessup. Basketball, baseball, and tennis keep him in perfect shape, and he has the bluest eyes of anyone I know. It's not his fault that I wish they were chocolate brown instead.

"Can we leave? Maybe drive out to—"

"You know better than that," he interrupts quietly. "Everyone would want to come with us as soon as we said we were heading out."

Everyone, of course, means our closest friends, but they're the same people I've spent the past few hours with—really, the past seventeen years with if I want to get technical. They're my friends, and I love them. Sometimes, though, I want to be just a girl with her boyfriend, not a girl, her boyfriend, and their dozen closest friends.

"Fine." I blush a little before suggesting, "We could go to one of the bedrooms . . ."

"With all of our friends out here?" Robert looks at me like I suggested we have sex on the coffee table.

"Just to fool around," I clarify.

He leans in and kisses me briefly, lips closed, and then he wraps an arm around my waist. "Come on."

For a moment I think he's agreed with me, but then I realize that he's headed back to the sofa. He murmurs in my ear, "We can do that at your house any day. Tomorrow, I'll meet you at Java the Hut, and then we'll go to your house for a dessert."

I nod. There's no way to say that it isn't really physical contact I want.

I want to feel swept away. I want to not sit here listening to gossip while Nate has sex in another room. I want to be wanted—and distracted. Instead, I sit next to Robert, our hands twined together, and resume the same routine.

"You totally missed it," Piper gushes. "You will never believe what Davey Jackson just did!"

Nothing ever changes, not here, not for me.

DAY 1: "THE ACT"

Judge

I SIT AND WAIT in my stolen car. The engine is still; the lights are off. I can't even listen to music. I don't want anyone to see or hear me.

I thought Eva understood me. Last night, she proved me wrong. She looked straight through me like I wasn't there and spent half the night paying attention to him, one of the countless people who will never ever deserve her. He's not right for her. *I* am.

When I see Eva walking away from the mostly empty parking lot and heading down the deserted street, I wish I had another option. I've been waiting for her to see the real me for so long, doing the things she asked of me so she would know I was the one for her.

I listened to every secret message she gave me. She was

like a goddess in my mind.

Maybe that's where I went wrong. The Lord ordered that "Thou shalt have no other gods before me." In my heart, I raised Eva up like a false idol. That was a mistake. Now I have to atone, not just for my sake, but for the safety of my future children. The good book says "I the Lord thy God am a jealous God, visiting the iniquity of the fathers upon the children." I have to protect the children I'll one day have.

"I'm sorry. I'm so sorry." I say the words quietly as I wait for her.

I picture her even after I can't see her anymore. She could've called Grace to pick her up tonight. She didn't. It would have been a sign if she had. I watch the signs. Eva Tilling—princess of Jessup, North Carolina—is alone. I made sure she would be, but I hoped we would be saved from this.

I turn the key, and the engine wakes. I turn on the stereo and shift out of park. My eyes burn, and my hands tighten on the steering wheel as I drive toward her. I flick the high beams on and turn the music up so loud that she can probably hear it now. I feel like I can hear the gravel crunch under the tires as I swerve onto the shoulder, but I can't, not over the music. I searched for the perfect song, "Lift Me Up," to tell her all the things I can't say. I hope she is listening. I know the Lord is.

I feel like my heart is beating in tune with the thundering drums, and I slam the gas pedal down before I can hesitate. I feel the thump, and through my tears, I see her hit the hood of the car and slide off.

I don't slow down. I can't. I can't even look in the rearview mirror. I did it, but it hurt. God, it *hurt* to sacrifice the one person I thought was meant to be mine. My Eva is bleeding along the side of the road. This was the only choice left to me.

I had to kill her.

DAY 3: "THE VISION"

Eva

MY MIND IS FUZZY. I hear unfamiliar noises, and I don't know why. My eyelids weigh too much, and I can't make them open to see where that awful beeping is. I think about sitting up, but if I can't move my eyelids, I surely can't move my whole body. I try anyhow. Someone grabs my arm, speaks softly in words I can't make out, but it doesn't matter.

All that really matters suddenly is that I'm falling.

I know I'm already on my back but somehow I still fall.

I fall into someone. I know it's not my skin I'm wearing even though it somehow is mine for the moment. The woman I am inside is waiting for her grandson, Ethan. He should have been here by now. My chest hurts. I have—no, she has—had this twinge all day, and even though it's probably nothing, it scares me.

Somewhere in my mind, I remind myself that this is not me, that I am Eva Elizabeth Tilling. I am only seventeen, and I have no children or grandchildren.

I try to pull myself out of her skin, but I'm stuck here. My heart hurts. It feels like the beats are going too fast, like I've been drinking nothing but caffeine for days, and somehow it keeps going faster and faster. My hands tighten on the arms of the chair. I need to get up, to call someone, to do something. Ethan isn't here, and I can't drive, and I think my heart is going to pound out of my chest.

I hear footsteps. He comes into the room. I look up to see a boy standing there.

His hands are on me, helping me not to fall so fast to the ground. I try to say something, but my heart stops racing. I feel it stop.

"Eva?" Grace's voice interrupts my death, pulling me back into my own skin with a snap, making me try to squirm away from the nurse who holds my wrist in her hand.

I feel her hand like it's burning me. I try to look to see if the skin is red, but I still can't focus my eyes.

"You're awake," the nurse says, before releasing my wrist to write something on the folded-up paper in her hand.

"Heart attack." I'm shaking all over and cold like I've just been wrapped in icy sheets. Every part of me, other than my wrist, feels frigid.

"No, sweetie. You're fine."

"Heart attack," I manage to say, even as I notice that my

heart isn't aching now. *Just a dream.* It was a dream. I'm not a mother, much less a grandmother. I don't know anyone named Ethan either. I can't remember what he looked like. I only remember the voice, the fear in it, and the way his hands felt strong while he helped slow my fall. I can see the whole thing playing over in my mind, can catalogue everything but his face.

"Your pulse is fine," the nurse says as she puts medicine into the tube that hangs from an IV bag beside the bed. "Your heart is fine, Eva."

"I don't want to die. So cold." I feel like I'm drifting again, and I'm scared, so I grab the nurse's hand. "Freezing."

"I'll get a warm blanket," she promises.

I'm cold, and I hurt all over. I close my eyes. I'm not sure how long I float in that nebulous state between awake and dreaming. When I hear the sound of footsteps, squeaky soles on the tile floor, I wonder if the pain or the footsteps woke me.

I look over at the white-clad woman. She moves a tube that hangs on the side of my bed and stretches to me. It's obviously an IV line, but I don't know why it's there—or why I'm here.

I feel the cold start to crawl up my arm as the medicine travels through my vein from my wrist upward. It's a disturbing feeling, one I'd like to stop, but by the time I force my lips open to ask the nurse about it, I'm alone in my room. My mind is encased in an ever-increasing fog, and I'm pretty sure the fog is because of that tube in my arm.

I'm not sure if moments or minutes pass before I ask, "Where am I?"

If someone answers, I don't hear it. Sleep or drugs make the fog and weight stronger, and I'm out again. When I wake the next two times, I try again to ask questions, but if anyone answers—or hears me—I'm not aware of it. All I know is that I hurt, and then I'm drifting away. Maybe that's why I dreamed of dying: I hurt from my legs to my head. Vaguely, I realize that between the hurt, the IV, and the nurse, I'm obviously in a hospital. I'm just not sure *why*.

In one of my moments of lucidity, I realize that I can't move my arms or right leg, but I'm not sure if it's from the medicine pumping into my veins or if there's another reason.

"I'm right here," Grace says from somewhere nearby. I can't see her, but I'd know her voice anywhere.

"Grace?" With far too much effort, I try to focus on the shape in the chair that is apparently my usually hyper friend.

"Rest. You're safe, sweetie. We're here," Mrs. Yeung says, and I realize that Grace's mother is somewhere beside her. "You just came out of surgery."

Grace hurries over to stand beside the bed. "You're going to be okay, though, and I'm here with you."

"Don't leave me, Gracie."

"I won't," she promises, and I am relieved. There's no one in this world I trust more than Grace Yeung.

"Everything is okay now," Grace says. She reaches out one hand as if she's going to brush it over my face, but she doesn't actually touch me. It's only the shadow of her hand that lands on me.

"You're going to be okay," Mrs. Yeung repeats.

I glance at her and then look back at Grace. She nods in agreement, and then I'm out again.

This time my dreams are a strange mix that may be a series of wakeful moments and unconsciousness. If not, I'm dreaming about nurses and Grace sliding a chair near the bed with a horrible screeching noise—which seems a bit unlikely.

"Why am I here?" I ask, possibly again, possibly for the first time. I don't remember if I've asked, but it's the most reasonable question after "where am I?"

As promised, Grace is still here. Mrs. Yeung isn't with her now, but that doesn't matter. The chair is beside the bed, and her voice is quiet as she answers, "They had to bring you to Durham. You're in Mercy Hospital. You were unconscious; 'head trauma,' they said, but you woke up late last night. This morning, you had surgery on your leg for a broken femur."

I nod.

"They had to delay the surgery a day, but they operated today. It went well," Grace says. "You're in a new room now. You were in ICU."

"Hazy."

"You're still coming out of the anesthesia. Plus, they gave you sedatives," she explains.

Time passes, and eventually, my head feels clearer. I swallow, trying to speak with a tongue that feels too thick and a mouth that feels too dry, before repeating, "*Why* am I here?"

Grace doesn't answer for a moment, so I watch her face

for answers. People are more transparent than they think. Even with whatever medicines pump through the IV tubes, I have enough clarity of mind to see the worry and the anger in Grace's face. Whatever happened to land me in this bed sent my best friend into a mix of emotions that she's trying to hide.

"Your parents really should be here to tell you this," Grace starts. Her lips press together in a judgmental way that's very familiar when my parents are mentioned. She's far more judgmental about my parents than I am. I *like* the independence I have because of their travel and work schedule.

I glance at the giant vase of flowers in the room and know that it's from them. There are other smaller arrangements, but the big one is orchids, my favorite flower. It's huge and overflowing. "They sent those."

"These were waiting when we got to your new room," Grace says, but she scowls again. Orchids don't make up for their absence in her book, but I'm sure they have a reason for being away. They always do. Most of the reasons boil down to them forgetting that I'm not actually an adult yet—not that I'm complaining.

"Why did I need surgery?"

"There was an accident," Grace says, her expression going from angry to gentle in a blink.

I grab her hand and tug.

She straightens her arm so our clasped hands rest on the edge of the hospital bed. She looks almost as tired as I feel. She squeezes my hand and stares at me. Her eyes are red and puffy, and I can tell she's been crying a lot and sleeping only a little. "I'm glad you're okay," she whispers. "I was so scared. You must've been terrified."

"I don't think I . . . I don't remember anything," I tell her. My voice wavers a little, but I'm not as upset as I probably should be. I feel sort of like I'm in a haze, which raises another question. "What am I on?"

"An antiseizure drug, a muscle relaxer, and . . . I'm not sure what else." Grace glances at the bag of medicine. "Sugar water or something for hydration. Plus sedatives and stuff from the surgery."

"Where's your mom?" I ask. I'd heard Mrs. Yeung earlier, but I don't see her.

When my parents travel, she's my unofficial mom. Truth-fully, she fills that function even when they're home, but when they're away, she has a signed power of attorney form for emergencies. My parents trust her completely—and for good reason. Mrs. Yeung has all the traits that "good Christians" in the South are supposed to have, including a few that my par-ents lack. She's a stay-at-home mom who gave up a career to move to our little backwater town in North Carolina with her husband when he got a chance at his dream job.

"She had to leave," Grace says. "We've been here a lot, and Jimmy had to miss a game already. She wanted to stay till you woke, but—"

"She was here when I needed her," I interrupt. "She's awe-some."

Grace scoffs. "Yeah, you say that because you don't live with her. The other day . . ."

I know that Grace is still talking, but I can't focus on what she's saying. Things don't add up. I remember leaving the coffee shop. Robert was to meet me, but he didn't show. We didn't argue at the party the night before. He was distant, but we didn't fight or anything. We never really fight. We're friends who've known each other since the cradle and decided to date last year, but honestly, we still mostly feel like friends who sometimes have sex. Fighting isn't an issue for us, so when he didn't show for our date and didn't answer when I called—or when I texted him—I was confused.

Both my parents and Grandfather Cooper were out of town. Grandfather Tilling was home, but he goes to bed early, so I didn't want to bother him, and I felt stupid calling Grace to come pick me up when it was only a couple miles to walk. Really, it would've taken longer for Grace to get there than it would for me to walk it.

"I was on my way home. I remember that. Robert forgot me or something." I look at Grace, as if her face holds the secrets I can't find inside my memories. Sometimes with Grace it kind of does. She's very readable. She squeezes my fingers, and I notice that I'm still holding on to Grace's hand.

"You got hit by a car when you were walking, sweetie."

"Hit? Like someone ran over me?" I try to remember, but I have nothing. It's a bright blur there when I try to think about it.

"Yes." She starts to tear up and adds quickly, "But you'll be okay. You hit your head; they call it a traumatic brain injury. That's why you can't remember things, and you have a broken leg, some bruised ribs, and . . . lots of black and blue."

But Grace looks down and won't meet my eyes, and I know there's more.

My mouth feels like the desert looks, and I have to swallow before I can prompt, "And? Am I . . ." I look down at my feet and quickly wiggle my toes. Then I glance at my stomach and arms. There's a bandage on my right forearm, as well as scrapes and cuts on my hands. The cuts aren't as bad on my left arm, but my right biceps is liberally decorated with slashes and dots. My left arm is scratched and cut, but nothing severe. Looking at my skin isn't going to tell me if there's something really wrong under it though. "Did I lose an organ or . . ."

"No! You still have all your organs; you're not paralyzed. You'll be fine," Grace hurriedly assures me. "They put a plate in your leg, but that's not going to mean much other than physical therapy. You hit your head pretty hard, and we were scared about that. You were out for a while, but you're *awake* now and seem okay so . . . that's good, too."

She's still avoiding saying something though. I know her too well for her to succeed at it. For someone so eager to dive into confrontation with most people, she treats me like I'm in need of sheltering. I take a deep breath and ask, "*And?* Just tell me."

"There was a lot of glass. That's all. You got some cuts, like on your arm. The big injuries were your leg and your head . . . your brain, really, but it seems like they'll be fine." She holds my gaze as if staring at me will keep me from reading whatever secrets she wants to hide. I know she'll tell me; she always tells me even when she doesn't *want* to do so. Earlier this year, when Amy blabbed to everyone at school that I had slept with Robert, Grace tried to protect me. She shielded me from the things people were saying, but even then, she gave in after a couple of days and spilled. I don't want to wait this time.

"Gracie . . . what *aren't* you saying?"

She sighs and hedges, "You're going to have some scars on your face. It's not really that b—"

"Mirror."

"Sweetie, maybe not yet."

"Mirror," I repeat, louder this time.

"Eva, let's just wait until you're feeling better, and it's heal—"

"*Please.*"

I watch Grace dig through her bag and pull out the little silver compact that her grandmother gave her for her sixteenth birthday. For a moment, Grace holds it in her hand, squeezing it so tightly that her knuckles look like the skin has grown thinner there.

She holds it out to me, and I don't let myself hesitate. I'm not vain, not really. I'm not the most beautiful girl in the world, but I've always been pretty enough to not be jealous or insecure. I have dark blue eyes, a smallish nose, lips that look pouty, and cheekbones that are defined without looking razor-sharp. I'm not opposed to wearing makeup, but I've always been happy that I don't need it.

I gaze at the reflection in the glass. The girl I see now *needs* makeup badly. Red lines crisscross my face. Dark blue stitches highlight some of them. As much as I want to, I can't look away from the tiny reflection of myself, and I'm glad that Grace's mirror is so small.

I reach up to touch the black-and-blue marks and cuts on my throat, but before I can, Grace grabs my hand. "No touching. The nurses said you shouldn't irritate the wounds. We had to keep your wrists restrained at first."

Even as she tells me that I was tied to my bed, which is disturbing on some basic level, I can't look away from my reflection. I dart my tongue out to touch the cut on my lip and promptly wince. I don't hurt like I should, and I know that it's because of the medicine coursing through my body. One particularly long cut runs from just under my eye to the side of my cheek where it curls under my ear and vanishes into my hair. That one has been stitched. Vaguely it registers that the ones deep enough to need stitches are the ones that'll scar the most. Some of the others are only shallow cuts like the ones on my arm, so I think they'll fade.

The tiny cuts vanish under the top of my shirt, and I look at my arms again. I was wearing a long-sleeved shirt when I walked home. Maybe that protected them a little, or maybe it was just how I hit the ground or how the car hit me. All I know for sure is that it's my face that took the worst of the impact. I glance back at the mirror, hoping for a moment that it isn't as bad as I first thought. It is though. No amount of healing is going to make these all vanish.

I close my eyes, and Grace takes the mirror from my hand. She doesn't tell me that everything is okay or that it's not as bad as it looks. She might try to hide things from me when she thinks it's for my own good, but she doesn't ever lie to me.

The day of the accident was the last day I was pretty.

DAY 5: "THE VISIT"

Judge

When the car hit Eva, the thump of her body was louder than I expected. It reminded me more of hitting a deer than a possum. I'm not sure why I was surprised. Girls aren't the same size as possums, but I suspect I thought more of her nature than her size. The initial thump of her body was followed by a thud as she fell against the car hood. I've dreamed about it twice since I hit her, since I thought I'd killed her.

I swallow and keep walking toward the entrance. No one looks at me any more than they do the nurses and techs that fill the halls at Mercy Hospital. I'm part of the scenery here. I'm nobody important.

Neither is she.

I can't tell anyone that though. They wouldn't understand. It's not that I need approval. I don't. I don't need a lot of things. What I *do* need is to see Eva. I've been thinking about it—thinking about *her*—since she fell. I have to know if she's really alive.

The article in the *Jessup Observer* says she is. I carefully clipped it out to save for my book, but after the fourth read, I needed a second copy because the ink was smeared and the edges were crumpled. I was careful with the second copy. Now, though, I hold the original clipping in my hands.

> **Eva Tilling, the granddaughter of both Davis Cooper IV (Cooper Winery owner and CEO) and of the esteemed Reverend Tilling, suffered multiple serious injuries after a hit-and-run earlier this week.**
>
> **Miss Tilling, 17, underwent surgery this week and remains at Mercy Hospital in Durham, where she was transported after the incident. She is in critical but stable condition.**
>
> **The victim was walking unaccompanied when she was run down by an as yet unknown vehicle. Authorities believe Tilling was only alone for moments after being struck when another passing vehicle saw her unconscious along the road and called 911.**
>
> **The Jessup sheriff's office is looking for witnesses to the incident. They said evidence has been recovered but declined to discuss specifics.**
>
> **An arrest has not been made at this time.**
>
> **The staff at the *Jessup Observer* would like to extend our prayers and thoughts to both the Tilling and Cooper families during this difficult time.**

I know the staff writer has to suck up to the Cooper-Tilling family. No matter what *They* do, they're always thought innocent. The paper is only one of the many things They control. I didn't realize it a few years ago, but I see it now: Jessup is owned by Them, the ones who support the crazy rules that govern every interaction in Jessup. I'm not ruled by Them, not now, not ever again. Eva wasn't either, but that changed. She became corrupt. I have seen it, dirt on her flesh where the corruption has begun to take root. She was the shining light, the proof that not everyone believed Their lies. Then she fell. She became just as guilty as the rest of Them, so I had to act before the corruption consumed her. It's like a disease, eating away at all that's good and pure.

I ran over her to save her.

I was willing to let her die in order to save her. I'm like Abraham with Isaac, willing to sacrifice the one I love above all others. Like Abraham, I lowered the knife—or car, in my case—but God spared my beloved one. Now, I am waiting, hoping, *praying* for a reward for my faithfulness.

I'm praying that her acceptance will be my reward.

As I approach the metal detector at the hospital, I wrap my arm around the large arrangement of flowers as I fish out my wallet with my other hand. I don't have an ID in it, but I brought an empty one so as not to draw attention. I drop it and my clipboard into the bin, and then I step through the arch with the flowers. The guard barely looks at me.

I look a little older than I am, and with the scruffy facial hair and hat, the guard probably assumes I'm in my early twenties. He sees the flowers and uniform, and he fills in the rest of the facts to match the image. It's enough for him to shift his attention to the next person. I gather my items and keep moving.

The flowers aren't ostentatious, but they're still large enough to be believable as a gift from the paper. My clothes are nondescript enough—black trousers, navy button-up, and a navy-and-white ball cap. My shoes are plain black, too. Nothing here stands out. Still, I tug the ball cap down a bit farther to shade my face and hold the floral arrangement up and to the side. I stopped in earlier to get a look around the lobby. A camera aims at the door, and another sits in the back far corner of the ceiling behind the reception desk.

A bored woman glances up as I approach the desk.

"Pediatrics," I say.

"Fourth floor." She motions toward the elevators.

A second security guard stands nearby, but he's not here to stop deliveries. Being the intersection of the east–west I-40 and north–south I-85, Durham has long been a high drug-trafficking area. It's not as bad as it once was, but the hospitals have security due to drug-related crimes.

Inside the elevator, I look at the flowers. We talked about the language of flowers in one of our lit classes because of *Hamlet*, so I know that Eva will figure it out. The flowers I picked are yellow roses (for apology and a broken heart), white roses (for silence and purity), red carnations (for passion), and white daisies (for innocence). The daisies were in *Hamlet* too, so I know she'll see them as a clue. She'll figure it out.

I've already removed the Harris Teeter grocery price tag, but I check again to be sure there are no other identifying marks that will ruin my disguise. I keep my eyes downcast in case there's a camera in here, too. By the time I reach the fourth floor, where Eva is, my hands are trembling a little, not noticeably enough that strangers would see, but I feel it. Intentionally, I step on the long piece of my shoelace as I walk, untying it as I approach the desk. I tied and retied it repeatedly to get the length right. I'd practiced as I walked around at home, too. Today, I'm doing everything right. Today, I'm not going to get impatient. It's hard though. I didn't think I'd ever see her again—aside from her funeral. I knew what I'd say *there*. I'd planned it. The words, the pauses, I practiced. I may change it some now that I have more time.

Maybe I won't have to say the words at all.

When I saw the article, when I found out she was alive, I knew it was a sign. God doesn't want her to die yet. I understand that now. I was hasty. I have spent the past three days thinking about the right path, praying for clarity and considering my options. He's giving me another chance, giving *her* another chance. Maybe I can make her see, and she can be redeemed. If I save her, she can live, and she'll be so grateful for all that I've done to save her.

I stop at the desk and tell the receptionist, "Delivery for"—I glance at the clipboard as if I don't know her name, as if I could ever forget her name, and read it—"Eva Tilling."

"That girl gets more flowers than the rest of the floor combined!" the woman says as she signs on the clipboard where I silently indicate. The sheet is very convincing. I ordered my own flowers so I could have a good model for my form.

Once she walks away, I glance at my shoe as if I am just now seeing that it's untied. No one seems to be watching, but you never know. I crouch, my posture allowing me to use my hat to hide my face as I watch her carry the flowers to a room. She taps on a door, and I finish tying the shoe as I watch her go inside.

Straightening, I glance around. No one pays much mind to delivery people. So many flowers arrive at the hospital. Why would they look at us?

I force myself not to hurry. We wouldn't be in this situation if I had practiced patience in the first place. Hurrying is dangerous. Slow and steady wins the race, especially in the South. My grandmother told me that so often that I'm sure she'd take a switch to me if she knew that I'd messed everything up by being impatient.

I glance inside Eva's room as I pass it. It's only a moment, a split second, but she's there. She's awake and speaking softly. If I didn't know better, I'd swear she was an angel. She's not though. She's one of Them. If I can't save her, she'll have to die. She's been spared for now, but I need her to understand. If she doesn't, she'll be a sacrifice at the altar of venality.

Like the rest of Them should be.

My mouth is dry at the thought of how close I am to her now. I could walk straight into her room and visit her, but I'm not ready to talk to her. Still, I needed to see her.

I wonder if she'll notice my name on the card. I listed several names—the editor, a few staff writers, and then I added my own in the middle. *Judge.* It's not the name I was born with but it's my true name, my *soul* name. I'm not really an executioner yet, and without Eva, I'm not a jury. Together, we could be a judge, jury, and executioner.

I'd despaired when I realized that she was one of Them. On the night I tried to kill her, I thought I would be always solitary. Now that she survived, I have hope again.

Outside, I pause to breathe the already thick air. Early summer in North Carolina isn't as humid as the heat of July and August, but the air is heavy already. The sweet taste of wisteria fills my mouth, and I wonder if Eva likes the flowers. They're not as sweet as the pale purple clusters of wisteria clinging to the trees. For her, I brought common flowers—like her, not truly special. That was my mistake before: I raised her up like a false idol. I know better now.

I cross the parking lot to the car I have today and slip on my gloves before I touch the handle. Like my uniform, it's not memorable, a dark blue, four-door sedan. I'll park it beside the one that has Eva's blood on it.

DAY 5: "THE DETECTIVE"

Eva

I'M ALONE. SO FAR, my friends are respecting my "no visitors" stance, and my parents are still stuck in Europe. Apparently, there was another volcanic eruption in Iceland that pretty much shut down all the flights in and out of Europe. It was nothing but smoke, ash, and gas, but Dad explained that when that same thing happened back in 2010, flights were cancelled or disrupted for over a week. I'm not counting on them getting here anytime soon. I don't need them to rush home anyhow. I've told them that several times. I told Grandfather Cooper the same thing when he called from somewhere in Alaska on one of his cruise-tour things.

Grandfather Tilling came by the hospital to sit with me, and of course, he had his congregation pray for me. It didn't occur to me to ask him or Mrs. Yeung to be here for the police visit I'm about to have.

Right now, I wish it had.

"Are you sure you're ready to talk to the detective, Eva?" my nurse asks again.

"Yeah." I offer the nurse a smile, but I'm not sure if it's encouraging with the way my cuts and bruises must still look.

"If it gets too much, you can stop the interview," the nurse says kindly.

My nurse helps me to sit up, and maybe's it's silly, but I have her get my brush so I can combat some of the snarls. I don't use a mirror because I can't stand seeing my own reflection. I'm not sure I ever want to see my face again. I certainly don't want my friends to see it. I'd like to cling to the image in my memory, not replace it with this one. Without a mirror, I can't put on even the little bit of makeup I might be allowed, so there's nothing to be done for my face.

When the police officer comes into the room, she looks at me the same way she looks at everything else: like she's taking mental notes. I realize that she's the first person other than Grace, Mrs. Yeung, and the hospital staff to see my face. I'm glad the detective isn't gawking at me.

"Hi," I say because I'm not sure what else to say. I've never been interviewed by a police officer before. I'd rather deal with the doctors than talk to the police.

"I'm Detective Grant," she says. Her hair is pulled tightly back in a knot, but it only makes her features more noticeable. She wears no makeup, but her skin is enviably perfect. I realize that I wouldn't have envied it before the accident, but now I'm looking at her and can't help thinking that no one will ever again look at me the way I'm studying her right now.

She holds out a business card as she introduces herself, and then drops it on the stand beside my bed between my lip balm and iPhone. "I'm going to record our talk so I don't miss anything," she starts. Once I nod, she turns on the recorder and continues, "Why don't you tell me what happened?"

"I don't remember much," I admit, feeling embarrassed at not knowing the details of what is probably the most significant thing that's ever happened to me.

She sits in the chair beside my bed. "Tell me what you *do* remember."

"I was walking home right after sunset, so it was still sort of light out." I feel idiotic as I try to explain what little I know. "My boyfriend wasn't answering, and I didn't want to bother my friends, and my parents were away, and really, I've walked home plenty of times."

"Did you see the vehicle?"

I think about it again. Dr. Klosky says it's normal for there to be memory issues with head trauma, but that doesn't do much to make me feel okay with it.

"I don't know," I admit.

She nods. "Were you walking on the side of the road? Were you wearing something visible?"

I try again to think back to that day, but the details aren't there. "I always walk on the shoulder," I say, sounding slightly desperate even to myself. "I don't remember, but I can't think of any reason I wouldn't do the same things I always do. . . .

Did they find me on the side of the road?"

"Yes. The driver who found you didn't see a car at the scene, but you were visible from the road."

I swallow. *I was visible. It was dusk. Someone hit me and left me.* As the facts and her tone register, it finally occurs to me that this might not have been an accident. The monitor that keeps track of my heart rate and blood pressure beeps. We both glance at it. I'm not sure what the numbers are supposed to be, but I know they're increasing.

My nurse today, whose name I can't remember, pops into the room and glares at Detective Grant. She does something with the monitor, and the beeping stops. "Do you need to rest, Eva?"

I suspect Detective Grant and I both hear the real question: does this police officer need to go away? It's not the detective's fault I'm upset, so I shake my head. "I'm okay."

"Do you want me to stay?" she offers.

"No. I'm okay." It's funny how we lie to be polite even when the evidence is present to contradict us. The monitor's recent beeping makes it very apparent that I'm *not* fine.

"I'll be back to check on you shortly," the nurse says, sounding a lot like she's warning us.

Once she's gone, I look back at Detective Grant. "I get where you're going, but no one would want to hurt me. I'm not bullied or a bully. It just doesn't make sense. This *had* to be an accident."

"What about your social life? Has anything happened

recently to cause waves? Any rivalries?"

I shake my head. "I don't do sports or clubs or anything. My boyfriend's on the basketball team, and my best friend does track. No enemies or dramas related to either of them . . . or anyone else really. My life is pretty routine."

"What about your family? Are you aware of your parents having any unusual upheavals or strange events? Threats? Anything at all that's stood out to you." She has one of the least readable faces I've seen, and her tone is level.

The questions still unnerve me, and the monitor starts beeping again. I don't need to look at it to know that my pulse is speeding. "Do you have a reason to think it wasn't an accident?" I ask.

My nurse comes back in. She folds her arms over her chest and levels a stern gaze at Detective Grant, who stands but doesn't answer me.

I look up at her. "I wish I could be more helpful. I just don't know anything. I remember walking, and I remember being here. Things in between are just fuzzy."

The detective nods. "Dr. Klosky spoke to me about your condition. He also said you're improving, so as you heal, you may remember more."

"I want to," I stress. "If I knew who did this to me . . . I'd tell you. I swear I would. They left me there. I could've—" I cut myself off before saying the d-word and shove that thought in a box. I *didn't* die, and I'm not going to die. My brain is healing, and my body is healing. Everything is going to be fine.

Detective Grant slides her hands down her already wrinkle-free trousers as if to straighten them. "If you remember anything, tell the nurses. They know how to reach me." She points at her business card. "So do you."

Once I'm alone again, my nurse satisfied that I'm calm and going to be resting, I think about what Detective Grant said. I can't think of anyone who wants to hurt me—or any reason why someone would want to kill me. What seems far more likely is that someone wasn't paying attention, hit me, panicked, and fled. Making a stupid decision in the moment seems infinitely more probable than murder. Maybe the driver is even out there feeling guilty.

It had to have been an accident. The alternative is too overwhelming to consider.

DAY 6: "THE PIPER-ETTES"

Grace

"How is she?"

"Do you know when she'll be back?"

The questions start the moment I walk into Jessup High School the next day. It's not that they're unexpected. Jessup has about twenty thousand people, which means that there are only two hundred or so students in my grade, which means they all have known one another since they were in preschool. Eva's family is the biggest employer in Jessup. Although the Cooper Winery itself doesn't have a huge staff, many of the businesses here are partially owned by the Coopers. They're the modern equivalents of aristocracy. Added to that, Eva's father is a minister's son, so the combination of Cooper wealth and Tilling modesty makes Eva a veritable princess here.

"How is she?" Piper Kennelly follows me through the

hall. Behind her are three of the "Piper-ettes," the seemingly interchangeable girls who are vying for her attention or Eva's. They stand silent but attentive. Much like Eva's, Piper's opinion matters.

"Awake. She's awake and through surgery. She's doing much, much better."

"I'm so glad!" Piper hugs me then, which is unexpected. I realize, though, that this is about Eva. I'm the only one allowed to visit her right now, so my status with Piper and her ilk just increased.

The bulk of the day goes a lot like that. It seems like everyone who sees me asks about Eva. People who are typically nice but not friendly to me are suddenly at my side like we're old friends. I almost hate them for their transparency.

"Tell Eva we asked after her," another girl calls out as I walk into my second-to-last-period course. I debate pointing out that I'm not Eva's servant, governess, or any other Southern cliché. I've learned though that such remarks tend to be the equivalent of fingernails on a chalkboard here, so I wave over my shoulder, hoping to keep a smile in place, and head into lit class.

In Jessup, American Lit focuses most of the attention on only *one* part of the country, and as much as I can appreciate Flannery O'Connor and William Faulkner, I'm pretty sure that there are giants in the field we're skipping—giants whose works would probably be useful to know before college. Thankfully, I can order critical editions online and study up on those. I'm not sure that Mr. Ellsworth would be much use with *non*-Southern lit anyhow.

I shake my head and glance at reason number two that I dread this class. Slouching in the back row is Robert Baucom. Eva's boyfriend of the past year is the epitome of everything I think is wrong with Jessup. His family, much like Eva's, is one of the first families of Jessup. He wears the clothes that speak of money and status, and he'll only date the kind of girls who can trace their pedigrees back to The War. If you told me—before I came here—that there were still places where social class and ancestry mattered this much, I probably would've laughed. Heritage, however, is no laughing matter in Jessup.

Despite my general loathing of Robert, I walk to the back of the room to try to talk to him. He's watching me approach with a flicker of nervousness on his face. He does that a lot, as if I'm a bug and he'd like to study me, but only once I'm safely under a jar. It stopped being creepy a while ago, but it's still irritating as hell.

He knows I've been opposed to Eva dating him, and although we've reached an uneasy truce, we're both very aware of the other's disdain.

"Robert."

He nods in lieu of replying. It's going to be one of *those* conversations apparently. Without Eva here to remind him that I'm not "the help," he tends to act like a dismissive jerk when he has an audience. At Jessup High, Robert always has an audience.

I ignore the curious gazes of the people on either side of him. Reid Benson and Jamie Hall exchange one of the looks that passes for conversation among this crowd, and Grayson Lane simply stares at me. Reid and Jamie are about the most vulgar boys I've met in Jessup. Around here, it passes for charm with half the school, or maybe it's their names that pass as charm, and the vulgarity is just overlooked because of it.

I smother a sigh and try again to talk to Robert. "I don't know when you plan to see Eva, but I thought we could check our schedules to make sure we don't overlap."

Robert shrugs. "I'm not sure. I have exams and things, and she isn't allowed visitors." He knows as well as I do that if he wanted to go Eva would see him.

"Seriously?"

He doesn't reply or look at me, instead busying himself flipping the pages in his book as if he's searching for a passage.

Reid coughs like he's hiding a laugh. I flip him off but don't look away from Robert. I force a smile and step closer. "Robert?"

He looks up.

"She could've died."

For a moment, he's silent. He seems to be weighing his thoughts, and I hope that he'll do the right thing. His friends, *Eva's* friends, are watching. No one is laughing now. The thought of the Tilling-Cooper scion dying is never going to be funny in Jessup, not even for a moment while a bunch of boys try to prove they're smart-asses.

"How is she? Really?" he asks.

"She's recovering, but she's lonely and upset. You visiting would help." I want to believe there's *some* good in Robert. I hope he'll show me that now.

Instead, he looks down at his book again and says, "I'll text her tonight."

And my good intentions about not arguing with him slip a little. "She deserves better."

Reid shoots me a quick secretive smile, but Robert and the other two boys are all ignoring me now. Despite being so crude, Reid usually seems like he's trying to be nice to me. He also seems increasingly convinced that he can charm me out of my clothes.

Reid doesn't even pretend he's interested in dating. As he so bluntly put it late one night after everyone had either passed out, left, or retreated behind closed doors, "My grandmother would have to mainline Xanax before she'd allow me to date a *non*-Southern girl . . . especially an Asian one." I couldn't decide whether to give him points for honesty or slap him for being an imbecile.

Mr. Ellsworth walks into the room, so I go to my seat. Listening to him drone on about the exam schedule is almost soothing. I don't understand a lot of Eva's friends *or* her boyfriend. Half the school seems desperate to let me know that they care about Eva—whether or not they do, I can't honestly say—but her actual boyfriend seems just as determined to be clear that he isn't going to worry about her. Part of me wants to stop and ask Reid to explain. He's been friends with them since birth so he must have some sort of insight.

Understanding Robert's idiocy won't fix it though, so I settle for hoping that this is the thing that will convince Eva to end things with him. If not, I may end up going native and spouting things like "cad" and "reprobate." If common sense won't make her see that he's a jerk, maybe some Jessup-isms will get it done.

DAY 6: "THE SURPRISE"

Eva

MY ROOM IS GETTING dangerously close to smelling like a perfume shop. Apparently my no-visitors lie was interpreted as an invitation to send arrangements. A few flowers are nice, but after a dozen or so bouquets the scent is nauseating. I blame the smell for giving me a headache and have the nurses give away all of them—except the orchids my parents sent. They called late last night—apparently after all these years they still can't master time-zone math. They think they can finally get a flight out, so I guess they'll be here soon—and I'll go home. I guess it's good. I'm already feeling caged.

I'm off the antiseizure drug, but I'm still on the muscle relaxer. I can even have narcotics too now that my brain seems okay. The doctors and nurses focus on my brain, my leg, and nerve damage. They tell me how lucky I am that I haven't lost any sensation in my face. They tell me how fortunate I am to be awake and seemingly not experiencing any mental degradation. They're right. I still asked them to hang a towel covering the mirror in the bathroom. The scars horrify me.

Robert still hasn't visited. He should know that I don't include him in my no-visitors request; Grace knew it didn't apply to her. Robert hasn't even asked to see me. Of course, I haven't asked him to visit either. I'm afraid of what he'll think. Although neither Grace nor my grandfather looked at me like I'm ugly, I'm not sure I want to see what Robert's expression is when he sees my face. Status matters to Robert. He has only dated girls who are pretty *and* from what his mother calls "the right families." My last name alone wasn't reason enough for him; it would be for her, but he's told me frequently that he likes the way I look. Maybe he's hoping that if he waits, I'll be prettier. I don't want to tell him how wrong he is.

I realize, however, that it doesn't make sense to flinch away from the nurses or the doctors when they do their rounds. They aren't flinching away from me. Living in the hospital means having someone come into my room to poke, prod, or check on me every couple of hours all day and all night. They're mostly nice people, trying to be quiet when I'm napping and not staring at the mess that's now my face. I suspect it's easier for them because they've seen worse—at least I hope they have.

It makes me feel like a lousy person for thinking that, and if my father heard me, there would be a lecture on "counting my blessings."

I hate thinking about all of this, but there's not a whole lot else to do in the hospital. I read. I watch television. I text Grace, Robert, Piper, CeCe, and a few other people. It's lonely, but I can't deal with most of them seeing me yet.

I don't even want to see me yet.

My nurse today, Kelli, is cool. She was here yesterday, too. She's the youngest nurse I've had, only a few years older than me, but she's not so old that she has that parent-vibe.

"How about a change of scenery?" Kelli busies herself opening the curtains, letting bright light pour into the room. "You could get the grand tour of Peds."

They aren't letting me walk yet because of the traumatic brain injury, but I don't want to walk either, so it works out just fine. "No thanks," I say.

"You're moping. It won't help to hide away in a dark room." Kelli levels a look at me that would do Grace proud. It's the keen gaze of someone who isn't going to accept my excuses or whining. I'm torn between smiling at it and wishing the day nurse was the one from two days ago. She didn't care that I was wallowing.

"Be right back." Kelli leaves, and when she returns, she's pushing a wheelchair. "There's a great view down in the lounge."

"Maybe later," I hedge.

Kelli crosses her arms over her chest and looks at me. "You're one of three patients I have right now, and I just checked on them. Now's a good time."

"Fine. Give me the grand tour."

I reach out to grab her arm, and she helps me as I turn my body ninety degrees on the bed so I can get down. Then, she steadies me as I lower my good leg to the floor. It takes longer than I think it should every time I do this, but at least I'm getting out of bed.

After Kelli helps me into the chair and hangs my IV bag on the pole, she quietly hands me a tissue. "Do you want something for the pain?"

"Nope." It hurts more than I expected, but I'd rather hurt than feel like puking. The muscle relaxers already make me queasy, and I'm trying to avoid as much of the pain meds as I can. I dislike the oxycodone they added on what they call "PRN" dose, which, I learned, just means "take as needed." As far as I'm concerned, it's *not* needed at all. I tried it, but it made me feel fuzzy-brained. Even without it my tongue feels fat, and my brain feels slow.

Kelli hands me the lap blanket Mrs. Yeung brought me. It's something she made herself, and I can tell that it's one of her more recent attempts. The stitches in this one are more even than the others I've seen. After I cover my cast and my bare leg with the puce and lime blanket, Kelli wheels me out of the room. It feels a little strange to be in public wearing a blanket, pajamas, and a robe, but it's either this or have someone bring me a skirt because jeans won't go over my cast, and even if they did, balancing on one foot to unhook jeans when I need to use the bathroom sounds like a bad idea. So, a nightgown it is.

The floor is flooded by natural light because of skylights and large windows, and the walls are decorated with photographs of nature. Huge potted plants—that I think are probably fake—add to the overall sense that the designers were trying to bring a little of the world outside into the hospital. The common area has chairs and game stations, racks of books, and a few tables. It's as inviting as it could be considering where we are.

"This is the playroom," Kelli says as she points to the left. "Over here is the Teen Zone."

I snort. I don't mean to, but I do. Then I quickly say, "Sorry."

"I didn't name it." She sounds unoffended, almost happy.

We're quiet as she pushes me through the hallway. Most of the patients' doors are closed. A few rooms are vacant, and a few have doors wide open with families visible inside. I try not to stare. I wouldn't want strangers invading my privacy. There are a few different types of cribs, and I guess that means that there are different ages of babies in them. That makes me feel sadder. It sucks to be in the hospital, but at least I'm old enough to ask questions and make some sense of everything. Babies can't do that.

Maybe Kelli senses my mood shifting or maybe she's just used to people sinking into a funk when they have more cuts on their face than Frankenstein's monster. Regardless of the reason, she starts talking again. "I hear that your friends can't come during the week, right?"

"Jessup is a long drive." I sound defensive, even though I try not to. I suspect that she already knows that I asked the desk to lie for me about the no-visitors policy.

"Maybe you can talk to some people here?" Kelli suggests.

I make a noncommittal noise because, truthfully, I'm simply not looking to make friends with the other patients.

Kelli wheels me past a kitchen and a laundry room, and then into a room that is a little bigger than the "Teen Zone." There are a couple of sofas, a few chairs, a coffee table, and a decent-size television. It's a slightly sterile version of the sort of living room that would be in most homes.

Another nurse comes around the corner. "You're needed at the desk."

"Do you want to go back or wait here?"

"Here."

She smiles like I did something wonderful and then points at a panel that's low enough to reach from a wheelchair. "There's a call button if you need anything. I'll be back, but page the desk if you're ready to go back to your room sooner."

I nod, and she leaves.

The window in the lounge overlooks a park. A group of about six people show up after I've been sitting there for a few minutes. They're playing some sort of group Frisbee game. I watch them. That's all I *can* do right now. It makes me feel pitiful, which pisses me off. God knows I'm not longing to chase a Frisbee. Sitting outside in the sunlight or taking a walk would be nice though. I can't do either of those things. I'm not sure when or if I will ever be able to either.

My leg was apparently broken in several places. My thigh—the femur, according to Dr. Klosky—has a plate screwed onto it now. He explained it. In time the bone would grow over the metal. Better that than having shards floating about and lodging where they shouldn't be; better a plate than not healing. Knowing all of that doesn't erase the sense of queasiness that comes whenever I think about holes being drilled into my bone. I'm not even letting myself think about the possibility of lingering effects from my brain being jarred, or the swelling that went down, or the couple days unconscious. If I think about it, I'm not sure I can stop at a few tears. I'm not sure where to direct my anger, but I'm fighting my temper more and more lately. It twists in and around the sorrow and disgust.

Suddenly, being in the lounge isn't as relaxing as it was supposed to be. I use my hands to push my chair closer to the call button, but before I reach it, I hear someone say my name.

"Eva?"

I look over my shoulder to see Nate staring at me in shock. I don't know why he's here at Mercy Regional Hospital *or* saying my name.

I stare at him as he steps farther into the room.

He drops onto the sofa across from me, careful to keep his distance from my extended leg, but near enough to talk without needing to be loud. "Hey."

The urge to reach up and smooth down my hair makes me shake my head. My face is a maze of cuts and stitches, and I'm wearing my pajamas and one of the world's least attractive blankets. My hair is the least of my issues.

"Hi," I say and immediately realize that my conversation skills are about as bad as my fashion sense right now. Nate is talking to me after all this time. I'm not sure I'd know what to say to him even if we were somewhere normal. I certainly don't know what to say *here*. I'm a little comforted that he doesn't seem to know what to say either; he just nods and looks at me.

After an awkward moment during which I consider pushing the call button repeatedly so I can escape, he asks, "Did you just get here?"

"Here?"

"Mercy." He stretches, tilting his head left and right as if he's been sleeping in an uncomfortable position. "I've been in the lounge the past few evenings, and I haven't seen you. Plus, those"—he points at my face—"look fresh."

I'm more than a little confused that he's not being a jerk like he has been for the past few years. I just don't know if I should ignore him.

Cautiously, I say, "I've been in for a couple days. Someone hit me with a car."

"That sucks."

I start laughing. It's not funny, not really, but it's such an understatement after everything I've been feeling that it seems hilarious to me. He stares at me like maybe I'm a little unbalanced, which only makes me laugh more. It takes a minute to get my laughter under control. By then, tears fill my eyes.

I sniff and wipe the tears with the back of my hand, but in

doing so, I bump one of the cuts on my cheek and gasp with pain.

"Shit," Nate mutters, and he's at my side holding out the box of tissues from the coffee table. "I didn't mean to make you cry."

"It still happens when I laugh—just like when we were kids." My voice is shaky, more from pain than tears. I'm not completely lying: I *do* cry when I laugh.

"I'm sorry," he says, his hand coming down on mine—and I'm . . . gone. I'm unable to speak. I feel the world around me vanish before I can ask whether he means that he's sorry for the past three years or sorry that I'm in pain.

I pull over, my tires crunching on the gravel. I wasn't drinking at all, but my vision is off. Something is wrong with me, and I'm afraid I won't make it to the house. I guess it's the flu or something, but I've never had the flu hit so suddenly.

My mother will be irritated when I wake her, but she'd be worse if I wrecked the truck.

I shiver as I get out of the truck.

With the help of the dashboard lights, I search the cab of my truck again, hoping that my phone fell out of my pocket and under the seat. The truck is clean enough that I know it's not there, but I don't see how it could be anywhere else. I had it earlier at the restaurant. I called Nora to talk to her and Aaron, but my brother was asleep, so I had Nora tell him I couldn't make it until morning.

I feel out of it, tired enough that I worry that I'm coming down with something. I need to shake it off. I can't carry germs to him. That's the last thing he needs.

I wonder if I have any more of those germ masks at the house. I'm fairly certain I have gloves. Even if I feel better tomorrow, I'll wear gloves and masks. Cystic fibrosis is hard enough for him to handle without adding colds or a flu.

"Eva?"

For a moment, I remember again that I'm not Nate. I'm Eva. Then the voice saying my name is swept away by a sharp pain in my stomach. Nate's stomach. I think about how I'm Nate and not-Nate. My stomach—Eva's stomach—shouldn't hurt, but I'm swept further into Nate, and it's all I can do to try to remember I'm not really him.

The stomach cramps become bad enough that I stumble and clutch the door frame of my truck. The pain is unexpected.

I pat my jeans pockets as if I would've missed my phone if it were there. It's not there. I can't call for help if my phone is gone.

My mouth feels like it's filled with something hot and sour. I'm not throwing up. Yet. My heart feels too fast.

Someone pulls up in front of me, their headlights shining in my face so I can't see who's in the car. I'm not sure if it's a helpful stranger or someone I know. There aren't a lot of people who drive along Old Salem Road. Aside from a few houses and the reservoir, there's nothing out this far. Mom always says that's the only reason she's willing to live at "the godforsaken end of the devil's elbow."

The lights make the person getting out of the car look like a silhouette. He's not a huge man. I can tell that. He could be a bigger woman. . . . I open my mouth to speak, but instead puke all over the seat of my truck. Something's wrong. Something more than the flu.

."Sick," I force out of lips that feel oddly numb.

The person from the car is beside me, but he—or she—isn't speaking. I can see jeans and tennis shoes, but when I look up, I can't see a face. It's there; it has to be, but I can't tell anything about it.

"You should've stayed away." The voice sounds almost familiar, but the person is whispering.

I'm shivering so hard that my face hurts from clenching my jaw.

My legs are shaking too, and I hit the ground. I'm sitting in a puddle of vomit. The person opens a bottle of what looks like Mad Dog 20/20, grabs my chin with a gloved hand, and tilts my head back. The alcohol pours into my mouth faster than I can swallow, and it spills down my shirt.

He takes my hand and wraps it around the bottle, and my muscles are too weak to put up much of a fight. I try, but it's about as effective as a toddler resisting a parent. My phone hits the asphalt beside me hard enough that the screen cracks. The stranger had my missing phone.

I try to turn my head so I can throw up on the ground instead of on myself, and the person helps me this time, turning my head so I can try to get whatever I ate out of my body. As soon as I'm done though, he puts the bottle back in my mouth. He gives me a break when I start gagging, but as soon as I've caught my breath, the bottle is back.

I need to get away. I need to get home. Then it hits me: I'm

not going to be able to walk anywhere. I blink blearily at the
silhouette crouched in front of me.

Then he helps me to the ground and puts the bottle to my
lips.

"Your blood alcohol should be high enough that they won't
ask a lot of questions," he or she says.

I feel like the world is spinning. I try to turn my head as the
bottle comes back, but the person holds my chin again. This
time when the Mad Dog gags me and the vomit comes at the
same time, there is no break. Tears fill my already blurry eyes as
I try to shake my head to get away, but it doesn't work.

I'm still shaking my head, suddenly aware of Nate saying
my name over and over. He sounds panicky.

I stare at him, and my eyes tear up. He's looking down at
me; he's not choking or vomiting. *What just happened?* I'm not
sure if it was a seizure or hallucination or what. All I know is
that he looks fine, but I'm suddenly freezing.

Then Kelli is there, stepping in front of him.

"Eva?" She squats down in front of me, and I look at her as
she asks, "Can you hear me? Nod if you hear me."

I can't stop shivering. I'm so cold that my teeth are chattering. I nod.

My gaze drifts back to Nate. He looks worried, and I want
to say something that will let him know it's not his fault that
I . . . what? Envisioned his murder? I don't remember hallucinations being on the list of things Dr. Klosky discussed.

"I don't know what happened," he tells Kelli. "She just
blanked out and started shaking. I didn't know what to do.

With my brother, I know—" He cuts himself off with a shake of his head and turns to me. "I'm sorry if I did something."

Kelli is taking my pulse. The feel of the latex gloves on my skin is still alien after over a week of it. I know now it's for my safety and theirs—not all of my cuts are covered. It still makes me feel unsettled, like I'm in some bad movie about contagion. I'm sure I don't have a zombie virus or bird flu or swine flu or whatever animal-named pandemic the next big outbreak will be.

"Is she okay?" Nate asks, drawing my gaze back to him. He's somehow better-looking to me with that expression of concern on his face. The last time I saw him look at me that way was when I slid into second base in a game when we were in elementary school. I still have a small, faded scar on my knee from that day. It was stupid, but I'd watched a game with my granddad and it hadn't looked painful when the players in the game did it.

"I'm fine," I try to assure them both. I hope it reassures me too, but so far it's not working. I feel incredibly unwell right now.

"Your pulse is good, and your pulse pressure is fine. Let's get you back to the room to check your blood pressure and oximetry." Kelli has that tone I've already come to identify as "something worries me but I won't let the patient know." Nate obviously recognizes it, too. He stares at Kelli a beat too long and then glances at me.

I sigh. There's no way I can tell them what I thought I saw.

I pictured Nate's *death*. Clearly, my brain injury isn't as healed as everyone thinks. My poor, battered brain caused me to hallucinate—and in a macabre way.

I pause when I realize I've started thinking of my brain as something separate from the rest of me and add that to the list of topics I'm not interested in pondering—or mentioning to anyone.

"What room?" Nate asks suddenly. He stares at me with the sort of intensity I've dreamed of seeing in his eyes—but for completely the wrong sort of reason.

I don't answer.

Kelli looks between us before telling him, "Nurses can't give that information out."

I take the coward's way out and stay silent. Right now I want to go to my nice, quiet room and try not to think of why I pictured him dying so vividly and awfully. I fake a yawn that turns into a real yawn, and Nate walks away without another word. *That's* the Nate I'm used to these days, the one who abandons me, not the one who sounds like he cares.

Kelli is quiet as she pushes my wheelchair back to the room. She does the same things the nurses do every four hours: check my pupils' reaction to light, my temperature, and my blood oxygen level. Everything is fine. She also checks my CSMs—color, sensation, and motility in my toes. Then, after she helps me up so I can use the toilet, she gets me settled back in my bed and piles several blankets on me since I'm still shivering. I think my quiet acceptance of her help makes her nervous, but I'm a little freaked out myself. In all of the things they've told me about TBI, there was nothing about horrible visions.

I *was* warned about less extreme issues like headaches, dizziness, ringing in the ears, and decreased sense of taste and smell. Then there are a whole slew of major worries, like issues with memory and speech, personality shifts, difficulty expressing and reading affect, and—one of my personal favorites—decreased coordination, because becoming clumsier is what every girl wants. Nowhere on the far too long list of things-that-can-go-wrong is vivid morbidity.

"Everything looks good, but I'm going to check in with the doctor on call to see what she wants to do." She flashes me one of the fake smiles that are meant to be reassuring, and then she heads out to the desk.

I close my eyes. I'm afraid I'll see Kelli dying, but thankfully, I don't. In my mind, I play out the details of what happened with Nate, and it's different remembering it. When it happened, I was more than picturing Nate dying. It was like I *was* Nate. I've never imagined being someone else, not like this and certainly not while they were dying. I feel embarrassed, but the more I think about it, the more I think I'm going to keep this to myself. I'm not up for being labeled crazy on top of "the Cooper-Tilling girl," "the scarred girl," and "the almost-murdered girl."

DAY 6: "THE GIRL"

Judge

I PRAYED ON IT for several days before I found clarity. The Lord wants me to teach, to make an example of Them. It's how I can save Eva. If she sees how fallible we all are, if she sees the truths that They want to hide, I can share all of my secrets with her. I understand now that the Lord spared her so she could learn. She's like me. She simply needs to understand.

I study Their kind, trying to find a worthy sacrifice. I need someone near enough to Eva that she'll care, but not so close that she'll be so grief-stricken that she misses the message. It's a difficult decision.

I need to do a better job this time too if I am to carry out my mission of change. If I'm to save Eva, I need to be able to do unpleasant things. She's worth it.

The fear of failure is almost debilitating. Failures don't

deserve happiness. My grandmother explained that time and again, and my father told me I'd never amount to anything if I put on airs. I touch the scar on my stomach from the last time he tried to teach me the lessons.

Something like guilt fills me at the memory, but then I think about how happy Eva and I will be if she learns *her* lessons. The image of her cowering on my floor like I once did before my father makes me cringe. I don't want to have to hurt her. Really, I don't. I don't want her to recoil from me. I want to *save* her so we can be together.

Dream Eva smiles and tells me, "I trust you."

My body reacts to the thought of her appreciating the time I'm spending to save her. I touch the scar on my stomach as I realize that she'll be grateful, not afraid. I push away my reaction to the thought of Eva looking up at me, accepting what I've done for her, understanding how it will be in the future. Later, I can close my eyes and think about it. I can picture her looking at me with that secret smile of hers. Right now, I need to concentrate on the work, not the reward. I look around the hallway at Jessup High, trying to decide which girl will be the best choice.

I don't want her to look like Eva. That would send the wrong message. It's not about looks.

I don't want her to be too close to Eva either. That leaves me with pretty much everyone but Grace and Piper. I smile at Piper as I walk past her. She's not the one; she's not as special as she thinks. I slept with her a few times during our freshman year, but she wanted to do the whole dinner-with-the-family thing, and that would confuse the relationship too much. I don't like to lie. I can when I have to, but I don't like to do it.

Eva is the only one who will ever understand me.

Someone here is special enough for this message, and I'll find her. She's the one who will help Eva see that They are corrupt, that They aren't better than us, and then she'll reject Them. She'll see the truth that I know, and she'll choose to be with me and only me. I'll leave the special girl with an amaryllis to help Eva see the message.

"Did you study?" Amy asks, interrupting my thoughts.

I shrug.

"I don't know why I ask. You never do." She pouts, and I shake my head at her. If I didn't know that the stories she spread about Eva were true, I might choose her as my message, but those things Amy said *were* true.

It was good and right that Amy spoke up. It should have helped Eva to see that They don't respect her; They only pretend to care about her.

I care.

"Hey!" Amy nudges me. She isn't really one of Them, not anymore. She used to be, but she dated an Undesirable. *They* aren't forgiving of that kind of thing. She thought she could ignore the rules, but her parents were already divorced and then she stepped out of line. Now, she's a girl only worth "dating" in private. She gives it up to anyone she thinks able to redeem her, but it only lowers her further and further from where she wants to be. She wouldn't be a good first message.

"Hey back," I say after a long pause.

"I hate exams. They make me feel stupid," she whines.

"You're not stupid. Plus, you're good at lots of other things," I remind her. She is, too. She has qualities that a lot of people don't appreciate. Amy isn't one of Them, not now. With Them I pretend, but Amy is real. I don't need to pretend with her.

She rewards me with a smile, ducks her head a little, and looks up through her lashes. It's the sort of coquettish things that all girls do—except Eva, of course. She's pure. Even though she's not a virgin, she's still pure.

"Can I borrow paper?" I pat my pockets and add, "And a pen?"

Amy shakes her head, but she still gives me what I asked for.

Without meaning to, I think of Dream Eva looking up at me much the way Amy is, accepting me even with my flaws, and my body reacts again. I know I can take care of that on my own later, but it's nicer with a partner so I lower my voice a bit and ask, "Hey, are you free after school?"

There's no doubt as to why I lowered my voice—this isn't the first time we've had this conversation—but she doesn't look at me like I'm dirty. She shakes her head. "Not today. Maybe tomorrow?"

"Maybe." I shrug again. "I have a project I'm working on, but if I can't find what I need for it, I'll call you."

The bell rings then, and we go into the classroom. I forget about Amy the moment she walks away. Maybe the one I need for the message is in this room. I slouch into my seat and look around, watching for her.

DAY 7: "THE BEST FRIEND"

Eva

THE NURSES ARE SUPER-ATTENTIVE the next day. The doctor on call the night of my episode saw no changes or alarming symptoms. Everything looks good. Admittedly, I haven't mentioned my hallucinations, but I haven't had any other hallucinations since then, so I opt not to bring it up.

The day nurse mentioned that Nate has stopped by the desk to ask about me. I keep my door closed in case he walks by. It makes me feel like a prisoner, but I'm not sure what to say to him. It feels like there are a lot of things between us right now that we *could* discuss, but I don't know if I want to start any of those conversations. I don't know why he's in the hospital, and I don't think I want to ask.

We were never anything other than friends, but he was my *best* friend for years. I learned to play baseball with him.

Our fathers were friends, and we were together after church a lot. Nate was my first kiss. Sure, we were nine, and it was my bloody knee he kissed, but still, he was my first. Then his dad left, and his mom wasn't big on church—a fact which made me jealous more than once—and then Nate changed. He stopped even looking my way when I saw him at school.

Until now.

By the time Grace arrives to visit that evening, I'm ready to pounce on her. Aside from the obvious—she's my best friend and I'm bored out of my mind and oh yeah, I saw Nate—I'm excited that she's here because she walks into my room all but hidden behind a big bag of clothes and snacks. Oreos stick out the top of the bag, and that alone would be reason enough.

"I love you," I say as soon as I see her.

She laughs. "Me or the cookies?"

"Both." I hold out a hand. "Gimme."

"A few days in Pediatrics and you sound like a toddler."

"Yep. Now gimme." I wave my arm as if it'll make the cookies come near.

Shaking her head and smiling at me, Grace relents. She lowers the big bag to the chair, opens the package of cookies, and holds them out to me. Better still, she also pulls out a small cooler from within the giant bag. "Mom thought it was criminal to have Oreos without milk."

The cookie is halfway to my mouth when I hear her. "Milk? She sent milk for my cookies? I love the General."

"More than me?" She holds on to the carton of milk.

I gesture to my leg with my cookie. "No taunting the injured!" When she hands me the milk, I add, "Maybe a little more, but it's too close to call."

She busies herself unpacking the clothes she brought while I eat Oreos and listen to her tell me how she'll never get through exams without me to study with her. I know she feels guilty admitting it, but Grace isn't a big fan of studying solo. My grades went up when I started spending more time with her, mainly because I felt like a loser just messing around online when she was working hard. So I studied instead. In exchange, she has my back when I'm dealing with the cattiness at school or tempted to have the entire pint of Ben and Jerry's. Some friendships work because they have so much in common; we work because we have so many differences. We fill in each other's gaps. That shouldn't have to stop just because some jerk hit me with his car.

"So why don't we study here," I suggest.

"You don't have to take the exams."

I shrug. "I *could* though, and you have to, so why not study together?"

"I could hug you . . ."

"Rain check. My arms are still tender."

She nods, and then goes over to the bag of treats. She pulls out a box of one of the sugar-filled, marshmallow-laden cereals that she finds disgusting and I love. She doesn't even lecture me on just how much exercise I'll have to do in order to counter the junk I like to eat. It hits me then: I'm going to be in a cast for weeks, possibly months. I *can't* exercise.

"Gracie!"

My best friend pauses as she's pulling out a bag of dried fruit and a box of some sort of sugar-free, preservative-free, flavor-free snack mix. "I'm not leaving you with just junk," she starts, clearly thinking I was objecting to the healthier snacks she brought.

"You can't." I gaze longingly at the cereal, all wrapped up in a bright child-friendly package. "Take it with you. My marshmallow cereal. Take it."

She tilts her head and gives me a suspicious look. "Take the *junk* away?"

I hold out my Oreos. "These, too." I shake the package. "I can't exercise."

"Sweetie, you hate exercise." She comes over to stand beside me. Her expression is clouded. "Remember?"

I feel a twinge of guilt. Personality changes are possible with TBI, and while Grace isn't making a scene over worrying about me, she is still aware of the possibilities. It makes me glad I didn't tell her about the hallucination thing.

"I remember. I just know I'll get fat if you can't make me run," I explain.

Clarity dawns on her, and she gives me a sympathetic smile. She also takes my Oreos. We're both quiet while she repacks some of the junk food she brought for me.

I break the silence by saying, "Thanks for bringing clothes."

Grace pulls out the skirts she and her mother bought for me. The first one is the sort of loud pattern that makes me wince visibly. It's the brightest piece of clothing I've ever owned. "Still think my mom is perfect? *She* picked this one."

I tilt my head. "It's not that bad. The General has fine taste."

Grace rolls her eyes, but she's smiling. We've been having the same discussion over her mother for at least eighteen months. She thinks her mom is overbearing; I think she should be grateful for having an attentive mother. Mrs. Yeung is awesome, and I'd wear a sack if that's what it took to back my stance.

"I picked this one." She holds up a solid brown skirt with a subtle peacock feather line drawing that starts at the hem and stretches over the bottom quarter of the skirt. The lines are in the same sky blue as the first skirt, but here, they're a burst of bright on a dark palate. It's exactly what I'd pick for myself.

She pulls out two more skirts, both more like the one she'd selected for me, and I know that she was responsible for keeping Mrs. Yeung's appreciation for bolder colors in check. "Thank you."

At the bottom of the bag are five short-sleeved T-shirts in various colors: pink, blue, black, gray, and brown. Grace doesn't unfold them, just puts them to the side. "These are pretty basic, but I figured you could use a few clean shirts so you aren't living in pajamas. Mom said she'd wash everything you have here now."

I hadn't thought about the state of my laundry until now. I had wanted some skirts because of the cast, but as Grace mentions my clothes, I realize that I'd have had to re-wear things if not for them. My parents are due back soon, but as usual when they're away, it's Mrs. Yeung to the rescue.

After a quiet moment, I blurt, "I saw Nathaniel Bouchet yesterday."

"The Jessup man-slut? *Here?*" She sounds more like Piper in this moment than I ever would tell her.

I simply nod.

"He actually seemed surlier than usual at school today." Grace shakes her head. "Which is saying something because when he's sober, he's about as friendly as a rabid dog."

"He was in class?"

"Yeah." She drags the word out like I've asked something stupid. "Every day this week I think, but text Piper or Laurel. They'd know for sure. I think Piper watches him even more than you do."

I know I'm blushing, but I try to shrug it off. Most people don't comment on the way I watch Nate. "I thought maybe he was a patient, too. When we talked he said he was in the lounge most evenings."

"So, let me get this right: Nate don't-talk-to-me Bouchet visited you, but *Robert* hasn't?" Grace pauses, looking at me as if I'll pick up the conversation.

"Nate didn't visit me. He was here, and we talked . . . it's different."

"Mm-hmm."

I motion toward my brush, which is on the nightstand. Grace hands it to me, and I busy myself brushing my hair. It's already become habit to brush it more often, as if frequency will overcome the fact that I refuse to look into a mirror to see the results. "Robert texts me," I say.

"About why he wasn't there the night of the accident?"

I pause mid-brushstroke. "No."

At that, Grace goes into a rant about Robert not deserving me anyhow, and how she "always thought he was an asshat"—which is nowhere near the first time she's said as much. I've given up on trying to explain to her that Robert is nice, even if he acts a bit stiff. He's been my friend forever, and while he's never been the sort to want to climb trees or go sloshing in the creek, he was the sort to listen to me when I was angry or to bring me a box of Krispy Kreme doughnuts when I was depressed.

I think about him while Grace repeats a lot of her usual complaints. I don't think he's "the one" for me, but he's a good guy even though she can't see it. Robert *gets* me. He's a Baucom. It's not quite the same as being a Cooper or Tilling, but if my grandfathers were selecting candidates for an appropriate match for me in Jessup, Robert would be on that very short list.

How do I explain Jessup traditions to Grace though?

When she takes a breath, I ask, "Who else is going to be willing to date me now, Gracie? Seriously, *I* can't stand looking at me."

"Oh, sweetie!" She grabs my hand, and I am gone.

I'm late. I know that Eva's fine without me there, but she's going to worry. I shove the rest of my books into my backpack. There are notes and photocopies, but I still don't have an answer.

"Good night," I tell the librarian as I walk past the reference desk.

She waves and smiles at me. I've been here a lot over the years, and the librarians are all sweet and very helpful. I wonder vaguely if there's a librarians' oath like doctors take. The thought makes me grin as I walk out the door.

"Eva? Eva!" Grace's voices echoes in my hospital room.

I shake my head and yank away from her.

"Are you hurt? What's going on? Let me get your—"

"No!" I can't tell her about my hallucinations. I'm too embarrassed. It's weird to hallucinate that I'm someone else.

"Shhh," she soothes. "You're freezing."

She pulls my blanket up and sits next to me on my bed to hug me.

After a few moments of silence, I whisper, "I look like something stitched together in a mad scientist's lab."

Grace doesn't miss a beat. "You'll get better. Your leg will heal, and the cuts will heal, and—"

"I know, but that won't fix how I *look*, not really." Tears start falling again. I don't have to ask for a tissue before she holds out the box of softer ones she brought for me. I dab at my tears because rubbing would hurt, and then continue, "I feel stupid for caring about this. I could've died. I get it. I'm lucky to be okay. I get that, too. But I hate that I look like this. I hate that even after these heal, I'll *always* look like something slashed up my face."

I take a deep breath, and then another one, and then a couple more.

Grace is quiet as I grab her hand and squeeze before saying, "I'm afraid to ask Robert why he hasn't been here because I don't want him to ditch me. We're more convenience than anything, and I knew we'd break up eventually, but I *like* having a boyfriend."

She holds my hand in silence for a few moments. Then she points out, "If he isn't here anyhow, does it *matter*?"

"He texts."

Grace holds my gaze. "If he were my boyfriend, what would you tell me?"

"He's an asshat," I say with a small smile.

"And?"

"You deserve better than an asshat," I add.

"And I'd listen because you're smart," Grace says. She taps her chin with one finger. "Wait? Who else is smart? Hmmm. I know this answer. Who is it?"

"Grace Yeung. Maybe I should listen if she offers me advice."

Grace's expression is serious, as if she's considering the matter, and then she nods. "You're right. I *am* pretty freaking awesome." She grows slightly more serious as she adds, "And I don't see any practical use for an asshat."

My laugh is watery, but it's there. Like so many other times in my life the past two years, Grace is the voice of reason in my life, the one who has my back.

"Eva, do the doctors know about whatever just—"

"Yes," I interrupt her with a lie. "I told them the first time it happened."

DAY 8: "THE CRUSH"

Eva

The next morning, I'm sitting in the common room reading. When I look up, I find Nate standing in front of me and let out a surprised squeak.

"You didn't see me." His voice lifts slightly as if this could be a question.

"True."

He pulls a rocking chair over toward me. It's one of the chairs that I've only ever seen moms with babies use, but he doesn't seem to care if it's unusual for him to use a rocking chair. He leans back and rocks in silence for a moment, so I dog-ear the page and close my book.

"Good book?" He nods toward the book I'm holding with both hands now.

"I like it," I say cautiously. It's an older book called *Story of a Girl* that I found on one of the shelves here. I've never read anything else by Sara Zarr, but I'll be looking to see if they have anything else of hers.

Nate folds his arms over his chest. "You used to read those Andrew Lost books and then the Warriors ones when we were in elementary school. I never got the cat ones."

I frown. It's hard to believe that Nate remembers my reading habits that clearly. It's been a long time. "The Warriors were good books!"

"I don't know about that. Andrew Lost was good though. I ended up borrowing some of those more than once." He nods as if he's said something profound. "So it's chick books now?"

"This isn't a 'chick book.' "

He leans forward and pushes the book flat so he can look at the cover. On it, a girl is staring out of a window, and the title is written in what could be lipstick or crayon maybe. "Story of a girl," he reads. "So it's . . . a story about a girl with a girl on the cover. Looks like a chick book to me."

I roll my eyes. "I've moved on since elementary school."

"It happens." He rocks a little. "I'm rereading the Andrew Lost series, actually. I dug them out after I saw you."

I frown, before realizing that he's watching me for a reaction. I don't know if he's joking or not. His expression hasn't changed, but I'm not sure why he'd be serious about reading a book series for eight-year-olds.

"My brother likes them," he says after a pause that's almost too long. "I've read the first three to him so far."

"Your brother?" I prompt in confusion. I know he didn't have a brother when we were friends. I don't think any of us knew or heard much about his family since then.

"Room 423." He gestures to the corridor on the opposite side of the common area. "I try to come most every night when he's in here. Aaron's mom works nights so she can be with him days. He has a sitter who's there when he sleeps. I try to go over to their house some, but when he's in here, I am here every night I can be."

"When does his mom sleep?"

"When Aaron naps, when I'm there, and she's usually home to catch a few hours before he wakes up in the morning." Nate shrugs like it's not a big deal, but his lips press tightly together and his gaze drops. "I try to go more, but *my* mom bitches about the drive and nags about my grades. Nora, she's Aaron's mom, gives me gas money so my mom can't bitch about that, too."

I stare at him, not knowing what to say. I remember his parents splitting up, but I had no idea his dad had another kid—or remarried. Whatever the case, Nate hasn't mentioned his father helping out. I debate briefly whether or not to ask, before deciding that since he's the one who brought it all up I might as well. We've gone from not talking at all to him sharing things that are extremely personal. I don't know how to make sense of it, but I figure that continuing talking is the only thing that I can do.

"What about your dad?" I ask.

Nate meets my gaze, and I resist the urge to shiver at the fury in his expression. "Aaron has CF, cystic fibrosis. The sperm donor couldn't handle Aaron being sick, so he walked."

I shake my head because there's nothing to say here that isn't harsh. I remember liking Nate's dad. He laughed and played with Nate like my parents never did with me. Mine were more of the "why don't you go play quietly or read, dear?" sort. I liked reading; I still do. But I think I would've liked wrestling on the floor, too.

It hits me as I'm staring at Nate that in my hallucination he thought about Nora and Aaron. He was concerned about worrying them. I gasp.

"Are you okay?" He leans forward but doesn't touch me.

"Twinge," I lie.

"Do you need the nurse?"

I shake my head. My hands clench the book, and I try to quell the insanity in my mind. Cautiously, I ask, "Have I met Aaron? Or Nora?"

Nate stares at me for a moment. "The memory thing, right? From your head injury?" He gives me such a sympathetic look that I wonder if *that's* the answer. I knew it, but then I forgot. Memory issues are common with TBI. Relief washes over me.

"No, you haven't met them," he continues. "We . . . stopped talking a few years ago. Do you remember that?"

I nod. I must have just heard their names somewhere. It's the only logical explanation. I guess if I'm going to have forgotten things, it's best that it was gossip I forgot.

"What do you remember about . . . us?" he asks.

"I missed you," I say. I thought I remembered everything up until the accident, but maybe I'm wrong. I look at him and continue, "I remember that you changed. We talked all the time, and then you were a jerk. Not all at once, but . . ."

"I'm sorry." He stares at me, and I'm not sure if he's the boy I used to know or the jackass I've seen around parties the last couple years.

I think back to the last night we spoke. "Then one night you were *awful*. The party out at Piper's parents' lake house? You knew everyone was watching us, and you acted like you didn't even know me."

He swallows and looks at me, not meeting my eyes, but gazing in the general direction of my chin. "I wish I could tell you that I'd already apologized for that and everything else before now, and you forgave me, but I'd be lying."

I nod.

"I *want* you to forgive me, Eva." He meets my eyes now. "I've wanted that for years, but . . . I know I'm only tolerated by your crowd these days. I couldn't walk up to *you*."

"I was the one who came to you that night," I remind him.

"Yeah, and I was a mess then. I just wanted to be numb, and beer and girls seemed like a good idea."

"Seemed?" I echo.

"I don't drink anymore." He looks straight at me. "Even so, what would they do if I walked up to you? Baucom, Piper, and the rest of them? Sober and at a party or at school?"

I'm not sure what to say. He is—like Amy Crowne—fine to be with in private or after a few drinks at a party, but he's definitely not considered date material or even friend material. He hasn't been since he stopped being a part of our crowd.

"Well, we're talking now," I finally say. "Are you going to ignore me later?"

"No." He rubs his hand over his head, just like he used to when we were kids.

"You still pet your head when you're nervous, Nate."

He pulls his hand away quickly, but he flashes me a smile I haven't seen in far too long. Then he says, "Aaron does it, too. He calls it 'helping to think.'"

I decide to let the other things go for a moment and ask, "How old is Aaron?"

"Eight."

I do the math. "So before your parents split . . ."

"Yeah. Hence Mom not being very supportive of all the time I spend with Nora." He reaches up to rub his head again, stops midway, and lowers his hand. "I missed you too, you know?"

I'm not sure what to say to that. If anyone told me before the accident that I'd be having a heart-to-heart with Nate, I'd have laughed at the thought. He's called a lot of things these days, but most of them are more along the lines of aloof, stoic, and mysterious. The person in front of me seems sweet and open. "You've been a jerk, ignoring me like I was chasing after you. I wasn't. You can't even look at me at parties or in the cafeteria or anything. It's insulting, and . . . ridiculous. Really, it's *ridiculous*."

"I know. I just . . . I was screwed up. I could've handled things better that night at Piper's and every other one after that when I saw you. I'm sorry, Eva."

Nathaniel Bouchet is an idiot. I'm not surprised by this revelation. I am, however, a little lost on what to say. It's hard to stay angry at him when he sounds like *my* Nate again.

"Eva?" he prompts when I don't reply.

"I'm in room 406," I say.

"I know." He grins briefly. "The nurses didn't tell me, but it was pretty easy to figure it out. Your door was the only one that stayed closed all the time."

"I like my privacy," I hedge. I'm not ready for total honesty.

"I still miss you."

My anger rekindles at that. I cross my arms over my chest. "We go to the same school, Nate. I live at the same house. You even saw me the *night* before the accident."

"What was I supposed to do? Walk up to you and the perfect people, and say 'sorry I ignored you for years; I was stupid. Now, let's go catch crawfish'?"

I remember Nate, super muddy on the bank of the creek, telling me that no one would even be able to tell we went into the water once we dried. I barely repress my smile before I say, "I don't catch crawfish anymore."

"You don't read Andrew Lost or catch crawfish," Nate says musingly. "Noted. What are we going to do when you get out of here then?"

I shrug, but I'm smiling at him as I do it. "Nothing, maybe."

He frowns and stands up. "I get it if you don't want people to know we're talking again—or if you don't want to talk to me. Piper and everyone would have fits, and Baucom probably wouldn't like me being around anyhow."

"It's none of his business who I'm friends with. He doesn't like Grace, either."

Nate looks at me like he's studying me, but I'm not sure what he's hoping to see. It doesn't matter though. I yawn suddenly.

"Past nap time?"

Without thinking I flip him off, and then promptly blush. "Sorry."

"Maybe I've missed your temper, too." He pauses and gestures at the wheelchair. "Do you need help back to 406 first?"

I shake my head. I hope I'm not blushing when I add, "But if my door's open tomorrow, you can stop by my room."

The smile Nate flashes my way reaffirms my earlier realization that he's dangerous. All he says though is "See you tomorrow," and then he's gone, and I'm left staring after him, trying to remind myself that he doesn't mean anything by it. But, somehow, even being friends with Nate is more than enough reason for me to smile so wide that the cuts on my face twinge worse than usual.

DAY 8: "THE MESSAGE"

Judge

I'VE FOUND HER, THE message. She is one of Them, not as bad as Piper but still one of the people who think they are superior. They live by class and name and none of it is *real*. They aren't better than anyone else.

Eva used to know that.

I open the pages of the photo album that I keep on the shelf beside my bed. It's one of those old-fashioned ones where the whole plastic layer lifts, and the photos are stuck in the pages. They sell them down at Harvey's Sundries. I like it even though it's old-fashioned. Not everything from the past is *wrong*—just some things. Caring whose family came first, worrying about what is owned by whom, those things are bad. Liking the simplicity of old-fashioned photo books is good. It's proof that I'm reasonable: I don't dislike everything that's outdated. I run my fingers over the first page, seeing Eva stare up at me. She's ordinary. That's why she was made for me. We're not like the ones who worry about status, not inside where it matters.

There are pictures of all of us from the time we were kids up to this year. She's talking to other people in some of them, so I cut up a few pictures and arranged them so we're close in *every* picture. That's the way we should be. Later, if she heeds the messages, we'll have new pictures where we are close like we should be.

Soon.

I feel a ripple of excitement at the thought of our future. When we were kids, I didn't appreciate what a gift she was. I see that now. No one understands me like she does. No one else can. Only Eva.

Slowly, I turn the pages, watching Eva grow older, seeing her skirts change to jeans. She smiles with more restraint in the newest pictures, as if she's pained by something. It's how I look in pictures, too. I hate the rules of status we all have to live by in Jessup; rules ruin everything.

In one picture from a party at the start of this year, Eva looks free. She has her mouth open in a laugh, and her head is thrown back. Grace is at her side. That's the secret in this one. Grace is someone the rules don't understand. They don't like her, but They don't have a good reason to reject her—not if Eva Cooper-Tilling declares her worthy. Eva's blessing would make the lowliest sinner worthy in Their eyes. Grace isn't from here, isn't even Southern, but she's the one who walks at

Eva's side. Sometimes I think Grace is Eva's Mary Magdalene, except that, unlike The Magdalene, Grace hides her impurity. I did one of those background checks they advertise online. I know enough about Grace Yeung to make friends with people on social media and check her out. I couldn't let just *anyone* around Eva.

Grace isn't as sweet as she acts. She's redeemed now. Like The Magdalene, she's stopped her whorish ways. She's perfect to walk with Eva. She used to be a whore, but she's been delivered from that; plus, she isn't connected to any of Them. If the messages don't help Eva see the truth, maybe Grace can help. I slide my fingertips over the picture of the two of them. I like the feel of the slick plastic of the picture album. It's not the same as bare skin, but I can pretend for now.

I wonder if Grace would let me touch her the way Amy lets me. Abraham laid with more than one woman; he had two wives. My breath hitches at the thought, and I look at their picture again. Eva would be my first wife, but she's too pure for some things. Grace isn't. I get frightened sometimes when I think of my future with Eva. How can we have a happy home if I have to be so careful with her? Maybe Grace is the answer. I'll pray on it. God's plans are often complicated. I'll wait for guidance.

"I'm sorry," I whisper. I think the path would've been clearer if I hadn't been impatient . . . and angry. I'll admit it: I was angry with Eva when I hit her with the car. I want so badly to make her see, to help her understand. I felt desperate, and I acted out. It'll hurt inside if I have to kill her.

But the thought of killing this one, the message, doesn't hurt. I feel excited, happy, and nervous. It's like a first date. I whisper a quick thank you to my Lord for giving me another chance, for trying to save Eva, and then I glance at the clock. I have time yet before the message.

My bedroom door is locked already. I wanted to wait until afterward, when the message was sent, but I can't wait. I'll have to atone later, but right now, I unbutton my trousers as I stare at their happy faces, and I let myself have a reward.

DAY 9: "THE NEWS"

Eva

It's PROBABLY A LITTLE silly, but I have Kelli help me into a skirt the next day. She grins like she knows exactly why I want to wear something other than my pajamas. She's right, but it makes me feel oddly embarrassed. Before the accident, I obviously didn't have what it took to attract Nate, so I can't imagine that I do *now*.

"I don't want to look slouchy. It's bad enough that I look like . . ." I gesture at my face. There really aren't words that describe what I look like.

"You're healing," she says gently. "I know the cuts look bad, but it'll get better."

"Right. Scars all over my face are—" I stop myself and take a deep breath.

Kelli shakes her head. "Try to remember that you're still healing."

She stands beside the bed while I pull myself into the skirt. She's there to steady me, but more and more I want to be independent. I need to if I'm going to go home, especially *my* home. Once I'm in she asks, "Do you need anything else?"

"No, just . . . leave the door partway open when you go."

"Soon, you'll be able to get to it yourself. You're doing great, Eva," she reassures me.

I feel a wash of happiness at her praise. I *am* doing well. I'll be ready when I'm allowed to go home. My parents are to be here tomorrow, and they'll see that I'm coping fine. I told them as much, and although I know I sounded convincing, they still suggested we hire a temporary companion for me. I know this is their way of trying to help, but I haven't had a sitter since I was eleven. I'm almost eighteen now and very accustomed to being on my own. They've never quite known what to do with me. They work hard and succeed, and when they think of it, they stop to say hello to me.

When someone taps on my door, I sit a little straighter, but I don't turn off the television. I pretend like I wasn't waiting for him, like I didn't get dressed a little nicer for him.

Nate walks in. He looks ridiculously good today. He's wearing jeans and a hoodie, which seems odd this time of year, but inside the hospital it's cold. Unlike me, he hasn't dressed any differently to spend time together. I try to remind myself that he's only ever going to be a friend, that he doesn't date, that he didn't look at me before the accident, that I'm just a girl he used to know. Then he smiles at me, and I'm grateful that I'm not still hooked up to the heart monitor.

"Hey."

I nod and mute the television. "Hi."

"Aaron's with Nora, so I . . ." He looks around the room. "Can I stay for a little bit?"

I nod again. I'm not sure why it feels different now that he's in my hospital room. Somehow the space seems smaller, and the fact that I'm sitting in my bed makes it all feel *more*. It's not like this is my real room or my real bed, except that right now they *are*. Being in the room with a bed and a boy—especially one who seems as awkward as I feel—makes me nervous. Maybe he doesn't know how to be with a girl he has no intention of sleeping with later. Maybe he'd be the same if he was here with another guy. Nate doesn't have friends. He has girls he has sex with at parties, and that's it.

"Classes ended. Only exams left," he says, his words seeming too loud in the quiet.

I refuse to just keep nodding, so I say, "I'm taking them when I get out."

"They're making you take exams? Seriously? That's fucked up."

"No. They said I could skip, take the grades I had currently, but I want to take them."

"Are your grades bad?"

"I'm holding all As, I think. I study with Grace now, so my grades went up."

He slides the chair closer to my bed and sits down before

he says, "Your dad must love that. Do you remember when he had his 'your duty' motivational chart?"

I make my voice low like my father's and say, "Verses inspire children." I can't keep a straight face as I repeat my father's reply when Nate's mother suggested that ice cream might be a good reward. He'd presented me with this awful laminated poster he'd made; the columns and rows listed my duties and reasons for doing them. It was one of the least effective parenting tools he'd tried.

"Not as much as sugar," Nate says lightly, and just like that, my awkwardness vanishes. It may have been years since we were friends, but we still know each other. That makes all the difference.

It's silent, but not awkwardly so, as he pulls an apple out of his bag. He holds it out to me, and I shake my head. "I'm good. Thanks."

He examines it as he says, "So poor Piper and the minions are beside themselves that you can't have visitors."

"*Piper* talked to you?"

"In public? Not likely. She watches me—kind of like you do—at parties and when she doesn't think anyone notices, but she hasn't spoken to me in public in years. None of them do anymore." He shrugs like it doesn't hurt, but I know better. "I still hear people talking, and Piper's never exactly been known for being *quiet*."

Talking to Nate is different from talking to most people. Almost everyone keeps to the rules about Unspoken Things.

It's a longstanding tradition in the South. Unpleasantness is best not discussed; delicate matters are hinted at, but not spoken. Nate and Grace are the only people I know who ignore those rules.

"She's a good person."

"Who thinks that you can't have visitors," he reiterates.

"I didn't want to hurt her feelings."

"She has feelings? This is the same Piper I know, right? Gossipy, perfect Piper?"

I frown at him. "We've been friends my whole life. Unlike *some* people, she's never turned her back on me."

"You're the rightful wearer of the crown she thinks sits on her obnoxious head. You don't want her here when you need people. Why do you even hang out with her?"

"She's my *friend*, Nate. I just didn't want her to see . . . I'm not ready for people to know how much I . . ."

Nate shakes his head as he peels a sticker off his apple. "You're still gorgeous, Eva."

I stare at him, blinking away tears, and in as steady a voice as I can manage say, "Don't lie."

"Jesus, Eva, you think you stopped being gorgeous because of a few cuts? Are you mental?"

"It's more than a few cuts, Nate."

He shakes his head, stands, and leans close to me. The apple he's holding drops onto the bed. "You're gorgeous. Trust me: I'm *not* going to start lying to you. I never lied to you—not when we were kids and definitely not now."

I'm looking at him, our faces inches apart, and I don't see a single hint of deceit. I don't get it. I've *seen* a mirror. I know that there are more than a "few cuts" on my face. "Are you kidding?"

"No. I think you're beautiful. You always have been, even when you were sopping wet from falling into the creek." He's still face-to-face with me, and he leans in and kisses my forehead. "Sorry I upset you, but I'm not taking it back. You're smart and beautiful, and only a fool wouldn't notice that."

"We may need to get you glasses," I murmur after he straightens.

He snorts and picks his apple up again. "My vision's just fine."

"So you're calling *me* a fool?"

"If the dunce hat fits . . ." He shrugs and sits back down.

I smile at him. Being complimented by Nate does good things for my mood.

It also makes me feel less crazy about what I'm about to do. "Can you do me a favor?"

"Sure. What do you need?"

I know the things I saw about him dying—that vision was just a hallucination, but I'll still feel better if I say something. "Just promise me that you won't drive on Old Salem without first checking that you have your phone."

"Okay." He drags the word out a little and looks at me like his agreement is also a question.

It's silly, and I'm sure it's a combination of my brain injury and the things the detective got me thinking. "The person that hit me that night might have seen me. It might not have been an accident."

Nate stiffens. "So you think it was on purpose?"

"Maybe. The detective wasn't sure, and I know it sounds crazy, but so does getting run over." I try to shrug like I'm not obsessing on the whole thing. "I just want you to be careful too."

He shrugs. "No problem. I'll promise you not to go to Old Salem without checking for my phone if you promise *me* that you won't walk home in the dark again."

"I'm not going to be walking anywhere. I'm on crutches," I point out.

"Not forever." He pulls out his phone. "Give me your number. I'll call you so you can add me to your contacts. Then, if you ever need a ride again, you can reach me."

When I don't reply, he adds, "I'll always have my phone with me since I just promised you could call me."

I grab my phone. "What's your number?"

I tap it in as he tells me, and then send him a quick text that says only, "Hi."

"Call or text if you need me," he replies.

I nod, and maybe it's silly, but I don't want him to think I'm foolish. "I did call Robert, you know. I didn't want to bother Grace, and my parents were away, but it wasn't that I *planned* to walk home in the dark. It was still dusk."

Nate goes so still that it's unnerving. "Baucom stranded you?"

I wish I could retract my statement. "He was busy or forgot. It's not like we're connected at the hip."

"Did he say that?"

"No."

"What did he say?"

"Nothing." I shrug. "I haven't really brought it up. He forgot or whatever, and I walked, and there was an accident, and . . ." I lift my hands in a what-can-you-do gesture. I know I'm ignoring the whole Robert situation, but I don't want to deal with it. Maybe he was going to dump me but now he can't. Maybe he's waiting to see what I say or what I look like or . . . I don't know. It'll work out though. We'll stay together or go back to being friends. In a town this small, that's just what happens. It's all very civilized.

Nate just stares at me, and I can tell that there are a dozen thoughts he's weighing and deciding not to say. I feel guilty. I get like that, guilty, when people look hurt or upset. I think it's why my parents think I can handle everything myself: I simply don't want to trouble anyone.

"It's not his fault," I say quietly. "I could have called someone else. I didn't. Neither of us knew some lunatic was going to smash his car into me."

The look on Nate's face isn't quite disdain, but it's close. "I don't want to argue with you. I just think you deserve to be treated . . . right."

When Nate sits silently for several moments, I murmur, "Thank you."

He smiles when my hand covers his.

I wait, fearing that I'll have another hallucination. I don't. Instead, I get Nate Bouchet looking at me with interest in his eyes. I remind myself that I have a boyfriend, but a little voice inside me also reminds me that Robert hasn't even asked to visit.

"I'm glad you're here," Nate says. He frowns. "That sounds wrong. I mean, I'm not glad you're *here*, just that it's nice to see you."

I almost laugh. I've looked in the mirror; I know what I look like now. I take my hand away from his and slide my fingertips over the blanket.

"Don't." He grabs my hand, and this time, everything is different.

The car swerves toward me, and I have to go off the road to avoid impact. I feel the truck dip and jerk as the front wheel hits the ditch. I'm braking, hoping the brakes don't lock up, praying I don't go into a spin, and regretting the lack of airbags. My brain is racing, rolling into thoughts that seem out of place. I wasn't going fast enough that the accident will be fatal, but I don't have time to be without wheels.

It's dark out, and there are no streetlights on Old Salem Road, but I know the area well enough after driving it every day the past year and a half. It's wooded along the road, but not thick. The front of the truck clips a tree, but it's only a sapling. I start to swerve farther only to jolt to a stop as I smash into a much larger tree.

After a moment, I unbuckle my belt, and shakily push open the door. I shiver as I stand outside my truck. My phone is in my hand, but before I can call anyone, a sharp pain in my stomach makes me bend over. The stomach cramps become bad enough that I stumble and clutch the door frame of my truck. I touch my stomach. I don't feel blood, but that doesn't mean I'm uninjured. Internal bleeding can be far worse.

My mouth feels like it's filled with something hot and sour. I'm not throwing up. Yet. My heart feels too fast.

A car pulls up in front of me, and I wonder if it's the car that ran me off the road or someone who saw the accident. The headlights shine in my face so I can't see who's in the car. There aren't a lot of people who drive along Old Salem Road, but there are a few houses and the reservoir.

The lights make the person getting out of the car look like a silhouette. He's not a huge man. I can tell that. Although he could be a bigger woman. . . . I open my mouth to speak, but instead puke all over the seat of my truck. Something's wrong.

"I'm hurt," I force out of lips that feel oddly numb. It's not that cold, but numb is the best word I know for this feeling. It's kind of like that tingling when you drink too much but aren't blacking out yet. I wasn't drinking, haven't in over a year. Hiding in a keg or bottle isn't going to make anything better, and I need to be strong for Aaron.

The person from the car is beside me, but he—or she—isn't speaking. I can see jeans and tennis shoes, but when I look up, I can't see a face. It's there, but I can't focus on any details. It's like a white fuzzy space where the features should be. My eyes can't focus there.

I'm shaking, and I think that maybe it wasn't the cold

making me shiver when I got out of the truck. The person takes my phone, and I'm grateful that he or she is going to help me call for help.

"Call my mom," I say.

My legs are shaking too, and I hit the ground. I'm sitting in a puddle of vomit. The person opens a bottle of what looks like Mad Dog 20/20, grabs my chin with a gloved hand, and tilts my head back. The alcohol pours into my mouth faster than I can swallow, and it spills down my shirt.

He takes my hand and wraps it around the bottle, and my muscles are too weak to put up much of a fight. I try, but it's about as effective as a toddler resisting a parent. My phone hits the asphalt beside me hard enough that the screen cracks, and I watch a blurry shape come down on it to stomp on it.

"Eva?" His voice, Nate's voice, draws me back into this moment. I am shaking all over, so cold that I can't speak at first. I don't know how or why I hallucinate like this, but I feel like my whole body is icy when it happens.

I yank my hand away from Nate.

"I'm sorry. I don't know what I did, but I'm sorry." Nate folds his hands together, pointedly not touching me now, and asks, "Is it the hand sanitizer? It burns in cuts. I know that. I just wasn't thinking."

"No."

After a few quiet moments pass, Nate says, "You're shaking."

"I'm okay," I lie.

It's not like I have any other options that make sense.

How do I say "either I'm hallucinating or I somehow saw your death"? I can't. I'm not overly superstitious, but I've always sort of thought that it might not be a bad idea to go along with the ones that are easy to manage. I don't step on dead folks' graves; I don't walk under ladders. I toss a pinch of salt over my shoulder to avoid bad luck; I only pick up pennies on the sidewalk if they're faceup. I'm not very fond of Friday the thirteenth, or really any thirteens, and I know that someday when I get married I will be wearing something borrowed, something blue, something old, and something new. For now, I stay clear of catching any bouquets at weddings, *but* I do stand in the group of girls and women. I may not be ready, but I don't want to risk being an old maid either.

My mind is still running over my tiny harmless superstitions when Nate asks, "Do you need a nurse?"

"No." I sniffle, and he hands me the box of tissues. I dab at the tears on my face, wincing a little as I get too near one of the unstitched cuts.

"Okaaay. . . . Tell me what's going on here because you were shivering and staring blankly, and right now, you look like you've been out on the slopes too long." He pulls off his hoodie and puts it on my lap like a blanket.

I smile at him and reach out to touch his hand, but he pulls back before I do.

"Eva, you need to tell the doctors if—"

"It's okay," I interrupt. "They know."

I repeat the lie again because I don't know what else to say.

I'm not okay. I'm hallucinating, scarred, and in a wheelchair. I'm really, really not okay.

We sit quietly for a moment until Nate says, "Do you want to turn on the news?"

"If you want."

Nate rolls his eyes. "I bet you still watch it for hours."

"Whatever." I can't argue though. It's true. I don't know why I like the news so much, but I follow bunches of news feeds online, and since I've been in here, I've watched everything from CNN to the Weather Channel to the local news on WRAL—even though it was mostly about the Raleigh–Durham area.

Nate reaches over and pushes some buttons on the remote, and the words fill the room. I'm not really watching it—Nate distracts me by simply breathing—but then I hear: ". . . and over in Jessup, seventeen-year-old Michelle 'Micki' Adams was killed in a car crash in the Jackson Road area. The accident happened early this morning when Adams' car overturned after going over an embankment. Indications here at the site"—the camera pans around the area, where skid marks are visible, and small bits of debris from the accident glitter in the sun—"are that Adams attempted to stop her descent after what appears to be a collision with an unknown car, but was unable to do so. She was rushed to Mercy Hospital in Durham, but was pronounced dead on arrival at 4:41 a.m., a spokesman for the hospital said. Police officials say that an investigation is ongoing, but are not commenting further at this time."

"No!" My hand tightens on his. Tears race down my cheeks. We've known Micki since we were in elementary school.

"Adams is the second Jessup teenager who has been rushed to Mercy Hospital in recent weeks. Eva Elizabeth Tilling, daughter of winery heiress Elizabeth Tilling née Cooper, was—" The broadcast cuts off abruptly as Nate clicks the remote again, stopping the horrible words.

We sit quietly for a moment. Micki is dead.

"I can't believe she's gone." Nate looks up and meets my eyes before he continues, "When we were in sixth grade . . . we were at a school dance, and afterwards, both of our parents were late. We were the only two left, and the chaperone went outside. I kissed her. Micki was my first real kiss."

"I know," I say just as quietly. "*Everyone* knew."

"Oh."

"Micki was so excited. Nathaniel freaking Bouchet kissed her." I do smile at the memory now. Thinking about that Micki—the one who was alive—is better. We weren't friends, but we talked. She was obsessed with her reputation, and it made her almost deferential to me. I didn't like it.

I'm not sure if Nate has noticed how much Micki has changed since then, and even though she still probably thought Nate was gorgeous, she wouldn't have kissed him now. I don't mention any of that. There's no reason to speak ill of the dead. All I say now is "She was the envy of half the class when you kissed her."

He frowns. "Why?"

"You were *cute*, Nate. Girls noticed. Micki had managed something that the others hadn't yet."

"I just can't believe she's gone."

"She's not gone. She's dead."

Nate nods.

Quietly, I ask, "Do you think it was an accident?"

"Maybe."

"She could've lost control or fallen asleep, but"—I falter, and my voice has an edge to it now—"I don't think it was an accident."

"So you think it's related to your accident like they implied?"

That's the question. If they're right, someone really did try to kill me—and they did kill Micki. This kind of thing doesn't happen in Jessup. There are crimes, but mostly mailbox baseball or drunk driving or fights. No one gets *murdered*. There are shootings and other real crimes in Raleigh and in Durham. There are drugs, muggings, and murders. Jessup is different though. Jessup is safe; it's like the town the '50s forgot.

Quietly, I say, "I don't know for sure. Newscasters always try to tie things together to make a story more sensational."

The room seems too quiet now, but I'm not sure what to say or do. Someone we know died. Someone might have tried to kill me. Those aren't thoughts that make conversation flow.

"Do you need to leave?" I ask after several silent minutes.

"Do you want me to?"

"No." I pause, swallow, and stare down at my hands before

saying, "I want you to hold me. It's probably stupid, and I know I'm safe, but I'm scared."

He stands and bends toward me, but then stops. "I don't want to hurt you."

I think he means my cuts and bruises, but it sounds like he means more than that. Either way, I catch his hand and pull him closer. He kneels beside me on the bed, and I rest my head against his chest as he hugs me carefully.

"Let me tell Nora that I'll be here, tell her about Micki, and then I'll stay for a while. Aaron will understand if I'm away for a couple hours."

Reluctantly, I release him.

He stands and leaves as soon as I whisper, "Okay."

While he's gone, my nurse comes in and helps me get out of bed and onto crutches. It's a very slow process, but it lets me have a few moments of mobility for things like going to the bathroom. I still ache in a lot of places, but I need to be able to do this in order to be released from the hospital. I'll have a wheelchair, but for a quick trip to the bathroom this is better.

I use the bathroom and brush my teeth. I'm back in the bed, and he hasn't returned yet—and it feels weird to be waiting in my bed for Nate. I tell myself that since the head of the hospital bed is raised, it's sort of like sitting on a recliner, but regardless of how it's shaped right now, it's still a bed, and Nate is still a boy.

He walks into the room, but he stops beside the edge of the bed. It doesn't make it any less awkward. I pat the space beside me, and he sits so his feet dangle over the edge. He's in a half-turned position, like he's trying not to be all the way in the bed.

"Put your feet up, too."

He is silent, but he does as I suggest.

"If you don't want to hold me, it's okay. It's probably weird. I just . . ." I shake my head. "I shouldn't have asked."

"It's fine." He moves closer.

I try to reach out to him rather than let him touch me first. The hallucinations seem to come when people touch my bare skin. I can't handle another episode, not tonight. I'm not fast enough to touch him first though, and his fingertips brush my shoulder. I brace myself, but nothing happens.

When I flinch, he tenses, arm not quite around my shoulders. "What?"

I look at him and see the wariness in his eyes. Rather than lie or admit my hallucinations, I reach up and grab his hand. After I pull his arm more firmly around me, I settle against him and feel safer immediately.

I feel guilty for it. Micki's dead. I shouldn't be thinking about how much safer I feel in Nate's arms.

After a few minutes, I glance at him and find him looking at me curiously. I reach up to touch his face. I watch him tense as I cup his face with my hand. It's sheer foolishness on my part, but I let my thumb stroke across his cheek.

He swallows, and I feel his throat muscles move under my fingertips. "What are you doing?"

"Touching skin that isn't covered with scars."

Although he doesn't pull away, he doesn't move toward me either.

After a few moments, I lower my hand. "Sorry."

"*I'm* fine with it," he says, but he still shifts a little farther away. "Baucom might not be though."

"No," I admit. "Robert wouldn't like it."

"Right." Nate moves so there is a gap between us.

I hate this. I don't want to talk about Robert or deaths or scars. I want to be normal for a minute. I want to be okay. I move closer to the boy who was my best friend for years, the boy I've *missed*, and whisper, "Don't move."

"Robert—"

"I'll warn you before I tell Robert I'm sleeping with the Jessup man-slut."

"You're *what*? Eva, that's not—"

"Hush." Offering him my most innocent look, I say, "I'm going to sleep. You're here. Ergo, sleeping with the man-slut."

"Jesus, Eva. You can't say things like that."

I put my hand over his mouth. "Shh. Sleeping now. I'll let you know if you live up to your reputation, although so far, I'm not seeing what all the fuss was about." I close my eyes. There's a lot wrong right now, far more than ever in my life, but I feel safer and *happier* because Nate's with me.

DAY 9: "THE SLEEPOVER"

Eva

"Miss Tilling?" My night nurse, Linda, is standing beside the bed.

I'm used to the nurses waking me in the night for vitals, so finding a nurse beside me isn't odd. What *is* odd is the body I'm curled against. Nate is still here, one arm wrapped around me holding me to his side. Worse yet, my hand is splayed out on his chest *under* his shirt. He hadn't put his hoodie back on, and his T-shirt rode up at some point, and I can see his bare stomach. If Linda wasn't watching me so studiously, I might take a minute to appreciate the sight, but she is watching.

I remove my hand from where it rests against his skin and hold it up to motion the nurse to wait. Then, carefully so I don't wake him yet, I move my leg off Nate, too. I'd rather he not know how I sprawled on top of him in our sleep.

He makes a grumbling noise when I remove my hand and my leg from his body, but he doesn't wake.

Silently, I extend my arm to her so she can check my blood pressure and pulse. Her lips purse, and I realize that she's about to go on my very short list of nurses I *don't* like. So far, almost every nurse here at Mercy has been amazing. Maybe it's because they work in Pediatrics; it takes a bit of extra awesomeness to work with sick kids.

After she finishes the rest of her check, she says, "Nate can't stay here."

It startles me a little that she knows his name, but he did say that his brother had been here a few times. It sucks that any kid has been sick often enough that the nurses know his family members. It also improves my opinion of Linda that she takes the time to learn that information.

"Boyfriends aren't—"

"Friends," I interrupt, a little too loudly. "He's my *friend*."

Nate rolls me back into his arms and trails his hand up my spine before he opens his eyes and blinks at me. He clears his throat before asking, "What time is it?"

Linda takes her gloves off and drops them into the wastebasket. "Almost midnight."

"Shit, Aaron—"

"Is fine." She softens a little more. "He's asleep. Andy played checkers with him and read a little. He knows you're here if he needs you. He's fine."

"Andy's his nurse tonight?" Nate asks.

He's still holding me, and it feels a lot less comfortable now that we're both awake and talking to my nurse. She's watching us with blatant curiosity, and it makes me decide to pull away from Nate. We might not be in Jessup right now, but nurses are as likely to gossip as anyone else—or, worse yet, tell my parents. The last thing Nate needs is a "talking to" from my father.

"A friend of ours died today," I say, drawing both of their gazes to me. "Nate and I were just sad and . . . we fell asleep. She was in an accident, and now . . ."

"Oh, sweetie, I'm sorry." She reaches out to touch me, and I flinch away before she can.

"Gloves!" I blurt. "The doctor said gloves so no one risks getting sick or . . . I mean, I'm *not* sick, but what if one of my cuts bled or . . . what if you had a cold you didn't know about . . . or something."

Neither Nate nor Linda points out that I'm babbling. Linda nods and repeats, "I'm sorry." I'm not sure if she's apologizing for reaching out without gloves or for what I said about Micki's death.

For a moment, no one speaks, but then Linda gently says, "Nate still can't stay in here." She looks at him and adds, "Stop by the desk so I know you've left Miss Tilling's room. Boyfriend or not, you can't sleep in her bed."

And then she turns and leaves the room. She doesn't latch the door behind her or even close it the whole way. I wonder if he feels as awkward as I do.

"I guess your reputation made it all the way to Durham," I

tease to hide my discomfort.

"Or they know that you're the daughter of Elizabeth Cooper-Tilling," he says in a less-joking tone. "I can't imagine Reverend Tilling or your father would approve of me sleeping with you . . . even if it was only sleep."

I cringe at the thought of my parents knowing that Nate slept here. "I'm sorry. If they find out, I can explain it."

Even though they're pretty hands-off on the parenting, I'm expected to follow the rules—those implied and those stated. I don't always. I've been to more than a few of the same parties Nate attends, and I slept with Robert with no intention of marrying him. I've always been careful not to get a reputation though, and I've never dated anyone who didn't go to church. I don't draw attention to myself, not academically or socially. Taking up with Nathaniel Bouchet would raise a lot of brows and lower a lot of voices.

He's said nothing, so I take a deep breath. "Still friends?"

He frowns before he pulls me closer. "Even if I was sure they would know I slept here, I'd still have stayed." His lips graze my temple, and he whispers, "You're worth the trouble, Eva."

I can't speak.

He stays holding me for a moment longer, and then he releases me and stands. As he moves away from me, I'm once more grateful for the darkened room. Hopefully, it hides the way I'm watching him. If we're going to manage to be friends, I can't let his words mean more than they should.

He rubs his hair, as if to smooth it down, and straightens his rumpled shirt. He doesn't meet my gaze as he does this, and I have a half-present hope that he's noticed me as more than a friend. Just as quickly as the thought forms, I dismiss it: I can't imagine anyone is ever going to find me attractive once they look at the scars and red lines that divide my face like an oddly drawn map.

"See you tomorrow?" he asks.

"I should be going home." I force my voice to sound as casual as I can make it. I don't want to assume he'll visit *there*.

"And . . . ?"

"I don't know."

"Okay." He gives me a little half wave and heads to the door.

Once he's gone, I sigh. I'm pretty sure that if not for the hospital part of the evening, Robert would consider tonight cheating. I could point out the truth: nothing happened, and I'm not Nate's type anyhow—especially now that I have a slashed-up face. It wouldn't matter. I was draped over the guy every boy at school thinks is a threat; that *would* be reason enough for Robert to break up with me.

I need to talk to him and soon, not just about Nate, but also about why he isn't visiting and where he was the night of the accident.

DAY 10: "THE PARENTS"

Eva

WHEN MY PARENTS WALK into my hospital room the next day, I'm a jumble of emotions. Micki is dead; Nate held me when I slept; I'm getting out of the hospital; my parents are seeing my scars. There's too much feeling wrapped up tightly inside me right now. My head throbs; my eyes fill with tears.

My father stands at the doorway, staring at me. His face is unreadable.

"Hi, Dad." I look away before my tears fall. "Hi, Mom."

My mother comes over, starts to lean closer, but then stops and kisses the air above my head. Quietly, she whispers, "I was so scared. I wish we could've been here sooner."

"I'm fine," I assure her as she straightens. "I told you that."

"Right." She nods, steps farther back, and folds her hands together. She's clenching them so tightly that her knuckles whiten. "I'll go to the nurses' station and tell them we're ready. I'm sure there are forms to sign."

Once the door closes behind her, my father lowers himself to the chair by the bed. He reaches out to touch me, and I don't think anything of it until his hand brushes against my cheek, and I fall.

I don't think I've ever been this scared. No, that's not true. When Lizzy told me she was pregnant, I was petrified. Her father didn't even know we were dating, and here we were with this to tell him. He could send her away, give my baby away. If he had suggested that, I'm not sure what Lizzy would have done. I smile thinking of her shock when I told her we should get married. I'm not sure how she could've thought I'd say anything else.

That was different though. That was the sort of fear that came from not being ready. I'm ready for this. I have been for months. Being ready doesn't mean death stops being scary, just that the fear isn't crippling.

The machines beside me beep and hiss. I wish I wasn't alone right now. I could let go then. I can't yet. Not until they get here. Lizzy and Eva will be hurt if they're not here to say good-bye.

A nurse comes in to check on me, but I keep my eyes closed. I wonder what it was like for Eva when she was in here after the accident. I should've been there. Lizzy wanted to go, but we couldn't get a flight.

The door opens again, and I realize that I was drifting again. "Lizzy?"

"I'm right here, Daniel."

She's walking toward me. Eva is behind her, but her little

ones aren't with her. I suspect they're in the hall with their father.
Even though I'm still sure he's not good enough for my baby girl,
he seems to make her happy.

I smile, and then I let go.

I waited, but I'm so tired. So very tired.

I gasp, and my father jerks his hand away.

"Eva!"

"Cold," I say, trying to minimize my shivering. "Sorry."
I smile, a nothing-to-worry-about smile. This hallucination
thing has happened frequently enough that I feel like I should
tell someone, but . . . not today. My parents are here to take me
home. They've pulled some sort of strings to get me at-home
examinations, and I'm afraid that if I tell anyone, I'll be staying
right where I am instead.

"Did I hurt you?" my father asks, and I stare at him,
reminding myself that he is not dying, but here at my bedside.
My heart still hurts. We aren't as close as I want, but he's still
my daddy. He's the one who taught me to ride a bike—and the
one who helped me hide my very bloody knees when I thought
I was more capable than I really was.

Tears are once more racing down my face. I really need
to get a handle on this crying problem, too. I force myself to
keep from chattering my teeth. I can't tell him. I can't tell anyone without sounding like I'm crazy, sick, or having weird side
effects. None of those things would get me home and back to
a normal life—or at least as normal as possible now that I look
like a failed science experiment.

"I was going to hug you and made the mistake of moving

my arm wrong," I lie. This is what we do now: we take turns lying to avoid hurting each other. I add a sort of truth to ease my guilt: "My ribs are still sore."

I slowly reach out to touch *his* arm.

"I'm glad you're home," I tell him, and this isn't a lie at all.

"We should've been here sooner. Your mother was ready to charter a boat, but that wouldn't have been any faster. I think the people at the airport were starting to draw straws to see who had to talk to us; we were there constantly."

"I told you I was fine. The Yeungs were here, and I'm in a hospital with great nurses. Honestly, I have some headaches and crutches." I shake my head, and then I lie horribly. "This is not a big deal."

My father nods, and I think that he means that he hears me, not that he agrees with me. Instead of pointing out my lie, he says, "I should check and see if your mother needs help. She's not always great with paperwork."

I nod, and I wonder if he realizes that I mean the same thing when I nod: I hear you, not I agree with you. I have a sudden almost crippling need to keep him here a little longer. "Dad? Wait, please."

"Do you need a nurse or—"

"No," I interrupt him, something I would never do typically, but this isn't an average day. "Thanks for keeping some of the news theories from Mom. I know you did, and I'm glad. I didn't want to upset her."

He nods. "She'll hear the rest soon enough now that we're

back. She'll hear about the Adams girl, and . . ." His words fade, and I know we're both thinking about the rest of that sentence, about the possibility that my accident wasn't an accident.

I mock-sigh to try to make things lighter and tell him, "Luckily, she still buys into that 'watching the news isn't lady-like' story that Grandfather Cooper fed her."

He smiles a little, and I feel a wash of relief that the hurt in his eyes is gone. "Are you okay while I go check on her?"

"Go ahead."

I think about my hallucinations, briefly considering the idea that they're real. I'm not sure if it would be a gift or a curse.

It's certainly not something I want to tell people about, but I also—for the first time—want to convince people to touch me, to test it, to see how it works. There seems to be a pattern to it. If there *is* a pattern, maybe I can control it.

I also wonder why I can't recognize any faces in the visions. I don't understand why all the faces are blurry to me—or why I feel like I'm actually *inside* another body.

Maybe the episodes are a combination of drug side effects and my own fears. After all, there might be a lunatic in Jessup who killed Micki and tried to kill me. That makes far more sense than the other thought, annoying, like an itch in the back of my mind. It makes far more sense than the idea that what I'm seeing is real.

That thought makes me feel sick, like I want to vomit, and I start to shiver.

I'm still queasy when my parents and Kelli come into the room. I'm glad she's my nurse today. Seeing her somehow makes me feel a little better. As a nurse, she deals with some pretty awful stuff, but she handles it and isn't falling apart like I want to right now. I want to be like her.

"Ready to get out of here?" She wheels the chair up to the bed and puts the brakes on so it doesn't slide when I go to get in it. "I know you're getting good with the crutches, but discharge requires the chariot."

"No problem." I return her smile.

Both of my parents step forward as I start to slide myself to the edge of the bed. My father reaches a hand out to rest on my mother's back without even looking at her. She steadies at his touch, but she still looks like she's strung too tightly and the slightest thing will cause her to snap.

"Can you pack up the last of my things, Mom?"

She seems to relax a little at having a task to focus on instead of watching me. I don't have a lot to collect, but there are a few odds and ends that need to be shoved into the box against the wall.

My father picks up the bag of clothes. His attention flits between us, but he says nothing as he watches me lower my foot, take my crutches, and move to the wheelchair. He accepts the first crutch as I release it to lower myself into the wheelchair, and then takes the second now that I'm in the chair. Kelli arranges my skirt over my cast, and I tuck the rest under my unbroken leg.

"Doing okay?" Kelli asks.

"So far, so good."

She nods. "You're going to hurt after the ride home. I know you don't like the pain medication, but if you need it, don't refuse it this time. There's a prescription for it in your papers and some pills in the bag for tonight."

"I won't take them."

"What medication?" My mother's voice is a little higher than normal. "You're refusing medication? The doctors have good reasons to prescribe the things they do." She folds her arms and looks at Kelli. "What is she to take?"

Soothingly, Kelli assures my mother, "The pain pills are PRN—so they are only administered when she requests them. She only needs them if the pain is unmanageable. The details are all in her discharge papers."

"I take everything that's *required*. It's the other stuff I skip; it makes my head feel fuzzy."

"Are you allergic to it? Why don't they prescribe something else then?" She's glaring at Kelli now. The odds and ends are already in the box at my mother's feet. She's quicker than I expected.

"No," I say as calmly as I can. "I'm not allergic. Narcotics have that side effect. They make you sleepy and slow, and I don't like it."

My father intervenes before she gets more upset. "It's fine, Elizabeth. We'll fill the prescription, and if she needs it, we have it. If she doesn't, we can throw it out." He catches my eye, and I know not to argue about picking the pills up. I'm fairly sure he also knows not to try to make me take them.

That's my father: the king of not making waves.

They walk quietly through the hall as Kelli wheels me to the elevator. Quietly, she tells me, "The shift supervisor told her about your friend's sleepover."

I wince, and Kelli gives me a sympathetic look. I'm not sure whether it's worse for my mother to know that Nate slept in my bed or that he did so because Micki died, and I was afraid. I'm not bringing it up either way.

We stop in the lobby, just inside the main door, while my father goes to get the car. It's a tense silence as my mother and Kelli both watch me—and each other. I let out a sigh of relief when my father drives up in front of the lobby doors.

Unfortunately, getting into the car is more challenging than I'd like. My parents debate whether it's better for me to be in the front seat or the back. The front reclines, but if I sit sideways in the back, I can stretch my leg out and keep it from hanging down. Kelli suggests that the latter is a better plan, and adds in a low voice, "I know you hate the pills, Eva, but you ought to take one today. No matter how carefully he drives, you'll hurt."

About ninety minutes into the drive, I decide she might have had a point. I haven't hurt all over like this in days. It sucks, but once I get home, I'll be more comfortable, and the food is certainly better.

Every bump and dip in the road brings tears of pain to my

eyes. I feel every bruise, the throbbing in my leg, and the ten-
derness in my ribs. My head aches too, and that seems worse
than all the rest.

By the time we get home, I hurt so much that my father
carries me up to my room. I hadn't thought about stairs, and
I'm in no shape to think about them right now. I wrap my arms
around my father and hope that I'm not going to throw up from
pain. Right now, I'm *beyond* willing to take one of those stupid
brain-blurring pills. If I don't, I'm not sure I'll be able to sleep.
My leg feels like it has a pulse of its own, and my head hurts to
the point that vomiting seems like a distinct possibility.

Once I'm settled with the medicine in hand, I realize how
much softer my bed is. I'd adjusted to the hospital bed, but
now that I'm home, I'm grateful to be on my absurdly soft mat-
tress with my down comforter and stack of pillows.

My mother fusses around me until my father convinces her
that what I need most is a nap. It's a little disconcerting seeing
them like this, but between the pills and general exhaustion,
I'm not going to be able to stay awake to ponder it. "I'm okay,"
I assure them. "Really. I'm fine."

My father says nothing, but my mother tucks the covers
around me like I'm a small child and says, "We'll be downstairs. Text if you need us for anything."

And that's all there is before I'm asleep.

DAY 10: "THE STALKER"

Judge

I DRIVE PAST HER house as I have for months, not so often that anyone would notice, but frequently enough to keep myself calm. Seeing a glimpse of her has always filled me with a sort of peace that is too hard to find. These past days while she was in the hospital, I had to pretend that she was inside, that there was a chance she could come to the window. Sometimes, though, I had to drive to the hospital in Durham. Being so far away from her for this many days has been more difficult than I could've imagined. I'm glad she didn't die. I'm not sure how I'll cope if she still has to die. The fear of her loss cripples me briefly, and I know that I have to do a good job. She *has* to understand the messages, and she *has* to obey them. Anything less will mean I have to finish killing her. I don't want that. I've never wanted that. She's made for me, my perfect match.

"And I was made for you," I tell her as I glance at the window of her room.

The curtains are pulled, and she's on crutches now, so I know she's not going to see me, but surely she feels my presence out here. Surely, she feels calmed by my closeness even if she doesn't know *why*. I imagine it, picturing her face turning toward the window in awe.

I do this for both of us. No one will ever know her the way I do.

They talk about her at school, repeating every detail as if They know her. I listen. It's all I can do right now. Eventually, They'll all find out about us, and They'll remember me listening quietly while They guessed and pretended to know things. They'll be ashamed at how They discussed the night I almost sacrificed her. They know nothing. No one does.

Someday when we are together as we were meant to be, I'll tell her about that night. I'll hold her in my arms, and she'll look at me rapturously as I tell how hard it was that night, how my heart hurt thinking I'd lost her forever, how my chest tightened when her body fell against the hood of the car. I'll tell her how grateful we should be that the Lord chose to save her. I don't know if she'll remember anything, but I'll tell her. She'll rest her head against my chest, and I'll kiss her hair when I tell her that she was spared so we can be as we were meant to be.

All of my fears are quieted as I picture the future. This is what I feel when we are together. Her proximity saves me.

The intersection near her house is empty, so I pause a little longer. Seeing her house in my rearview mirror is like a closing prayer. I can pause and exhale, and the grace of the moment will carry me through the day ahead. Everything is right in this moment.

The past week has been harder because I didn't have those rare flashes of togetherness at school. There, we talk in the corridors. Sometimes, it's only a smile, but I can tell by the way she smiles at me that she feels the special connection we share. The first time I was shocked, but over the past year, I've felt our love grow. She knows me, knows things that no one else would understand. Someday They will know about how far I've gone to protect and cherish Eva.

"Soon," I whisper.

DAY 11: "THE EX-BOYFRIEND"

Eva

I WAKE AT HOME, in my own bed, and it makes me feel closer to normal. I'm still in bed trying to decide if I'm ready to face the world when Nate texts to ask if I want company later. I do, but I'm not sure how much time I can spend with him before there's trouble with Robert.

Instead of replying to Nate, I text Robert: "I need to talk to you. Come see me."

"Exam this afternoon."

"I know. Need to talk. Now or tonight?"

After a few minutes, he replies, "Video?"

I sigh. It's better than texting, but it's not how I want to have this conversation. I want him to *want* to see me, to want to hold me, to hand me a tissue if I cry. None of that seems to matter to him. I don't want him to see my scars, but I need to see him.

"No," I text. "Come over. Am home."

After a few minutes, Robert replies, "k."

Now that he's coming, I feel a burst of panic. I wish that my face was healed enough to use cover-up. My face is still a mess of bruises and cuts, and I feel nervous about my appearance.

Now that I have a plan to talk to Robert, I reply to Nate. "I'm home. Mom knows you were at hospital with me. Sure you want to come here?"

His reply is instant: "Yes."

I can't stop the smile that his reply evokes. Nate is coming to my house. We sort out the details, and I start the laborious process of getting out of bed and downstairs. I'm only as far as returning from my bathroom when my parents walk into my room.

"Eva Elizabeth Tilling!" My mother has both hands on her hips. "What on God's green earth are you doing?"

"Umm . . . going downstairs?" I don't mean it to sound like a question, but it does.

"You're on crutches!"

My father smothers a bark of laughter at my expression or maybe at my mother's posture. "Why don't I carry you down?" He turns to Mom. "We'll be right down, Lizzy."

Once she's gone, I convince him—after a few minutes of debate—to let me try the stairs. He only agrees under the condition that he walk backward down the steps in front of me. It's a slow process, and I suspect that he's using all of his patience to do it my way instead of carrying me.

My mother scurries into the kitchen to set out breakfast, and once we are all seated, she pours fresh-squeezed juice. It's odd. We aren't the sort to have breakfasts like this. Grabbing fruit or cold cereal before I leave for school is my usual routine. Sometimes on weekends we all sit down together, but even then, Dad is typically lost in the paper or a magazine and Mom is often working on one of her to-do lists. We have a "no tech at the table" rule—so my iPod and my mother's tablet are banned—but old-fashioned pen and paper are fine. Today, there are no newspapers, magazines, or lists in sight. We sit awkwardly exchanging glances.

"Did you sleep well?" my mother asks.

"I did. Did you?"

My mother frowns. "Of course we did! We aren't injured, and you're home safe now."

My father's lips twitch briefly, not quite smiling. "I think Eva was making small talk, dear."

"Oh." She scoops fruit salad into a bowl and admits, "I'm a little distracted." She pauses, but when no one asks why, she continues, "Trying to figure out the new schedule."

"I'm fine, Mom. There's food in the fridge, and I'm good on my crutches."

She smiles at me in the way that says it's cute that I'm clueless. "I know."

I think I'm making my parents a little uncomfortable with the way I quickly reach out to touch them when they reach toward me even a little. I don't understand the hallucinations, but I *do* realize one thing—being touched seems to trigger them. I don't want to see my mother's death, and I'm not sure if I'll see my father's again if he touches me. Either way, I won't chance it. My head is pounding already.

"I have your pills," she starts.

"Tylenol is enough."

Before she can overreact, my father reminds her that they are PRN, patient requested. She's mollified, but she sets alarms in her phone for the Tylenol and the sedative they still want me to take. I'm not entirely sure how many days of her hovering at home I can handle. I'd much rather she go back to work with Dad at the winery.

After my father leaves and my mother wanders off to another part of the house, I stretch out to nap on the sofa until Robert gets here. It's possibly the least comfortable place I've slept in years, but I still manage to doze. Unfortunately, I sleep fitfully, waking expectantly several times. There are no nurses to wake me, but I think I've become accustomed to the frequent interruptions and wake as if they are still happening.

When my mother checks in on me and discovers that I'm awake, she sits primly across from me in one of the stiff but pretty floral-patterned chairs and announces, "I think the thing to do is to get your ideas for hiring a companion."

"Grace can be here some," I suggest. "You're here in the evenings."

"Eva." That's all she says, just my name, but she also gets that look—the one that says she's inflexible. I know resistance won't help this time. A companion is inevitable.

"Fine."

"Thank you." She rewards me with the smile that usually works on people, but I'm wise to my mother's seemingly innocuous ways. She's never a bulldozer like Mrs. Yeung can be, but she *is* a well-bred Southern woman. That means that she's been trained in making the world bend to her will since she was born. Her aunts and the church ladies all stepped in to help the "poor motherless dear," so she was *extra* indoctrinated into the rules of being a gently bred Southern lady.

"Does Robert have any plans for the summer? Or the Kennelly girl?"

"I'm not sure," I hedge. "Robert is coming over this morning."

"Good!" She beams at me and leaves again.

Right now, I sort of hate that my parents like him, deeming him "a sensible boy, just like his father and uncle." He's fine, I suppose, and being with him is nice. My family likes him, and we have fun when we go out. I owe it to the both of us to try to talk about whatever's going on instead of just ignoring it.

Maybe he just feels guilty for not answering the night of the accident or maybe he's afraid to see me when I'm injured— or maybe time apart has also made him realize that we're really not much more than friends.

I call Mom back, and with her help, I brush my hair again,

change into a nicer shirt, and even put on earrings. My lips are cracked from so long in the dry hospital air, so I've been using a lot of lip balm, but for this, I use gloss with a little color. I can't put on foundation or concealer, but I could do my eyes— if I was willing to look into a mirror. I'm not.

When he arrives, I notice that my hand is shaking. I hear his voice as my mother greets him, and I watch him saunter into the room. He's looking at me with the startling blue eyes I've missed, but the slow smile he usually gets when he sees me is missing. Instead, he's staring at me in a sort of shock, and I know that I must look worse than he expected.

"Damn, Eva!" He presses his lips closed as soon as the words are out, and I know he regrets saying it. He tries again, saying only, "How are you?"

"Better." I try not to notice that he's looking down rather than at my face. I tell myself that it's hard to blame him: I still don't like to see what I look like right now, and this is the first time he's seen my injuries. "How are exams?"

"Not horrible." He squirms in his chair. "What's up?"

There's an awkwardness that makes me want to give up and forget we tried to talk, but I need answers so I ask, "Where were you the night of the accident?"

"Eva . . ." He looks up then, meets my eyes, and immediately looks away.

That's when I realize there's another reason he won't look at me. It's not just my battered face; it's guilt. I'm ready for answers now though; I need to know, so I continue, "You didn't answer my calls or texts *after* you stood me up."

After a quiet moment, he asks, "Do you really want to do this now?"

"What don't you want me to know?"

He sighs. "You're not going to let this go, are you?" When I shake my head, he says, "I was with Amy."

"Crowne?" My voice is steady although my chest hurts. I want to scream at him, but I won't. I *can't. I am Eva Elizabeth Tilling*, I remind myself. *I don't scream or yell.* The voice in my mind sounds a lot like my mother's right now. Apparently, her lectures on propriety did sink in.

Calmly, I ask, "You were with Amy Crowne and that's why you left me waiting?"

He nods silently.

It's not that cheating hadn't occurred to me as a possibility, but really? With *her*? The girl who told everyone I was a skank, who lied and said that I wasn't a virgin when I slept with Robert, the girl who told everyone that I slept with him in the first place?

When I don't say anything, he adds, "It wasn't like I knew that not showing would lead to . . ." He lifts a hand and gestures.

"Almost dying? Being unconscious? Getting sliced up and having a broken leg?" Maybe I'm not screaming, but I've raised my voice. I sound like someone else. I'm not sure who. *I* am polite and even tempered: reasonable Eva, responsible Eva . . . but right now, I'm also cheated-on Eva.

"Eva," he starts again. I look up and meet his eyes, and he continues, "I made a mistake, but I didn't cause this. You could've called someone else. I'm sure Grace—"

"Fuck you." Tears blur my vision. I swear I've cried more in the past week than in the past year. "You could've told me you weren't coming instead of leaving me there. You could've at least texted." I wipe at my cheeks and wince at the pain. "And afterwards? You should've told me."

He looks aghast, as if I'd just suggested his father was a closet Democrat. "I didn't want to break up while you were in the hospital."

"Were you going to break up with me?"

He goes perfectly still, and I know him well enough to tell by his expression that he's debating how truthful he should be. After a moment, he says, "No, but I figured you would break up with *me*. It's not what I want; it was what I was trying to prevent. Amy threatened to tell you about us that night if I didn't. That's where I was. I was trying to convince her not to tell you."

"For how long?"

"Does it matter?" Robert's tone is evasive.

Pieces start clicking into place for me. Even as I hope I'm wrong, I say, "That's why she made such a big deal over me sleeping with you."

"I didn't want to pressure you," Robert says.

When we were dating, I *was* grateful that he wasn't trying to get in my pants. Now I understand why. "The whole time we were dating, you were sleeping with Amy?"

"No. Not the first few weeks, but . . . when Amy came up to me at the party, that one you couldn't make, it just made sense. I've always liked her, but I couldn't *date* her. My parents would be furious, especially since I was dating *you*. They think you're perfect."

"I see."

"I broke it off though. I told her the other week that we were done, but she showed up when I was getting ready to leave to meet you that night, and she was just being crazy. She's not usually like that, but she threatened to tell you, and to tell my parents what we had done. Dad would get it, but Mom would be upset. Everyone knows about Amy's past."

Despite everything, I feel bad for Amy. We aren't friends, but she doesn't deserve this any more than I do. My voice is still level when I ask, "Did you tell Amy that?"

"I did." He pauses, glances at me awkwardly, and then adds, "Just so you know, I was careful. I used a condom every time. I wouldn't risk us that way. She went on the pill, too."

"So what do you propose? I know about her now."

"I don't know. I figured you'd be yelling at me by now, but you're not. You're still *you*, just with a messed-up face now." He pauses. "I can be a better boyfriend, Eva."

My "messed-up face" hurts from how tightly I'm clenching my jaw now. Robert is an idiot. I stare at him in a sort of disconnected shock. I understand the importance of reputation, of the pressure not to be "bad," of not failing our parents. It was one of the things we had in common, but I don't get how that evolved into this mess. I can hear in his voice that he cares about Amy. There's a softness there that I'm not even sure he notices.

"What do your parents think about the accident? Did you tell them?"

Robert laughs as if I'd made a joke. "I told them I had a flat. They, umm, think I've been visiting you."

I don't need to ask where he went when he was too guilty to visit me, but lying to the Baucoms about it.

"You should apologize to Amy," I say as calmly as I can. "And me. You should apologize to me. I deserve an apology."

Robert isn't the first guy to date someone on the side, and he's certainly not the first to date a girl in secret because of her reputation, but that doesn't mean I agree with it. Jessup is still the sort of place where name and money matter too much; I know the whole world isn't like that, but our town still is. I don't want it to be like that, and I thought Robert agreed with me. Obviously, I misunderstood.

His beautiful blue eyes are wide, and I wonder if I'd have forgiven him if not for the accident. Girls forgive boys for cheating all the time. Some keep doing it as adults. Robert's dad has a long-term relationship with a colleague that Robert and his mom both know about, though no one ever mentions it. I don't want to be one of the women who thinks it's fine to "look the other way."

"I can't do this," I tell him. "We're done."

"People will think I broke up with you because of how you look," Robert says, and I'm not even shocked that his objections are about other people's perceptions. He doesn't tell me that he'll miss me or argue that we share something special.

"Tell them I broke up with you."

"Can we, umm, at least break up as friends?" Robert asks.

"Sure," I snap. It's not like there's much option in a town the size of Jessup. Our families are friends; our friends are friends. There's no way to avoid being around each other, so we'll do what everyone does after they break up: we'll put on masks and be polite. I can't start pretending today. I'm not so much hurt that we failed, but I am hurt that he cheated and lied to me. I meet his eyes and say, "We'll be friends, but I need time, Robert."

"Okay . . . I'll just say that you needed space because of the accident," Robert adds. "We're friends, and then maybe if you change your mind—"

"Good-bye, Robert." I close my eyes for a moment, and then raise my voice to say, "Mom? Can you help me upstairs? Robert is leaving." I look at him and add, "Now."

He leaves before she arrives. When Mom comes into the room, I say with as little emotion as I can manage, "Robert won't be around anymore, Mom. We broke up."

She puts her hand to her chest as she lets out a little gasp. "Just now? His mother told Jillian Dawson that he was with you every day at the hospital. We took comfort in that."

"He lied."

"Oh." She folds her hands together and waits.

"He cheated on me," I say, trying not to let my guilt and anger show. It's ridiculous that I feel guilt at all. It's not like it's my fault he cheated, but I still feel it. It's like this idea that maybe if I'd done something different, he wouldn't have cheated. I know it's not true, but logic isn't the same as emotion. Pushing my guilt away, I add, "He was cheating, and that's where he was the night of the accident—with her."

"Oh, baby!" She's off the chair and beside me in a blink.

I reach out to wrap an arm around her before she can touch me, avoiding the risk of falling into another hallucination.

She's expecting tears, but this time I'm not crying. I did that already, and I refuse to cry over Robert again. I rest my head on my mother's shoulder, and I feel an unexpected comfort at being hugged.

When she pulls back, she's wearing her Intense Focus expression, the one that scares people into agreeing with her or donating to her cause du jour. "I'm going to call Celeste right now. She needs to know what her boy did."

"No." I catch her hand in mine and squeeze. "The other girl doesn't deserve this. She's . . . not someone Mrs. Baucom would approve of."

My mother's stern expression softens. "You're nicer than I ever was. If your father had cheated on me, I'd be damned if I'd let him hide his shame."

Hearing my mother cuss always amuses me. She does it

so rarely that it makes me smile every single time it happens. "It's not about him. It's about me and about her," I clarify. "Everyone's already going to be looking at me because of the accident. I don't want more attention."

After a moment, she nods, and I loosen my grip on her hand.

She doesn't remove her hand from mine. "I won't tell Celeste he cheated, but I won't lie and say he visited at the hospital"—she reaches out with her other hand and cups my face gently—"and neither should you." Then she stands, affixes a smile, and says, "How about I get you something to eat? I had LeeAnn make up a bunch of your favorites. She left a fruit salad and a tossed salad, too."

Our cook, LeeAnn, comes in twice a week and makes a series of meals that are then labeled and stacked in the fridge. It's like having fresh home-cooked meals, and my mother seems to enjoy the illusion that she prepares them because she *does* put them in the oven or microwave herself. Plus, with LeeAnn doing the cooking the meals are healthier and tastier. My mother has the ability to tackle a lot of things, but cooking has never been one of her skills.

"Fruit salad sounds good."

She leaves and heads to the kitchen, and I can't resist the urge to text Grace immediately. I give her the quick rundown. "Robert slept with Amy. Broke up with him just now."

"Want me to beat him up?"

I smile and reply, "Let me think about it."

"Love you."

"You too." I don't know how a few short texts can make me feel so much better, but they do. Everything is less overwhelming with a good friend on my side.

DAY 11: "THE LIES"

Grace

I TRY NOT TO obsess over Eva's texts from this morning, but it's hard when I see Robert slinking through the hall with Reid and Jamie. Robert looks less arrogant than usual, or maybe that's just wishful thinking on my part. Nate is watching them, too. I shove my history book into my locker and force myself not to speak or look at them.

"Yeung," Reid says as they pass.

Robert, of course, says nothing to me, and Jamie doesn't seem bright enough to initiate conversation unless there's a keg, a drunk girl, and a dark corner. Then, he'll nod and mutter, "Want to?" Sickeningly, it seems to work for him.

I pull out my Spanish book and look at Nate again. Eva texted that she and Robert broke up, and from the way Nate is watching Robert—and the way Robert doesn't notice—I've already figured out that Robert is unaware of Eva's renewed friendship with Nate. What I can't decide is whether Nate's anger at Robert is because he's crushing on Eva and upset that she's hurt, or if he knows about the breakup already.

"My dad said that Micki's death and Eva's accident had to be caused by the same person," Piper says as she walks up to my locker with several of the others. They murmur a mix of greetings in my general direction.

"It's possible, I guess," I say. The idea isn't too much of a stretch: two teen girls from Jessup in car accidents with no witnesses? It's a little too coincidental.

"What does Eva think?" Piper doesn't add "because that's what we will think too," but I know that's her motivation. Half the girls in our class seem to share DNA with parrots. The other half smile and nod. I suspect they have opinions, but Jessup isn't a hotbed of independent thought.

"We haven't really talked about Micki," I tell them.

"Will she be home by the funeral?" Jessica Greer, one of the Piper-ettes, asks.

The others watch. Laurel Dawson and Bailey Owens whisper to each other, but they're as likely to be talking about this as shoes. CeCe Watkins seems utterly unconcerned by the drama, but she is still waiting for my answer like the others are.

"I'm not sure," I say. I don't want them to know Eva is home in case she isn't ready for a deluge of visitors. "She's doing a lot better, but . . . we haven't talked about it."

"I'll ask Robert," Piper says. "I know he's been visiting

her during the week. His mother was complaining about how much time he's spent there. She thinks he blames himself because he had a flat that night."

My mouth opens as I turn to stare at her, wondering what to say. Jessica and Bailey both nod, mutely agreeing with Piper.

"She's lucky." Piper pushes off the lockers and quickly amends, "I mean, she's not *lucky* because the accident was just horrible, but she's lucky you both care about her so much."

"Right." I nod my head.

I see Nate standing nearby. He's staring at the girls, and I realize he must have heard Piper's remarks. "I'll catch you later," I murmur, and then call out, "Hey, Nate?"

He meets my gaze, and I concentrate on looking at him instead of letting my attention drift to Piper or the other now wide-eyed girls. I'm not worried about being seen talking to him. I've never been under him, and I have *no* intention of changing that, especially since it's obvious that Eva has a thing for him. When I'm standing directly in front of him, I ask quietly, "Did you hear them?"

He tips his head slightly and then glances at Piper. "You probably shouldn't stand here too long."

"Because the Piper-ettes will think I'm chasing you?"

He nods once.

"I'm not a sycophant, so I'm not particularly concerned about what they think."

Unexpectedly, he laughs, and for a moment, I get why Eva and half the girls in school look at him like he's a god. He's beautiful when he laughs. He's still an emotional train wreck, but at least he's an attractive disaster.

"You're certainly a step up from the asshat."

"We're just friends," he says quickly.

"You and the asshat?"

Nate rolls his eyes. "You're about as funny as she is."

"You want funny? Watch this." I hook my arm through his. "Walk with me to our exam."

Once we pass the gossips, Nate looks down at me. "That's your idea of funny? Your reputation—"

"Will be just fine," I interrupt.

"You don't know what they can be like," he says in a low voice. "Amy Crowne used to be one of Piper's friends. I grew up with them. It doesn't take a minute to end up worth no more than the muck on the bottom of their shoes."

I'm a little shocked to get a glimpse of the person Eva sees. He's trying to protect me, but I don't think he realizes how much he's sharing. He was one of them. Now they don't even talk to him. Whether he says it outright or not, there's bitterness there.

"I don't care if they ignore me," I admit just as quietly. "I'm only around them because Eva's my friend. Soon I'll be applying to college, and then I'll be gone, and none of these people will be anything but vague memories."

I release his arm as we walk into the room.

"The joy of not being a native Jessupite," he says, softening the bite of his tone with a quick smile.

I watch him stalk to his seat and drop into it. The girls who aren't looking at him are staring at me with blatant curiosity on their faces.

Reid and Jamie look at me and then at Nate. He glares at them and very pointedly doesn't look at me at all. Everyone is tense after Eva's accident and Micki's death. I can't imagine that's going to get any better once they hear about Eva's renewed friendship with Nate and her breakup with Robert.

DAY 11: "THE JOB"

Eva

I'm STARTLED WHEN THE doorbell rings, and nervous when I hear Nate's voice. The awkwardness of my mother talking to Nate is enough to make me want to cringe, but he's here, and there's no way around it.

"How are your parents, Nathaniel?" she asks as they walk into the room.

"Mom's doing fine," he says.

"And your father?"

"I have no idea." Nate shrugs. "I guess he's alive. He sends child support for my brother; that's all I care about where he's concerned."

I'm sure my mother is flipping through her copious mental files to recall details about the Bouchet family. I'm not sure if Nate meant to lead the conversation into awkward areas, or if he simply didn't steer away from them. I'm almost sure he wasn't aiming to be confrontational, but as I watch him, I realize I might be wrong. His body is tensed for conflict.

"His father has another child, a little boy named Aaron," I supply helpfully.

My mother hears the unspoken words—that there is a different mother—and I can see the moment where she recalls the cause of the Bouchet divorce. She smiles politely at Nate and lets the subject drop.

"Can I get you anything to drink or eat? I was just going to bring some snacks in for Eva."

"Do you need a hand?"

"No." She pats his shoulder in that weirdly faux-affectionate way of women far older than she is and motions toward the chair across from my uncomfortable sofa. "Have a seat and visit with Eva. If you tell me what you'd like, I'll bring it in with hers. I was getting her some fruit salad, but there are sandwich fixings, too."

"I just ate, but thank you."

My mother nods. "What would you like to drink? I have sweet tea, sodas, juice, and milk."

Like any properly raised Southern boy, Nate knows not to refuse again. The first refusal is how one says "no need to go bothering over me," but a complete refusal would be an insult. He smiles at her and says, "A glass of water would be great if you don't mind."

"Lemon?"

"Whatever's easiest," he replies.

She nods and leaves us there. We're both silent as her heels click across the floor. There's an elegance to the way she moves that even seems to permeate the sound of her footsteps. I'll never be like her, but I think she's mostly come to accept that truth.

Nate sits quietly across from me. "Are you okay?"

I debate how much to tell him. "I broke up with Robert this morning because he was cheating on me. That's why he wasn't there the night of the accident."

I look up and meet Nate's eyes. He's staring at me, and I see the temper he had when we were kids. The two of us were both short-fused then, but I know that he's made as much progress as I have on that front. Right now, however, he looks like that progress is about to slip away.

"I'm okay," I add.

"Did I mention how much he didn't deserve you?" Nate asks. "I'm sorry though. Cheating is . . . my dad cheated on Mom *and* on Nora. I don't get it. Baucom will figure out that this other girl isn't worth even half of your little finger."

"She's not all bad, but he's not dating her either." I decide not to tell him outright that the girl is Amy. She has been treated as unfairly as I have. All I say is, "She's not the sort of girl one dates, apparently."

"I reserve the right to veto any future boyfriend choices, Eva." He frowns again. "Actually, I can't think of anyone in Jessup good enough for you. We may just need to veto dating in general."

"And here I was thinking that my father might have issue with us hanging out. You keep saying things like that, and Dad will be thrilled to hear that we're friends again." I smile at him. "I expected a little more rule-breaking and trouble-making. I'm starting to suspect that all the stories about you are lies."

He swallows, looks down, and then quietly says, "Sorry to disappoint you, but most of the rumors are very true, Eva."

I blush, thinking of the things I've heard.

"I was a stupid drunk. I got into too many fights and accepted ridiculous dares, *but* I stopped drinking when I figured out that I wasn't going to be able to be here for Aaron if I kept partying."

"I was teasing," I say cautiously. "I didn't mean . . . I'm sorry."

He shrugs. "Sore subject, I guess."

"There seem to be a lot of those."

"Still worth the friendship?"

"Definitely."

He nods and leans back into the chair as if he's going to find a more comfortable position by moving. I don't have the heart to tell him it's impossible. The furniture here isn't designed for comfort.

"I saw Grace this morning," he says after a moment. "She talked to me . . . in front of Piper. I tried to tell her that she shouldn't, but she hooked her arm through mine and paraded down the hall like she was escorting her prize hog to the state fair. I'm expecting to be blue-ribboned any minute now."

I smile at the image of Nate winning a "best of" category

at the fair, but then have to quickly steer my thoughts away from the things I've heard he's best at. Those are not thoughts to have about him, especially with my mother due to walk into the room any moment. Nate might not notice the lingering looks I can't seem to stop giving him, but my mother is like a bloodhound when it comes to figuring out who's interested in whom. It's one of the few things I hear my father tease her over: she predicts relationships the way some people predict the weather.

"You need to tell her not to do that again. People will think things about her, and it's"—he shifts position in his chair again—"awkward to explain to her, but I don't want people giving her trouble. She seems like a nice girl, but . . . you know how people are about girls who talk to me in public."

"You *do* know I'm not going to ignore you in public," I point out evenly.

The clatter of my mother's heels heralds her return. I don't turn to look at her; instead, I watch Nate. He tenses as she approaches, and I'm reminded how different things are from the last time he was at my house.

"Do you have summer plans, Nathaniel?" She sets the tray atop the coffee table, hands me my bowl of fruit salad, and then hands him his glass of water. A twist of lemon garnishes his glass. Even now, during her post-accident hovering, she's still a polite hostess.

Mutely, I take a bite of my fruit salad to keep from saying something regrettable.

He sits straighter as he replies, "Jobs aren't as easy to come by with my schedule limitations."

"Limitations?"

"I watch my brother when his mother needs help, but her schedule changes—sometimes at the last minute. He has CF, cystic fibrosis, which sometimes means complications." He sips his water and then carefully sets the glass on a coaster. "Sometimes he's fine though, so I have some applications in already. Nora found a summer camp last year that Aaron liked, and if he doesn't get sick, he'll go there during the day."

My mother sits in the other chair, so we are seated in a loose triangle. She's to my right, and he's to my left. The whole thing feels unsettling to me. She's brought herself a glass of sweet tea that I know from experience has enough sugar in it to make my teeth ache. Considering my sweet tooth, that's an accomplishment.

"That's good of you to help with him," my mother murmurs.

"Someone has to, and our father can't be bothered." Nate shrugs like it's not a big deal, although his tone makes it abundantly clear that it is. "My brother deserves a family, and Nora works a lot of hours so she can provide for them."

"Nate's very devoted to his brother," I interject.

My mother looks from me to Nate and smiles. "I'm not sure how I didn't put the pieces together when the nurses talked about 'Nate,' " she muses. "So you're the same young man who was there with my Eva at the hospital. After all these years, you turned up when she needed you."

"It just happened." He shrugs. "I visit Aaron, and when I saw Eva, I figured she could use a friend."

My mother sips her drink. "The nurses spoke highly of you."

This time, I can tell that it's not the uncomfortable chair that's making him squirm; it's my mother's very polite words. He was born and bred in Jessup, which means that he can see the cunning in my mother. He's obviously not sure where she's going with this yet, and neither am I at first.

Then she says, "So if you had a position with flexible hours . . ."

It clicks, and as much as I like the idea of having a way to keep Nate close, I quickly interject, "Nate's probably looking for something more out and about, Mom."

She waves her hand at me as if to shoo away my objection. "Eva was heartbroken when you stopped visiting her when you were children."

"I was an idiot," he says. "I'm going to be here for her now though." He shoots me a look I can't read. "She was my best friend, but things got messed up in my life when my parents split."

"Despite your father's example, you seem like you're turning out well. You're certainly shouldering a lot of responsibility," my mother says. "The nurses told me that you were instrumental in Eva's mood improving."

Right about now, I wish the sofa would rip open and

swallow me. My mother has moved from polite Southern woman to bluntness tempered by a sweet voice. I close my eyes for a moment as I try to push away the mortification that I'm feeling.

Neither Nate nor I say anything, so my mother continues, "Tell me more about your brother."

Nate doesn't seem the least bit put off by my mother's order. "Aaron's a great kid. The cystic fibrosis means he has to constantly be on guard for infections, and he has treatments and medicines. He doesn't have diabetes so far, and he's doing well. There's no cure, but there *are* treatments. A lot of people with CF live into their thirties or older." He pauses and scowls. "Our sperm donor, however, can't be bothered to raise a kid with a health issue. He says it's too 'hard' to see Aaron, as if what's hard for *Aaron* doesn't matter. I'm not going to turn my back on my brother. When he wants me around, I'm there as much as I can. It's harder because they live over in Durham, but the drive isn't horrible and Aaron's worth it. I'm *nothing* like my father."

"I can see that," she says mildly.

Nate sounds so passionate that it would be impossible not to see how much he loves his brother. It's no wonder that Nate has no friends at school. So much of his time is given to his brother.

"Nate is reliable, but he's also busy," I point out.

My mother doesn't even acknowledge that I spoke. She continues, "I need to hire someone to help Eva when I'm at the office. You were a help to her in the hospital, have experience with injured or ill children, and of course, you look strong enough to help her. Plus, she obviously trusts you or you wouldn't have been sleeping in her room"—she glances at me now—"which your father won't hear about . . . as long as you don't keep trying to object to Nathaniel's accepting the job."

"Mom, you can't *blackmail* me by threatening to tell Dad." I cross my arms and glare at her. "I don't need a caretaker, and even if I did, you can't bully someone into taking the job."

"It's fine, Eva," Nate interjects when I take a breath. He turns to look at my mother. "I can't do it if Aaron gets sick. If he needs me, either he comes here with me or I'm off that day, depending on how he feels."

"That's reasonable." She's studying Nate, and I can't help but think she looks far too happy with herself. "Can you start the day after tomorrow?"

"Sure."

"I expect Eva is planning to go to the funeral, and she'll object to her father or me taking her. It's graveside, which means it'll be more difficult to navigate her wheelchair. I don't think Grace is strong enough."

"You're willing to let me go without you?" I interject. My mother is attentive to every funeral, wedding, baby shower, or significant anniversary of the people we know in Jessup.

"I can go if you don't mind, but I thought you might want space." My mother watches me as she speaks, and I can tell that there's more going on here than I understand. This feels like a test of some sort, and I don't know the right answer.

"I'll take her." Nate's answer breaks the sudden silence. He glances at me. "If you want to go . . . I was going anyhow, but if you don't want to go, it's fine. You just got home."

I don't want to go, don't want to see anyone yet, and I really don't want anyone to see *me*. I have to go though. Fear won't keep me at home.

"Grace is coming too," I tell him.

Nate nods. "I figured." He glances at my mother then. "The problem is travel. I'm not sure how comfortable Eva would be in my truck."

"Nate can drive my car," I suggest. "That way Grace can ride with us, too."

"Perfect!" my mother says with a small hand clap, obviously pleased that we've played into her hands.

I know my mother isn't plotting against me, at least that's my usual theory, but as I look at her satisfied expression I worry. At the same time, I'm relieved that I'll see Nate more, glad he'll be with me at the funeral, and grateful that he's seemingly unconcerned about my mother's gleeful expression.

After my mother excuses herself to check in on her work email, Nate and I exchange a quiet look before he says, "She maneuvered both of us without blinking."

"You don't have to do this." It feels weird to realize that my mother is going to be paying Nate to spend his days with me. My family hiring him to spend the summer with me is awkward. I suggest, "She can find someone else, you know?"

Nate is quiet again. In our years apart, I think I'd forgotten how often he retreats to silence. Not for the first time, I think that his reputation as enigmatic at school is a cover for his tendency toward quietness. When he speaks, his words are measured. "I need the money, and I like seeing you."

He holds up a hand when I open my mouth, so I stay mute as he adds, "Plus, it gives me a way to explain being here that doesn't make people think the wrong thing about us."

It's my turn to be silent, but I suspect I seem more sulky than mysterious.

He stands, looks at the dishes, and muses, "I'll need to ask your mother to show me around. Figure out meals and what all I'm to do."

"Right." I try to smile. Being around him is confusing. He keeps saying and doing things that make me think he's interested in me, but then, he retreats.

Now that Robert and I are through, I can admit that I'm really *not* content with platonic friendship with Nate—which is why my voice comes out sharp and I snap, "Leave the dishes today. You're not on the clock yet."

An expression I can't read crosses his face.

"Would it help to think of me as your combo butler and maid?" he half teases. He smiles, and I can't help smiling back at him. I need to work harder at suppressing my crush, or I'll lose him completely.

"Maybe . . . but we'll need to discuss your uniform then." I pause and look at him as if I'm considering the matter seriously.

"I might as well get *some* pleasure out of having a sitter, and you're not horrible to look at."

He shakes his head.

"I'll see you and Grace the day after tomorrow," he says, and then he leans down and kisses the top of my head, further blurring lines that I'm already having trouble seeing.

DAY 12: "THE SACRIFICE"

Judge

TOMORROW, I'LL SEE HER again. They probably think I didn't care enough. If They knew how much I *do* care, They'd be shocked. I bet not even Reverend Tilling prays for her as much as I do.

Since I sent the message, I've been waiting for a sign, some proof that she understood. I've seen nothing.

Perhaps the message wasn't clear enough.

Sin and status are sure ways to death. It's so obvious. Maybe Micki was too vague. She wasn't filled with sin. She clung to her status, but she guarded her chastity. Maybe a second message, one on the nature of purity, will help.

I drive past Eva's house on the way to the grocery. Grandmother wants some special cheese for some dish that no one will eat. Every so often she decides to pretend she can still cook, so I volunteered to go to the grocery. She'll be asleep by the time I'm home, but I'll tell her I was back early. She'll cover for me without prompting if anyone ever asks. An alibi will matter this time.

I text Amy while I'm at the grocery. "Busy?"

"When?"

"Now."

"Pick me up at DQ in 15."

I smile. She's a good giver. I'm glad we'll get a chance to spend a little time together before the message. I was sad that she wasn't available a few days ago, but yesterday we went to the old summer kitchen out on the Kennelly place.

I check the cooler in the trunk where the asphodel I bought is waiting. It's an odd flower, harder to get at the grocery, so I drove almost all the way to Durham to buy it. Amy deserves it, and later, Eva will understand what I'm saying with it. I slip on my gloves and bring the flower into the front seat.

My smile doesn't fade as I drive to the parking lot beside the ice cream shop. I'm a little late, but Amy is used to it. She never lets her parents see who's picking her up. Her mother is a believer in changing their lot in life by way of marriage. It worked before, and since the divorce, she's determined to try it again. My grandmother detests the Crowne family because of it. She calls Amy's mother a "social climber." I have to wonder if my father took a climb on that reputedly well-frequented ladder. He's discreet, but he explained it to me years ago: there are girls you fuck, and girls you marry, and it's best not to confuse the two.

I turn on the cell phone jammer I keep in the glove box right before I pull into the lot, and then I cut off my lights. I trust Amy, but it's important to be cautious anyhow. Privacy helps avoid questions.

I picked this lot because someone broke out the street lights here. I could explain it if they saw us—Amy has plenty of boyfriends—but I won't have to explain. There's no one around the darkened lot to see me.

Only a few moments pass before the car door opens, and she slides into the passenger seat. I'm moving before the door is even closed.

"Jerk," she mutters.

I reach over and put my hand on her bare knee.

She flinches at the feel of the gloves on her skin. "That's new."

"Shhh." I take my other hand off the wheel for a moment and hand her the asphodel. "For you."

"It's . . . unusual." She examines the flower as I slide my hand up until my fingertips are wedged between her thighs.

"Open up."

She complies.

When I don't move my hand after several moments, she starts to close her legs.

"No." I tighten my grip on her leg, not enough to bruise but hard enough that she lets out a small cry of pain. "You're generous."

"You could ask," she mutters, but her hand is in my lap

now and she unfastens my trousers quickly. Her other hand holds tightly to the flower.

I don't look at her. Instead, I think of Eva . . . but she wouldn't do *this*, not here in the car. She's better than this, special in a way that no one else can be. I think of Eva in the backseat watching us.

"Stop." I put my hand over Amy's. "Not like this. Not tonight."

She obeys, and we're silent as we drive to Scuppernong Park. I park, cut off the engine, and reach into the backseat. On the floor is a bottle of wine—from the Cooper Winery, of course. I like to drink it when I'm with Amy. It makes me think of Eva, helps me feel like she's with me.

Once I open it, Amy and I pass the bottle back and forth. I put on a condom before I guide her hand back to my trousers. "So it's not messy."

She giggles, but doesn't argue. "And the gloves?"

"It's something I read about," I say. I don't mention *where* I read it.

I know her body well enough to distract her before she thinks too much about it. A few minutes later, we're both panting. "Will you? No one else does it like you. I've missed it."

In my mind, I realize what a sacrifice I'm making. I'm giving *this* up so Eva can be saved. I tangle my hand in Amy's hair to urge her down. When she starts to remove the condom, I yank her away.

Her yip of pain makes me guilty and excited all at once. "No. Leave it on."

"But—"

"Please. I just want tonight to be different," I whisper.

She sits up and stares at me for a moment.

"Come on," I beg. "I want to pretend. We could be strangers tonight."

She frowns. "You're fucked up."

"But you like it." I start pulling her back toward me, and this time she doesn't resist.

Afterward, I remove the condom and stuff it into a bag that I brought with me. Beside it on the floor is a tiny pill and the wine bottle. I slip the pill into the wine, lift it like I'm drinking so I can dissolve the pill into the wine. I would never drug a girl to get her naked. That's wrong. I don't want Amy to hurt though. If there were anyone else who could give the message, I wouldn't do this.

I hand her the bottle and tell her, "Here. You can drink the rest while I take care of you."

Her eyes widen, and I realize she thinks I mean something different. I've been too careful not to leave any fluids so far, so I can't do that. I put the bottle to her lips and use my gloved hands to make her happy before the pill kicks in.

"Serious afterglow," she mumbles after she reaches satisfaction. Her words slur, and she slumps to the side.

I realize that I'm crying silently when she loses consciousness. I'm proud that I gave her happiness before that happened. I'll miss her.

Quietly, I get out of the car, go around to her side, and scoop her into my arms. I bring the asphodel, too. I walk to the edge of the lake and lower her to the ground. "Thank you," I whisper. She can't hear me, but I still need to say it. I have manners.

I remove her shirt and break the wine bottle on the ground beside her. I watch to be sure Amy doesn't move. Then, I tuck the asphodel under her, so the water won't wash it away.

She's unconscious, facedown at the edge of the water. Then, I pick up a piece of glass and start to write a message on Amy's back. I keep one hand on her shoulders to hold her steady as I push the glass into her skin. She cries out as I carve the words, but she doesn't move away. She can't, but I still whisper comforting words to her as I carefully spell out FOR EVA. JUDGE.

I turn Amy's head so she's facedown in the water, and I hold her steady. I could've left, left her alone for her death as I did with Micki, but Amy means too much to me for that. I stay at Amy's side as she inhales the water, shudders, and dies.

Then, I carefully peel off the gloves and incinerate them on the ground. After they stop burning and melting, I use the piece of broken bottle to push the remains of the gloves into the water and tuck the glass into my pocket to save. It's harder to walk away from Amy than it was from Micki. I glance back and whisper, "Thank you."

Someday, I'll tell Eva about this moment, and she'll understand how deep my love for her runs.

I sacrificed a friend for her. I wouldn't do that for anyone else.

DAY 13: "THE VEIL"

Eva

I FEEL LIKE I'M getting ready to face an attack instead of a funeral. I know that most of my classmates will be there, and as guilty as I feel for wanting to skip it, I really wish I could. I want to pay my respects to Micki, but I don't want to talk to anyone. I certainly don't want them to see my slashed-up face. I'm not ready. I'm not sure I ever will be.

I pull on the long black dress my mother set out this morning. It seems strange that we wear the same size, but she's really not that much older than me. Maybe that's why motherhood has always seemed a little confusing to her. She was almost my exact age when she got pregnant with me, so she's still young enough to be thin and have clothes I'm not embarrassed to wear. If anything, I look *better* when I borrow from her closet. This dress is no exception.

"I can do this," I repeat as I try to avoid the mirror my mother refuses to cover. I'm fairly sure I'm lying to myself; I'm not at all sure I can handle today. Going to the funeral feels too weighty. Micki was my age, and she's dead. The suspicion that her death wasn't an accident, that maybe the same person hit me, was a topic of discussion in today's *Jessup Observer.* What if the newspaper is right? If my accident was meant to be a murder, will the killer try again? Will he be there watching me? My stomach turns at the thought that the person who did this will be there—gloating over Micki's death, over my scars, over the growing fear.

I sit in my wheelchair trying not to let my fears paralyze me, when my mother comes back into my room. "Try this."

She holds out the black veiled hat. I accept it and hold it by the brim.

"It'll hide your face," she says gently.

It's not the sort of thing I've ever worn. Mom was raised with a more conservative, Old South attitude. I blame some of it on her decision to stay in Jessup and not go to college. Of course, I can't criticize her too much: that decision was made because she was pregnant with me. Grandfather Cooper continued to treat her like a child, and my father—and *his* father—were much the same. Between Grandfather Cooper, Grandfather Tilling, and my father, my mother was treated like a sheltered Southern woman of an earlier generation. She wore pearls and tasteful clothes, poured tea, and volunteered like it was a career.

When I meet her gaze, she adds, "I know you don't like attention, so I thought this might help."

I nod. "Braid my hair first?"

She pulls my wheelchair backward so she can sit on the chair that I usually use for reading. I feel like a child sitting in front of her while she brushes my hair. She's gentle, and the rhythmic tug of the bristles makes me close my eyes. I could probably do this without a mirror, but for the funeral, I'd rather it look as good as possible. This will be the first time my classmates see me, and I am terrified.

"The veil works today, but you'll need to face them after this," my mother instructs. "I agreed with the nurses lying so people didn't come to the hospital, but you need to move forward. They won't all be great, but you'll know who your friends are." Mom's voice is matter-of-fact. "The longer you stall, the harder it'll be. I know a little about this, Eva."

I hear the soft clatter of the brush being lowered to the wooden table beside my chair. I stay silent as her fingers start separating my hair into chunks for braiding. Oddly, it occurs to me that this is the closest I've felt to her in years. She's not a touchy-feely person, but right now, I feel like a little kid.

"When I was pregnant, even though I was married before I was showing, it was hard walking around Jessup. Their eyes would go from my face to my stomach to my hand, like they were saying 'Lizzy . . . the pregnant one; yes, she did get married.' It was true, but I don't think I ever felt *small* before that." She tucks in stray tendrils of my hair as she talks. "I was a brat. Daddy bought me what I wanted, spoiling me the way he'd have spoiled Mama if she hadn't died. Every girl at school wanted to be me, and every boy wanted to kiss me."

I'm tempted to speak, to ask questions, but I'm afraid that if I do, she'll stop talking. She so rarely talks about being a teenager, so I don't say a word. I listen.

"A few of them did kiss me, but your father . . . he was different. The preacher's boy, trying to prove he wasn't a good boy, and we were careless. We had so much fun, but there were consequences." She sighs, and I'm not sure if it's regret or longing for those days when she and my father were young. She smiles at me then and continues on, "I knew Daddy wouldn't let me date him seriously; not even being the preacher's boy would overrule your father's lack of 'proper breeding'—until I turned up pregnant."

"I'm sorry," I whisper.

"Why?"

"You wouldn't be stuck with Dad if—"

"Hush, you." She leans forward to see my face. "I loved your father. I still do. I didn't mean to trap him, but I wouldn't change a thing. I have you and him. This was exactly what I wanted then—and still is. The only thing I might've changed was how young I was." My expression must be as disbelieving as I feel because she adds, "I love you, Eva. I'm lousy at being a mother. I try, but you just never seem to need me. I'm not sure you ever did. You always seemed to know what you wanted, and no matter what I said or did, you marched off to do whatever you felt like doing. When you were little, you and Nathaniel—"

"Nate," I interject.

"You and *Nate*," she continues, "were such little hellions. I swear you sweated mud. I'd buy you the perfect little dresses that I loved as a girl, and you'd go outside and wallow in the mud like a piglet. It made me so crazy. I didn't understand you." She laughs a little. "I probably still don't. I never knew what you needed, so I listened to what Daddy and the Reverend suggested. Even when their advice was in opposition to each other, I tried to listen. I didn't want to mess up at this. I try not to push you, but I'm not sure I can keep this distance between us. Knowing you were in the hospital and I couldn't get there . . ."

She'd finished the braid at some point while she was speaking, and now her hands slide over my hair in a caress.

"I knew you couldn't get there, and I was okay," I promised.

"You're *always* okay. It makes it hard to know when you need me." My mother sniffles, and it's so out of character that I turn to look at her. The impeccable Elizabeth Cooper-Tilling looks heartbroken. Instead of grabbing a tissue to dab at her perfectly made-up eyes, she swipes the back of her hand across her face, and then wraps her arms around me. I lean back against my mother and close my eyes as she hugs me and sobs.

"I'll do better." She's not hugging me so tightly that it hurts, but she's not letting go. "Maybe I can ask Grace's mother. You like her, right?"

"Ask her . . . ?"

"How to be a good mother," she clarifies, like it's the most obvious thing in the world. "I bet she has ideas. She could be my mentor."

I smother a laugh, but I know she's not joking. She has the tone that I've always associated with one of her volunteer projects. If her new focus is motherhood, I'm not sure what that will mean for me—especially if we get confirmation that my accident was not random.

"I'll have her over for tea, and we'll get started." My mother settles the hat on my head and drapes the veil over my face. In an instant, the world is dimmed by black gauze, and her fingers arrange it so it looks artful and natural.

When she holds a hand mirror in front of me, I don't feel like looking away. The veil hides the cuts and yellowed bruises. I smile before murmuring, "Thank you."

"This is just the start, Eva. I'm going to be a new mother. I'll do everything right," she promises. She smiles at me for a moment, and then she adds, "I need my planner. We'll need a schedule for meetings with Mrs. Yeung, and then mother-daughter events." She pauses, clearly thinking of the lists in her mind already. "We should have a brainstorming session to figure out what I can do better, and what activities we should set up. Maybe Grace could help, too. She's so smart and out-spoken. I'll see what day works for the four of us to get together this week."

And then she's off, and I'm left sitting in my room a little alarmed, but also a little amused. The idea of my mother and Mrs. Yeung together should terrify me. Mostly, though, I feel happier than I have in a while—at least until I think about going to a funeral . . . and the murderer who waits somewhere out there. Fear fills me, and I can't help feeling overwhelmed.

When my mother goes downstairs to wait for Nate, I debate telling someone about my hallucinations. Despite only being back in touch with Nate for a little over a week, I'm tempted to tell *him*. The problem there is telling him that I imagined his murder. I'm not sure how I feel about that. It isn't the sort of thing that sounds sane or like a reason to become closer friends. I don't want to tell my parents or the doctors though. They'd overreact, and I'd end up with a bunch of tests or back at Mercy Hospital. I'm still thinking about what to do when I hear his voice downstairs.

I smile as I listen to him and my mother talk. I feel a little like a creeper, but luckily, Grace arrives while Nate is still going over my mother's undoubtedly copious notes on taking care of me. Unlike Nate, she doesn't stay downstairs with my parents.

When she walks into my room, she gasps, "What are you wearing?"

"A dress."

"On your head, Eva." She walks closer, gently closing the door behind her.

I flip the veil up to bare my face. "I like it. I'm not ready for the stares."

She reaches out to brush my cheek, and that's all it takes. I fall into what looks like a continuation of the same hallucination of Grace I had before.

The streetlight I parked under is out, but there are no other cars nearby so I feel comfortable walking across the parking lot. All of these articles I've been skimming have made me jumpy. No one knows what I'm here researching, but too much time with my thoughts makes me nervous.

I pop the trunk to toss my bag in. Quickly, I drop it in there and reach up for the trunk lid to close it.

That's when it happens. I feel a thump on the back of my head. I open my mouth to scream, but a hand comes over it. I bite down so hard my jaw hurts, but the person holding on to me doesn't let go.

I try dropping my weight like they tell you in street defense class. A hand on my back shoves, and I fall into my own trunk. My legs scrape against the car, and I feel like I can't breathe from the force of the fall.

Blinking against the pain and trying to push myself out, I look up and see someone standing there. Then the trunk closes, and it's all dark.

I'm shaking so hard that I feel like I'm going to be sick.

"Eva?"

"I saw you get shoved in a trunk," I whisper. "I saw Nate die, and my dad, and you."

"What? Eva, what are you talking about? You're scaring me." She looks over her shoulder, and I realize she's going to call for someone.

"No!" I grab her arm. "Please . . . just take my hand. I need to know."

My best friend is looking at me like I've taken a leap into

the land of needing massive meds, but she doesn't question me yet. She simply does as I ask.

I'm braced for it, ready to fall back into her death, prepared to stare at the face of the person who shoved her into a trunk. Grace's hand touches mine—and nothing happens.

"Again," I say desperately.

Silently, she pulls her hand away and then after a moment I reach out to touch her again. It doesn't work. I'm still here in my own skin, not in the middle of her death. I don't know whether to be grateful or not. The hallucinations are starting to feel too realistic and fit too much of a pattern for me to keep thinking that they're medical or simply my fears at work in an overactive imagination.

"It's not working," I mutter.

"*What's* not working?"

And in that moment, I make the decision. There's no one I trust more than her. "Since the accident, when people touch me, I see their deaths," I say.

Her mouth gapes open as I quickly fill her in on what I just saw.

She says nothing.

I stare at her face as she squats down in front of me, but despite the pain I see in her eyes, I have to keep going. "I think they may be right—the police, the newspaper. I think there's a killer, Gracie. First me, then Micki, and then he's going to go after you or Nate. I couldn't see his face when he struck me. The killer, I mean. I couldn't see it when I saw him attack you or Nate either. If I can't see who it is, how do I stop him?"

I realize I probably sound crazier than I'd like, but right now, I can't keep telling myself that this is a side effect or something. It *feels* real. If it is and I ignore it and they . . .

I don't even finish the thought. It would destroy me.

Grace crouches down in front of me. "Are you dizzy? Headache?"

"Every day," I admit.

Mutely, she continues studying me from where she is crouched in front of me. I know the sort of thoughts she's probably having because I've had them since this started. She's likely thinking my TBI has lingering symptoms that the doctors ought to hear. She might even be right. I am willing to admit as much, saying, "I know I had a head injury. Maybe it's some sort of symptom. I want it to be, but . . . Tell me you'll be careful, that you won't walk out of the library alone, and that you'll help me try to figure this out."

"Of course I will," she says. "Whatever it is, I'm here. You know that."

I do. I can count on Grace, and she can count on me. If I'm wrong and these are hallucinations, we'll deal with it, but if they're not—if I'm seeing deaths before they happen—I'm going to figure it out. No one is going to hurt Grace or Nate if there's anything I can do to save them. That alone is reason for me to see where these visions lead me.

DAY 13: "THE ADMISSION"

Grace

I REALIZE MY FACE is readable to Eva. Sometimes, I find it helpful. Right now isn't one of those times. Eva is the closest friend I've ever had, and I'll let her see my supposed death if she wants, but I don't think it's real. Carefully, I say, "Everything I've read on TBIs says that there are a lot of weird symptoms, that different patients can have widely different responses. My guess is that you have some injury to a part of your brain that's making you think you're seeing these things."

"I'm not crazy, Gracie. I thought I was at first, but I think this is real."

"I don't think you're crazy," I correct her.

"But you don't believe me," she adds. It's hard to see the hurt in Eva's face, but we don't lie to each other. It's a rule between us. No matter how weird or cruel the truth is, lies are banned.

"I don't think you're crazy *or* lying. I just think there's probably another explanation. When you say you see our deaths, does it look like we rot or fall or something? Maybe it's an optical problem," I suggest. "Maybe when you look at us, what you're seeing is a distorted image from optical damage."

Eva laughs in a way that sounds like tears are just as likely as laughter right now. "No. Not at all. It's like I fall into someone else's body. I feel things, and I hear them, and I *know* things as if I am that person, as if I'm inside of them." She goes on to summarize experiencing a heart attack, alcohol overdose, and some sort of chronic health issue, and then adds, "It only happens if it's skin-to-skin contact and the other person initiates it. At least that's what I think so far. I thought I was hallucinating, but . . . it keeps happening, and it feels so *real*."

It's hard to believe that she's developed some sort of precognition powers from her accident. I don't believe in those sorts of things. It simply doesn't make sense.

"I couldn't see his face," Eva says. "The killer, I mean. I couldn't see it when I was in Nate's death or yours. I can't see anyone's faces when I'm in people's deaths. If I can't see who it is, how do I stop him?"

My closest friend is staring at me, waiting for some sort of answer, trusting me to know how to help her make sense of something that doesn't make sense, so I say the only thing I can. "I don't think that's your job, stopping him. *If* there is some homicidal maniac, *if* you're really seeing deaths, I don't know . . . we find a way to tell the police what you know."

"How do I tell them who he is if I can't see him?"

"If it *is* real, we'll figure it out. I'll start researching anything that could be related. We can take it to the police as evidence."

"You can't!"

I raise my hand and continue, "I'll only research from home—because even though I'm not sure I believe that you're really having some sort of precognition in seeing deaths, I promise I won't go to the library alone. I can use the remote log-in at the Jessup library."

For a moment, Eva is quiet. She folds her arms over her chest. "Maybe, we start to test it. I'll try with you and Nate, and then once we figure some of it out, we can try on other people." She shivers so slightly that I could almost think I'm imagining it until she says, "I don't want to see you die, but someone *killed* Micki. Someone tried to kill me. I have to do *something*."

"So what? We convince people to touch you? That shouldn't be too hard." I'm mostly joking, but she's not.

"Yes!" Eva smiles at me and says, "Just small groups. Piper, Jess, Laurel, and CeCe for starters. I can come up with excuses to have them touch me without being weird." She pauses and swallows. "I get cold when it happens, like I'm out in freezing weather with no coat, so I can't do too much. I shake all over."

"Eva, sweetie, maybe that's because it's a seizure or something." I reach out for her hand, but she jerks away. "Doesn't it make more sense that it's medical?"

"I don't know. That's why we're testing it." She has a resolved look on her face, and I'm not sure there's a lot of room for discussion. This is one of those cases where Eva will get her way, and the rest of us will cooperate. I don't think she realizes how spoiled she sometimes is, but if she pitched this idea to everyone at school, they'd line up to obey.

"Fine," I say. "We'll try your plan. If it doesn't prove anything, we're talking to the doctor. Promise?"

Eva nods, relief apparent in the way her body seems to relax. She grabs my hand and squeezes. "Thank you."

I squeeze back, and we sit listening to the hum of voices downstairs for a moment. Then I prompt, "What was the *other* secret you wanted to tell me?"

"Two others, actually." She blushes faintly and has trouble meeting my eyes. "Mom hired Nate to be my caretaker, *and* in her mad desire to implement a Be a Better Mother mission she's going to arrange mother-daughter days for us."

She's not going to distract me from the news about Nate by telling me about her mother. That tactic might work on the Piper-ettes, but I'm not one of them. Nate is the only boy to leave her flustered, and I hope he's finally going to admit that whatever he's trying to work out in his life would be easier with her by his side. I know the class thing is an issue in Jessup, but it shouldn't mean they can't at least date.

I laugh. "Isn't there some 'fox guarding the hens' saying around here that fits this?"

Eva shakes her head. "Nate doesn't see me that way . . . and did you miss the part about General Yeung and Ms. Southern Decorum teaming up?"

For a moment, we lock eyes, and then I say, "Immovable object, meet unstoppable force."

"They could take over a small country if they join forces," Eva says with a hint of awe in her voice. "My mother wants to learn how to be a better mom, and she's decided that your mom is the one to teach her."

For the first time I can recall, I'm genuinely impressed with Mrs. Tilling. It's hard to admit when you're not doing a great job at something. It's probably harder still to admit it when the entire town seems to think your family can do no wrong. "Good," I say. "Maybe it'll be what you two need. I know you make excuses, but I also know that you've wished you had the General for a mom. You confessed it after you killed that bottle of wine at Piper's party last year."

Eva blushes, and then promptly flips her veil down as she mutters, "Drunken admissions shouldn't be used against friends."

With an eye roll, I reply, "Wrong. If they were used in front of the subject of the admission, that would be different." I lower my voice and tease, "For example, mentioning you leering at man-slut while he was—"

"Shhh!" Eva's gaze darts to the closed door, and she

whispers, "He could be outside the door for all you know."

We exchange another look and start laughing. Somehow, everything feels a little ridiculous right now, and I suspect that it's because everything is all so serious. Micki is dead; Eva was hit by a car. Now, after broken bones, lacerations, and a brain injury, she thinks she can experience other people's deaths. Focusing on her crush and our mothers' frightening efficiency is easier.

I check the time. "We need to go soon. How do we get you downstairs?"

"Carefully." Eva flips her veil back up and motions to the door. "Open that, grab my crutches, and let's go."

I comply, and once we reach the top of the stairs, Eva looks at the bannister for a moment.

"Put the wheelchair brakes on for me, and hand me one of my crutches," she says.

Once she has a crutch in hand, she hoists herself out of the chair and leans on the crutch. "Now I just need to—"

"Eva, we discussed this!" Mrs. Tilling is standing at the foot of the stairs now. Her hands are on her hips, and the look on her face is fierce. "And having Grace help you no less."

"Let me guess: you're not to do this on your own?" I whisper.

Eva offers me a sheepish look. "I am perfectly capable of it."

Nate is already halfway up the stairs looking at the two of us with an expression of irritation that rivals Mrs. Tilling's.

"Are you trying to get me fired?"

"I can do this," Eva insists.

He puts an arm around her. "Give the crutch to Grace."

I expect her to argue, but after a moment, Eva sighs and hands me the crutch. Nate lifts her into his arms like she's a bride, and Eva loops her arms around his neck. With no visible effort he carries her downstairs. At the landing, Mrs. Tilling stands with her arms now folded over her chest and an assessing look on her face. She walks over to the front door and opens it, and Nate carries Eva out to her car.

Miss I-can-do-everything accepted his help with far more tolerance than I would expect. I follow them with the crutches in hand. Mrs. Tilling fusses over Eva, who's in the backseat, and Nate stares at Eva with an intensity that is near embarrassing to witness. At least, he does until he catches me watching him. Then, his face becomes blank.

"I'll grab her chair," he says flatly as he walks past me.

I slide into the front seat and turn around to smile at Eva. "Between Nate and me, you'll be well guarded from curious onlookers today."

Mrs. Tilling shoots a grateful smile at me before she turns to Nate, who has returned with the wheelchair. "Do you know how to fold it down or should I get my husband?"

"I've done this before," he says with what sounds like sadness in his voice.

A few minutes later, he's in the driver's seat adjusting mirrors and the seat. We're all silent as he drives toward the cemetery for Micki's graveside service, and I wonder if he's thinking the same thing I am: this could've been Eva. We could've lost her. The thought makes me reach back for Eva.

Eva reaches up and takes my outstretched hand, and we stay that way until we reach the cemetery.

DAY 13: "THE FUNERAL"

Eva

WHEN NATE PARKS AND cuts off the engine, I release Grace's hand. My heartbeat feels erratic in my chest, and I have the sudden urge to beg them to keep driving, to not stop here, to escape the stares and questions and grief that wait beside Micki's still-open grave.

"Are you ready for this?" Grace asks when Nate goes to the trunk to get out my wheelchair.

"No."

The trunk closes, shaking the car with the force of it.

"Do you want to go back?" Grace twists in her seat to face me.

"Yes, but I'm not going to."

Nate opens the back door on the passenger's side. I sat with my back to the driver's side door so my broken leg could stretch across the backseat, but I can't get out that side. Once the door is open, I use my hands on the seat and my left leg to slide myself to the door. I pause at the edge of the seat when Nate asks, "Would it be okay for me to lift you?"

"I can do this. Just make sure the chair brakes are on."

"They are."

Grace is standing behind the chair, and Nate is at the open car door. When I start to stand, his hands go to my hips. He steadies me, and I gasp.

"Are you okay?"

"You startled me." It's not really a lie. He *did* startle me, but that wasn't why I gasped. I like him touching me.

"Sorry. I'll warn you next time," he says.

He helps me into the chair, and I pull the veil down over my face again.

"You don't need that," he whispers. "You're beautiful, Eva. Remember that."

He's so at ease that it's frustrating. I want him to feel the same adrenaline rush as I do, but he seems completely unmoved by touching me.

I tug at the black gauze, making sure it covers as much as possible, and then I put my hands on the arms of the wheel-chair. It still feels a little unnerving to be in the chair, as if it could topple and spill me out. I'm sure Nate is careful, but we're outside and there are rocks and things.

Grace steps around the side to straighten my skirt. She stays to my side as he pushes me up the path to where the service will be starting soon. It's a little ridiculous that I'm coming in like some grand old matriarch. All that's missing are gloves and heavy jewelry.

My nervousness spikes at the sheer sense of exposure I feel in being outside. Not only do I need to face my classmates, but I worry that the person who hit me is here. Logic says that's unlikely, but in so many of the crime television shows my father likes, the criminal likes to appear at places to enjoy his or her victory. Attending Micki's funeral fits that. My hands tighten on the arms of the chair as panic wells up in me.

"What if he's here?" I ask.

"Who?"

"The man who did this to her . . . and to me."

Grace and Nate are both silent for a moment, but then she says, "We don't even know if it's the same person."

"It has to be," I insist.

No one replies.

Nate continues pushing me up the path in silence. As we get closer, I can see the awning that covers the rows of folding chairs and the coffin. There are so many flowers that even though we're outside the smell is cloying.

It's like an audible ripple when we get near. Even with the veil over my face, there's no doubt who I am. If the broken leg didn't give it away, Grace's presence would. No one approaches us, but there are more than a few surreptitious glances. I'm grateful for the veil. Even without my healing cuts and bruises, I'd still feel uncomfortable at the way people are watching us.

When we reach the chairs, Grace pulls one back to sit beside me, but Nate stays standing like a sentinel behind me until I whisper, "Get a chair, please."

Mutely, he pulls a second chair back so he's on my left side. The two of them have flanked me, and we're in the back of the crowd. I feel like this is as unobtrusive as I could possibly be, but still there are furtive glances.

Nate doesn't touch me, and neither does Grace. I suspect his reserve is a combination of worry over my reputation and habit in public. Grace's distance seems odd until I realize that I'd told her that being touched causes the death visions. She's likely just being cautious.

I reach out and take both of their hands. Nate startles a little at my touch, but I grip his hand tightly so he can't pull away. He knew Micki, and no one else here is going to remember to offer him any comfort. Grace might not have been friends with her, but she's had more than a little worry the past couple weeks because of the person who—I believe—did this to Micki and to me.

We are still sitting like that, with me holding a hand on either side, when the service begins, and we stay that way through the whole thing. My hands tighten on theirs when Micki's coffin is lowered into the ground, but I don't cry out loud. I can't here. Despite all the tears I've cried lately, today my face is dry.

Afterward, when people are starting to leave, I wish I could run away. They mean well, but as my classmates come toward me, I feel trapped. I don't ever like to be the center of attention. I reach up to be sure the veil still hides my face.

"Oh my God, Eva! Are you okay?" Piper half breathes the words. "I didn't know you were out of the hospital!"

She's reaching out to hug me, but Nate grabs her arms before she can touch me. He raises his voice a little so the others who are now clustering near us can hear him. "Please don't touch Eva. She still has injuries."

No one responds, but I see several people eyeing him and me like they are figuring out some juicy tidbit. Before he can say anything else—like the fact that he's there as a job—I say, "Thank you, Nate."

"I should've thought of that," Piper says awkwardly. "I'm sorry, Eva. I just missed you." She motions around her. "We all did."

I can tell she's hurt that she didn't know I was home, so I reach out and squeeze her hand. "I missed you too. Luckily, I slept constantly, so it was easier for me."

Nate snorts. Piper smiles at me though, and I see that she believes my little lie. Nothing about this was easy, but I'm here with my friends and I know what they want me to say. They want assurances that everything is fine, so I give it to them. "I'm doing better. Still a little beat up from the accident, and you know"—I gesture at my leg—"a broken bone, but I'm fine."

"Do you remember us?" Lisa Mitchell asks from where she stands behind a few people. "I heard you had amnesia."

"Just about the accident itself." I smile at her, but realize that between the veil and the distance she probably can't tell that I'm smiling.

Robert speaks up then. "Did you decide if you're coming to the funeral breakfast?"

He moves to the front of the crowd of about ten people who are still standing here all around me. He lowers his voice as if he's trying to be confidential, but he's clearly not because his words are a lie. "Sorry I couldn't bring you today. I'd already offered to take a couple people. I could give you a ride to the breakfast if you want. They could ride with Grace and Bouchet."

Everyone is staring at us, and I want to hit him. I won't. The cemetery is no place for violence. I can see the pleading in his eyes, the request not to embarrass him, but I'm not going to cooperate. If he had avoided putting me more in the spotlight, I could've let it go. He didn't though. This isn't what *friends* do.

"We broke up, Robert. Why would I want to ride with you?"

He opens his mouth, but before he speaks, I say, "Don't. Not here. Not now."

He turns and walks away. Everyone else stares at me silently. The already awkward moment grows unbearably tense, and I'm grateful for the veil shrouding my expression— and my scars.

"Piper, could you do me a favor?"

"Of course!"

"Tomorrow or something, come see me." I reach for her hand again. "I've missed everyone."

I realize as I say it that it's true. They're not perfect, but neither am I. They're my friends, and if there is a killer out there, I don't want him taking any more of them from me.

DAY 13: "THE SUBSTITUTE"

Judge

I DON'T KNOW WHEN Eva's presence started making me feel this twist of excitement and anger, but when she showed up at the funeral with Bouchet and Grace, I had to force myself not to go to her. They stayed on either side of her like bodyguards. She doesn't need them; she needs *me*.

I spent the entire time trying not to stare at her; I still want to, but I can't. They wouldn't understand. I blame the Jessupites who treat her like she's special. She's not. She's just like me. Once she understands that, she'll be saved. I'd hoped Micki would teach her. I'd prayed on a clear message, but here she is acting like They want her to act, pretending that some people are better than others.

Sometimes I felt like Amy understood the truth. She was good that way, but there was a thread of corruption inside her body, too. I think her mother created the appetite for filth, but it was fertilized by all of Them. She let so many of Them touch her. They left their own seed behind, and in time, she would have been roiling with corruption.

When I left her to be cleansed by the water, her body was purified. I smile as I think about saving Amy. I left a flower and even words this time. Sharing the truth is slower than I'd like, but being impatient was no good. Eva is worth slow, steady lessons. I feel like I imagine the best teachers do—considering my lesson plans and hoping that my star student will understand the importance of the material. I have to try different strategies though; I remember that talk we had freshman year on "learning styles."

Running over Eva wasn't clear enough. It wasn't really a lesson, if I think on it. I was hasty. Killing Micki should have been a clear lesson. I left an amaryllis there. *Pride goeth before the Fall.* We learned that in church and in something we read in school. I sent flowers to the hospital. Now, I've written words *and* left flowers. Each flower is a message. There are words, and flowers, and they say the things I can't tell her in person yet. Eva's smart. She'll see the lessons soon, and then she'll change.

"Thy will be done," I pray. Silently, I add, *"By me."*

From my left, Grayson elbows me. I guess I was talking too loud. If he understood that I can talk to God Himself, he wouldn't act like that, but he doesn't know. Someday, maybe I'll tell him.

"The funeral's over," Grayson mutters.

I guess he wasn't reprimanding me for being loud. I let my gaze dart to her, noticing the black veil she wears. I know that her humility is because of my hitting her with the car I'd stolen from the Phillips Garage. Maybe hitting her *was* a lesson, too. God's hands guide me in mysterious ways.

"Thank you," I whisper silently. I know God listens, and I've realized over the past weeks that He speaks, too.

I watch as our classmates surround her. Her face is hidden behind a veil, but that's allowed. It's modest. So much changes every day. I have to study it all, look for the clues and plan my next messages.

Teaching is hard.

If she doesn't understand the message I left with Amy, I'll send a gift to her house.

"Let's go," Grayson urges.

That police officer is standing at Eva's car, and I duck my head to hide my smile. It would be wrong to smile at a funeral, but I fill with excitement. They found Amy. They saw the message.

I glance at Eva one more time. I know she's been taking medicines because I ran over her. It might be making her too confused to understand. I hope not. I hope she understands.

I wonder if Eva will call me, if she'll realize that I am her teacher, if she'll know that I alone can judge the unworthy and worthy. It's God's work I do, and by His hand and His secret messages, I've chosen her to be my helpmate in this mission.

To the rest of the world she'll be common, but to me—and only me—she'll be special. I'll treat her like she deserves, cherish her, protect her, and she will look at me with love.

"Let's go out by the lake," I suggest. "It's hot enough that maybe there will be some girls we can pick up."

Grayson gives me a look of shock. "We're at a *funeral*."

"So . . . no?"

"I didn't say that, just . . . have some respect." He shakes his head.

"Micki's dead, and we should live life to its fullest. She can't." I glance toward Eva's car. "Micki was a virgin; she'll never get to have that kind of joy."

"You're kind of a freak," Grayson says, but when we get into his car, he drives us toward the lake. The thought of being with a girl near where I sacrificed Amy makes me repress a shiver of excitement. Maybe someday, I'll bring Eva to the very spot. We can make love while the water flows over us. Today, though, I imagine the police have it all blocked off while they look for clues I didn't leave. Today, I'll find another girl, a substitute for the girl God made for me.

DAY 13: "THE PICTURES"

Eva

"I NEED TO GIVE my respects to Micki's parents and then go home," I tell no one and everyone after Robert leaves. Murmurs of acceptance and wishes of health come from my friends, and then Nate is pushing my chair over to the grave where Micki's parents stand sobbing.

"Thank you for coming," Mrs. Adams says.

I'm not entirely sure what I say to them. It's as if I'm on automatic pilot at funerals: I say the words that I've been trained to utter, and they nod politely. They mention the beautiful flowers my family sent to both the funeral and their home (which I knew nothing about) and the very generous donation in Micki's memory (I'm not even sure which charity). I realize that the over-the-top donation and flowers were how my mother coped with her willingness to let me go without her.

I always hate funerals, but this one feels worse than usual. Micki was my classmate, not the grandparent of a classmate. I want to tell her parents that I'm sorry that she died, that I'm not sure why I survived, but there aren't rules for those admissions. Instead, I reach out and take Mrs. Adams' hand and squeeze.

"I'm sorry," I say as steadily as I'm able. "She was a great person."

Mrs. Adams cries more at my words, and Mr. Adams folds her into his arms. "Thank you," he says. "They'll find who did this to you two. They have to."

I nod because there are no words here that work, and Mrs. Adams lifts her face from her husband's chest again. She's a strong Southern woman. Her breakdown is brief. "You be careful," she orders. "Tell your friends, too."

"I will."

Another woman is coming over to talk to the Adamses, so Nate wheels me away as they turn their attention to the other mourners. Once we're a little farther away from them, Nate says, "Let's get you home."

As we near the car, I see Grace standing next to Detective Grant. The look of fear on Grace's face tells me far more than the impassive expression the detective wears. Something has changed, and for a moment, I'm terrified to find out what it is. My fears increase as Detective Grant says, "I'm here to see you home, Eva."

"What happened?" Nate asks.

"And you are . . . ?"

"Nathaniel Bouchet, a friend," I supply for him.

"And caretaker," he adds. "Mrs. Tilling hired me." He reaches past the detective to open the car door. "Grace, grab the crutches from the trunk."

It's almost funny how quickly Grace goes to do as he asks. I don't need the crutches, but she needs a focus in the midst of whatever panic is riding her right now. I'm not sure if it's the detective's presence or if something was said before we reached them.

Detective Grant stares at Nate appraisingly for a moment, but she doesn't say anything. She simply stands near us. I realize, though, that her attention is not on us directly. She's scanning the area, studying the lingering mourners, and I know that whatever she's going to tell me includes confirmation that the accident wasn't really an accident.

Once Detective Grant elicits Nate's assurances that he will drive us straight to my house, she adds, "I'll follow you. Give me a minute to get in the car."

Grace and Nate are silent as she walks away. Whatever she knows now is obviously reason enough for her to decide that I need to be escorted to my home. Of course, talking about an ongoing investigation in a cemetery would be strange and awkward. More so because the funeral that just ended was probably for a victim of the same criminal.

"Did she say anything to you, Grace?"

"She just asked where you were, who you were with, and that was it really." Grace twists so she's able to look over the seat at me. "She relaxed when she spotted you. Something has to have happened."

"It could be that she was just not wanting to talk at the graveside. Bad taste and all." I flip my veil up finally. I'd become so comfortable with it that I'd almost forgotten about it.

Nate looks into the rearview mirror, and I meet his gaze. "Don't play stupid, Eva. Not with us."

Immediately, Grace opens her mouth to object, but I say, "Sorry."

He's right. I do that. I pretend to be a little less smart, a little less observant. It lets me blend better. I take a breath and say, "Fine, I'm betting that they got their lab results back or a witness or some sort of proof that my accident wasn't an accident. She is escorting us home. That's a little bit of a clue that there's more going on than worrying about bad manners."

We're quiet again. I lean forward a little to touch Grace's hair, and she reaches back to close her hand over mine. I'm a little surprised at how quickly she's adjusted to my "let me touch you first" rule, but she's my closest friend. She trusts me even when I seem a little crazy.

When we reach my house, my father immediately comes outside. The trepidation I was already feeling spikes. Unlike the detective, his face is very readable right now. He's at the car door almost before the engine is off. I look past him to see Mrs. Yeung standing with my mother on the porch, too.

"The General's here," Grace says from the front seat.

"This is worse than we thought."

Dad opens the door. "Slide over here. I'm going to carry you inside."

"I can—"

"No." He motions me forward with his hand, and there's something in his expression that makes me decide not to argue further. He turns his head to the side and says, "Grace, go inside now."

The Southern male attitude that says girls need protecting is in full force right now, and I realize that my father is afraid. It's not a familiar look on him. "It's going to be okay," I whisper as he scoops me up. "Whatever it is. It'll be okay."

He says nothing, but his lips press together tightly like he doesn't believe me.

As soon as we're inside, Mrs. Yeung grabs Grace into a fierce hug.

My mother and Mrs. Yeung both look like they've seen something horrible, and my mother is reaching out toward me. I quickly put my hand on her arm before she can touch me. I think it's that first contact that matters, and I cannot bear seeing her death, especially right now when everyone is so tense. My falling apart like I seem to when I have those visions would be the last thing they all need.

Nate walks in behind my father, and Detective Grant follows him. I hear a click, and look back to see that, oddly, my father has thrown the bolt on the door. I don't think I've ever known him to do that during the day.

"If you let me know what time to come tomorrow, I can get out of the way," Nate tells my mother in a low voice.

"You need to stay, Nathaniel." My father is using his no-nonsense voice now, and I'm getting more freaked out by the moment.

Detective Grant must realize it because she interjects, "Let's all sit down."

Mom leads the way, and then she immediately slips into her hostess mode. She fusses over me first, and once she's sure I'm comfortable, she turns to the others and offers to fix refreshments.

"Lizzy," my father murmurs.

When she looks at him, he suggests, "Why don't you bring everyone some of that lemonade you fixed earlier."

She nods and flees to the kitchen, and my father relaxes a little. He catches my eye and says, "She's not sure what to do."

"That's perfectly understandable," Mrs. Yeung pronounces, and I'm struck by the differences. The General looks likely to attack someone. My father is trying to manage everything, and my mother wants to look after all of us.

"Eva, we have reason to believe that the accident was an attempt on your life," Detective Grant says baldly. "I've discussed the particulars with your parents, but what you need to know is that we will do everything in our power to find the perpetrator and keep you safe."

"Is this because of Micki?"

"We believe her death was also connected," the detective

answers. Her words confirm my theory, but they don't actually answer the question I just asked.

When we say nothing, Detective Grants says, "Let's talk about flowers."

"Flowers?"

She nods once. "What about in the hospital? What flowers did you get? I remember seeing a bouquet. Who sent it?"

"My parents. They sent orchids."

She watches me with a concentration that seemed less daunting in our first conversation. "Anyone else?"

"The newspaper, some teachers, a few people from church, people from the winery . . . I didn't really keep a list of names. After the first few, I just asked the nurses to give them to other people."

"Did you keep the cards?"

"No. I wasn't thinking." I feel guilty, but I just didn't want the flowers. Quietly, I tell my mother, "I'm sorry. I should've kept names, so we could send thank-you cards. I was just sick of all the reminders that I was hurt, and there were other people that might enjoy them, so I asked the nurses to give them away."

"I'll need you to write down every name you remember."

"Okay."

Detective Grant's gaze settles on all of us in turn as she asks, "What can you tell me about Amy Crowne?"

No one speaks, but both Grace and Nate look at me.

"She didn't send flowers," I say warily.

"Did you get along with her?"

I realize from her carefully blank expression and follow-up question that Detective Grant didn't think Amy sent flowers, which could mean then that the detective thought Amy was somehow involved. I might not like her, but I can't believe that she could do this.

"She's not a killer," I say. "There's no way she could've killed Micki. She doesn't like me, but I don't think she'd have run over me either."

I think about the death visions of Grace and Nate. My impression was that the killer was a man. I'm not sure of height or race or anything. The more I think about it, the less sure I am about gender.

My mother walks back into the room with a tray of drinks. She looks calmer now, and I wonder whether it was having a moment to compose herself or having a focus. Either way, I am glad she's less tense. My father stands and gives her his seat next to the detective. He stays behind her chair, much as Mrs. Yeung does with Grace. Grace and I sit facing the detective. Nate stands with a hand on the back of my chair, so he can look at the detective too.

"Miss Crowne is not a suspect," Detective Grant tells us. "What is your relationship with her? All of you." Her attention shifts from me to Grace and Nate now.

Grace says, "We aren't friends. She spread some . . . stories about Eva earlier this year, and I told her to stop."

"I think she's in my fourth-period class," Nate offers. "I've talked to her at parties, but not alone." He looks at me some-what awkwardly, and I feel bad that my parents are in the room, especially as he adds, "I've never been alone with her."

"She was promiscuous," Grace clarifies the unspoken things for the adults. "A lot of guys *were* alone with her."

The detective nods. "Eva? What about your relationship with Miss Crowne?"

"She slept with my boyfriend . . . *ex*-boyfriend. He was with her the night of my accident, so she couldn't have been involved." I feel myself blushing. "Robert just told me. His parents don't know because she's not, umm, the sort of girl he'd be allowed to date."

"Do other people know about Robert's relationship with her?"

I think about it, and I have no real answer. "Maybe Reid and Jamie. Probably Grayson. They're his closest friends, and they probably would've hidden it from me. Amy would have a better idea who knew. Robert said she was angry that he wasn't going to date her openly." I look at my mother. "Don't say anything to the Baucoms. Please?" Then I look back at the detective. "They were fighting about it the night he didn't show up to get me. That's where he was when I got hit."

"I'm with Eva on this. Amy's a gossip, but she wouldn't hurt anyone." Grace shakes her head. "What did Amy say?"

The detective shakes her head. "Nothing. We think she was the latest victim."

"Is she . . . where is she?" I ask. The waver in my voice says the part I don't want to say aloud: something about the detective's tone makes me suddenly sure that Amy isn't okay.

The detective ignores my question and opens up the case on her iPad. "I need you to look at some things, Eva." She turns the tablet so I can see a strange flower. "Can you tell me what this is?"

I shake my head. She moves to a picture of another flower. This one looks sort of like a lily, but not quite. "No," I whisper.

"Asphodel and amaryllis. Do they mean anything to you personally? Are there any secret clubs at school or anything at all that would tie to these that you know?"

I want to laugh at the idea of secret clubs, but I can't, not with the growing fear that something awful happened to yet another of my classmates. I look away from the iPad and meet Detective Grant's gaze. "They're pretty, but that's all. They don't mean anything to me, and there are no secret societies at Jessup."

"Are you familiar with the idea of flowers being a language?"

Grace says, "Like in Hamlet."

"English class last year," Nate adds helpfully.

At this, the detective perks up a little. "Did the whole grade level read it or just your section?"

"All of us, and they're doing it this year, and they did it the year before us. Maybe before that, too."

"So whoever did this goes to Jessup High?" Grace interjects, and I shiver at the realization that my attacker—the killer—is at my school. I can't imagine anyone I know being this sick.

"It's possible, or they know someone who does."

"Which is pretty much all of Jessup," Nate says.

I am a little relieved by his point. The thought that someone I know is responsible makes me feel even worse. I'm extra comforted that it's summer. I don't know how I could sit in class thinking that someone in the room tried to kill me and Amy and *had* killed Micki.

Detective Grant draws my attention back to her by asking, "Do these words or anything about them mean something more to you?"

She opens up her tablet and turns it so I can see a close-up of three words in an odd red font on a kind of beige paper: FOR EVA. JUDGE.

I stare at them as the reality of what I'm looking at comes clear.

It's not a font.

It's not paper.

"That's skin," I whisper.

"Yes."

"*Amy's* skin?"

She nods.

Grace makes a choking noise. Nate reaches out, and I take his hand. I'm not sure when he moved closer to me, but I'm immeasurably grateful that he did. He feels like an anchor holding me steady, keeping me from sinking into the sickness that threatens to engulf me.

"Someone wrote that on Amy's body?" I can't force myself to say the correct words. They *cut* it into her body.

"Yes."

I reach out and flip the tablet cover closed. I can't look at it. No one should look at it. Ever.

"She's dead, isn't she?" I swallow before I can continue. "Whoever killed Micki and Amy did it because of me? They're trying to say they did this for *me*? How does that even make sense? Someone tried to kill me, and now he's killing my classmates, and saying it's *for me*?" My voice grows shriller as I speak. "What am I to even do? How do I even—"

"Nothing," she says. "You do nothing. You're to stay safe and tell me when you think of anything, anything at all, that you think of about your relationship with or related to Amy Crowne or Michelle Adams."

I nod because I don't know how to speak around the sudden tightness in my throat. It hurts to think that someone did this because of me. It hurts to imagine Amy or Micki suffering.

"Does the 'Judge' part mean anything to you?" Detective Grant asks.

"If I wanted to judge her, it would be because she slept with my boyfriend." I force the words out carefully. I don't want to say them, but I don't want to lie to the detective either. I swallow to try to keep my throat from feeling like it's closing.

I don't look at anyone other than the detective. "Plus, she told people I slept with him . . . with Robert earlier this year. They were already sleeping together then. I had no idea, but that's all we have in common: Robert. I didn't know about her, but he said she was angry about him not breaking up with me."

"Could Robert do this?"

"Kill two girls in our class, and try to kill me?" My voice is getting shrill again. "No! No, he couldn't. He's not like that."

"Not even to make amends with you?"

"How would killing them make *amends* with Eva?" Grace sputters. Her hand flings into the air in a gesture of frustration, almost as if she can't stop the motion. It stays there, upraised with her fingers splayed open, as she half yells, "Are you crazy?"

Mrs. Yeung catches Grace's hand and holds it. "Are you done with us, Detective?"

At Detective Grant's nod, Mrs. Yeung tells my parents, "Someone will escort Grace to your house so the girls are able to see each other." She looks at Nate. "You can bring her over if my husband or I can't, but I trust all of you"—she gives the three of us a stern look—"to stay together. No slipping off to the parties you don't think we know about."

Grace startles, but Nate says, "I won't let them out of my sight when I'm here."

My father shoots Nate a look of approval before offering, "Why don't Nate and I walk you out to your car?"

Mrs. Yeung nods. "Let me text David, so he knows I'm on the way."

After they walk out, the detective sits quietly for a moment. Then she says, "Did Michelle also have a relationship with Robert?"

"Micki?" I want to laugh at the absurdity of that. "She wore a purity ring, and she meant it. The only way she'd have been with Robert would've been after a church-made vow of forever. I'm pretty sure she never even dated. No one at Jessup was up to both her standards *and* her parents' standards."

"The Adamses have a history of marrying within their station," my mother offers mildly. "Prenups and fidelity clauses are required, and Micki wouldn't have risked dating anyone her father didn't approve of. I expect she planned on finding a husband at Duke in a couple years."

The detective looks at my mother for a moment, and then merely nods before telling me, "You need to be careful, Eva. No going out alone." She turns to my mother. "How sure are you of Mr. Bouchet's honesty?"

"We've known him since he was in elementary school. His family was here all the time when the children were younger." Mom clasps her hands tightly together, and I can see by her expression that she's thinking carefully. "He's a good boy."

"I trust him," I interject. "I was with him when we saw the news about Micki. He was shocked and upset."

The detective nods. "If anything he says or does alarms you or if *anyone's* actions alarm you, you contact me immediately."

"We will," my mother promises. "We want you to catch this person. This . . . killer."

"We all want that, Mrs. Tilling." The detective stands, and my mother shows her to the door.

Then I am left alone in my house thinking about the words carved into Amy's skin. I thought that Micki's death tore me up, but I am horrified by Amy's. It's disgusting, what he did to her.

I hope she was already dead when the killer cut her.

I start to think of my classmates. I can't think of anyone who could do this. Maybe they're wrong to think it's a teenager. Teachers? I picture Mr. Sweeney and Miss Ferguson. They're not killers. I'm pretty sure Mr. Sweeney couldn't kill a bug much less a girl. I start to picture my friends and classmates. I picture Robert. No. There's no one I can think of who would do this.

None of it makes sense to me. Micki did nothing to me, and although Amy slept with Robert, that's not reason enough to wish this on her. Neither of those things explain why the killer attacked *me*. I sit on the sofa trying not to think that someone wants me dead—someone who has now killed two girls I know.

DAY 14: "THE FLOWERS"

Eva

I SLEPT HORRIBLY AFTER Detective Grant left. I don't remember most of my nightmares, just vague images from the death visions I had of Nate and Grace's possible ends. I think that Amy and Micki's killer is the same person who pushes Grace into her car trunk and makes Nate choke on liquor. I have no actual proof—just a feeling. The odds of *two* killers in my small town seem impossible. Truthfully, even one seems impossible, but I know there is one. We all know that now. What I don't know—and need to figure out—is what it has to do with me.

As I lie in my bed, thinking over what I know about the visions and murders, I realize that there is one more thing I do know: I can't see faces in my visions. I'm not sure why that is. I can see them in my own life, but when I fall into someone's death, the sense that's least reliable is vision—or maybe cognition. I grab my laptop and I try several search terms, but it's not until I enter "face blind" that I get useful results: prosopagnosia. Basically, as I read I learn that some people can't recognize faces, even people they see regularly and know. Prosopagnosia is either inherent, or it's acquired from a brain injury. Although my brain injury didn't cause me to have trouble recognizing faces in the waking world, it has in my death visions. I try a few more searches, but not surprisingly, there aren't any articles that explain altered perceptions in death visions. The most useful information I have is that people with face blindness—prosopagnosics—have to use other characteristics to identify people. The bit that I learn isn't much, but I'm not sure where to learn more. I can't expect any insight from my doctor, especially as I'm not interested in sharing my new ability.

I spend a few minutes thinking about it, and then I close my laptop and start slowly working my way downstairs. Some coffee and food will help me think. At the very least, it'll distract me from this nightmare for a few minutes. I thump into the kitchen, where I find my mother. It's odd seeing her so determinedly domestic, but it's also comforting. If there was ever a time when I was willing to admit to needing some extra TLC, this is it.

She puts her hands on her hips when she sees me and *tsks*. "Why didn't you call for help? Your independent streak has to be some latent Tilling gene."

"Says the black sheep of the Cooper clan," I tease without thinking.

She stops moving, her hand midway to the pitcher of orange juice, and I wonder if it was wrong to try to tease her. I thought we were trying to be closer. I thought it would be okay. Hurriedly, I start, "I'm s—"

My apology is lost under a snort of laughter. She's laughing in that unrestrained way that I've so rarely seen, and I can't look away. My mother is beautiful when she's *real* like this. In the midst of everything that's so very wrong, I'm exceptionally grateful for this moment.

"Oh my goodness, Eva," she says a few snorts later. "No one—and I do mean no one—has the sheer nerve to mention that other than Daddy. I swear they all think the whole of Jessup is going to go all cattywampus if they bring up my checkered past."

She grabs the handle of the pitcher of orange juice and sits down; her poise is already returning, and if I hadn't just heard those very unrefined noises, I would've never guessed that she had laughed. The pitcher and two glasses are in front of her, and she watches me attentively.

I pull out my two chairs. I sit on the first, and I raise my leg to prop it up on the second chair. "You don't *seem* much like a troublemaker, but I figure my 'difficult streak' has to come from somewhere."

My mother smiles. "I was determined to be my own person, and after years of Daddy having so many of the church

ladies lecturing me on my manners and my dress and everything under the sun, I had a fierce urge to prove I wasn't a
good girl." She shakes her head. "I don't imagine it makes a
lot of sense considering who I ended up with, but I just wanted
to be someone other than Lizzy Cooper, daughter of the great
Davis Cooper IV."

"I get that." I stare at her, wondering how I didn't know
this before. "I feel like that sometimes. I'm his granddaughter,
your daughter, and granddaughter to the Reverend Tilling."

She sighs. "I'm sorry. You seem so confident all the time
that it didn't occur to me that you felt that way."

"I'm fine. I just hate the way people watch me. It'll be
worse now when the news about the killer gets out."

"They'll catch him," my mother says, and it feels somewhere between a wish and a promise.

We sit quietly for a few minutes, and I realize that despite
all the wrong happening now, I have some *right* with my
mother. Our peace is interrupted by the doorbell, and we both
startle at the sound. For a moment, I see my own fears in her
eyes, but then she pats my hand.

I brace myself for the vision, for falling into her death,
but nothing happens. There is no death, no slipping into her
future self, and I'm speechless at the absence. I don't *want* to
feel her die, but I don't understand why it didn't happen.

Then her hand is gone from mine already, and she's heading to answer the door.

A few moments later, she returns, carrying a vase of flowers and a small package wrapped in brown paper. Her hands are shaking as she sets them on the counter.

"There are flowers," she says, pointing out the obvious. "There are flowers here at our house."

I look at them. A gladiolus and a scarlet lily are surrounded by honeysuckle. It's an oddly beautiful bouquet, but it fills me with horror. The package that came with it is too small to be chocolates. If it were from a friend, I'd think it was jewelry. It's about that size. Part of me is oddly distant, trying not to get scared. I think of my friends, of the death visions that I now suspect are real, and I am resolved to figure this out. I have clues the police won't believe.

My hands tremble as I look at the bouquet. The killer knows where I live, knows I'm out of the hospital, and sent me flowers. After talking to the detective, I know these flowers are a message.

"I'm calling her now," Mom says. Her phone is already at her ear, and she walks out of the room as she begins to speak: "Detective? This is Mrs. Tilling."

My mother's voice grows faint as she walks farther into the house, and I debate what I'm about to do. I need to know what's in that package. I don't want my mother to open it and find something awful there. I think back to every police procedural I've watched with my father. I don't want to destroy evidence. So far, the delivery person and my mother's fingerprints are on it.

I get up, grab my crutches, and hobble to the walk-in

pantry. There in the far back, beside the tinfoil and storage bags, is an unopened package of the thick yellow gloves my mother wears if she hand-washes any dishes. I balance on one foot as I open the plastic bag and put on the gloves.

Once I've hobbled to the counter, I carefully open the small white envelope with my yellow-gloved hands. It's a standard card, one of the "thinking of you" ones, and on it are five letters in tight block print: YOURS.

My hands are shaking as I set the card aside and turn my attention to the tiny box. Visions of severed fingers or ears fill my mind, and by the time I open the package, I'm expecting something gross. Inside the tiny box, which is actually a white cardboard jewelry box, is a dead cicada.

I don't get it. The killer sent me a dead bug. It's clearly a message, but I have less than no idea what it means. Is it a threat? Is it something else?

When my mother returns, I look away from the bug in the box to tell her, "I need my laptop."

"What are you . . ." Her words fade as she comes to stand by my side. "He sent you a *cicada*?"

"I need my laptop," I repeat.

She looks down at the card and gasps. Suddenly, my mother hugs me with one arm, and again, I don't fall into her death.

When Nate arrives a few minutes later, I'm at my laptop typing. I hear my mother explaining that she's not going to work.

"You're going to work, Mom," I call out. "Dad needs you there. I'm fine here with Nate. Promise!"

She doesn't answer me, but her voice is a quiet hum in the background as she brings Nate up to speed. I'm copying and pasting possible meanings for flowers and cicadas and the word "judge." I remember from class that there was a book in the 1800s that was supposedly all about the official flower meanings, but I'm guessing that the killer uses the internet if he's anyone younger than thirty.

Gladiolus: "I'm very sincere," preparedness, flowers
of the gladiators (Note: Dedicated/serious in his
crazy?)

Red lily: "high bred" or "high souled" (Note: Online it's
called a "scarlet lily," but the orange one means
"hatred." I think this is red/scarlet though. He
either is saying I'm high bred, or he is, or it's to
be orange and he hates me.)

Honeysuckle: united in love, devoted love, fidelity
(Note: He's telling me he's a creeper. Figured
that out already without the flowers.)

Asphodel: regrets beyond the grave, I follow you to
the grave, remember me after the grave (Note:
Who had the asphodel? Micki or Amy?)

Amaryllis: pride, pastoral poetry (Note: guessing it's
not the poetry. So who is he calling prideful? Or
is he saying he's proud of what he did?)

Cicada: regeneration, change, rebirth, longevity,
    patience, immortality
Judge: to form an opinion, to try, to weigh in, to find
    guilty or innocent; an authority
Yours: What's mine? The flowers? The cicada? The
    blame? The killer? All of it???

In a separate file, I jot down what I remember of the death visions, the deaths that already happened, and prosopagnosia. I add my notes that prosopagnosics use voice, clothing, hair color, walk, and other details to identify people. Maybe that's the trick I need to try in my visions. I'm still staring at my notes, googling other meanings on the flowers, and flipping between them when Nate comes to stand behind me. He looks over my shoulder at my screen listing the flowers and says, "I'm sure the police already started looking up what the flowers he left with Micki and Amy meant."

"I can't *not* think about it." I look back at him. "The killer carved my *name* on Amy's body when he killed her. He killed Micki and tried to kill me. And now"—I motion to the counter—"he's sending me flowers and dead bugs and cryptic messages."

"I know." He looks so calm that I feel better just having him near me. "That doesn't make it your fault."

As much as I want that to be true, it feels like it's somehow my fault. I save the document and close my laptop. I don't say anything, but Nate knows me. Even though it's been far too long since we were kids, I don't think I've changed so much that he can't figure out that I disagree with him.

He pulls out the chair my mother had been using and sits down. I reach out for his hand before he takes mine. It's more forward than I would be, especially if we are truly just friends, but I feel like my seams are loose. I'm afraid that he'll touch me, and I can't bear looking at his death. I thought I was holding it all together, and I'd planned to test my visions, but last night I realized that I'm ready to fracture.

"They'll catch him," Nate says.

"Everyone keeps saying that, but Amy and Micki are dead."

His hand tightens on mine, and I'm reminded of those weird days between death and funerals. In Jessup, my family makes a lot of appearances at the homes of the grieving. My mother has an almost pathological need to take covered dishes to mourners. Dad says it's because she lost her mother so young. Looking out for the grieving makes her feel less helpless, but being inside the house where death is clinging to every thought makes me feel lost. There's a hazy sense of being out of time and place in that grief window—sort of like being in the hospital. I feel desperate to talk about something, *anything* other than death, but it's there in every room and under every word. It's inescapable.

It's all part of why I hate funerals. They're so heavy with awkward desire to talk about anything other than loss, but the guilt of doing so makes it impossible. It's suffocating—and there will be another one in a matter of days.

"We'll have to go to Amy's funeral," I think out loud.

Nate's expression is stony. "There's a killer who's obsessing on you. I'm not sure going to Amy's funeral is a good idea."

"I agree," says a voice from behind me. I look over my shoulder and see the detective standing there with my mother.

"You can't stop me," I point out, calling upon my television police knowledge. "I'm not even a material witness. I'm allowed to go anywhere I want."

Detective Grant's lips twist into a smile of sorts. "Everyone I've interviewed describes you as sweet and almost meek. I'm not sure they were right."

I tilt my chin upward and stare at her. "I'm not going to live in a cage because of some sicko."

She walks past me to examine the flowers, the card, and the cicada. She doesn't touch them, telling us, "A tech will be by to collect these shortly."

I push myself up, using the table for leverage. Nate wraps an arm around my waist to help steady me. I reach for my crutches and pull away from him.

"I wore gloves," I point out.

"You shouldn't have opened them at all," the detective chastises me.

"Nathaniel, why don't you help Eva out to the sofa," my mother says.

I can't disobey her. There's nothing else to say to the detective right now, and I won't learn anything new by staring at the dead cicada, the tiny card, and those horrible, beautiful flowers. I meet Nate's gaze and nod. I'm not sure I'll ever be able to feel safe again. I want to lock everyone I know and love, and even those I only like, here in the house with me, and we can wait while the police catch the killer.

The sheer weighty terror of it all creeps up on me. Someone tried to *kill* me. Someone feels such vile things for me that he—or maybe even she—wanted my life to end. There's no way to make that kind of wrong feel okay. It's such a big violence that it killed Micki and Amy. Their deaths feel like my fault.

And it makes me sick.

What did I say or do that made this crazy person fixate on me and my friends?

"Are you doing okay?" Nate settles on the uncomfortable chair to the left of the sofa, near enough to reach me if I need anything but not so close as to make me nervous.

I'm nervous anyhow. I need to figure out who's killing girls in Jessup, and to do that I need to tell Nate my secret. I can't research anything without him knowing why I'm trying to solve it.

"If you touch me, I see your death," I tell him before I can back down from the impulse. "Since the accident, I see people's deaths. I thought it was just hallucinations, but . . . I think it might be real, and I'm terrified."

Nate stares at me with something like sympathy in his eyes. He's still staring at me when my mother walks into the room.

"The detective is leaving, and I have to go to the police station with her. I'm swinging by the office *briefly* to pick a few things up, but I'm not staying," she says. "I'll lock the door behind us. The alarm is set, the company is monitoring it as a top priority, and the police will do drive-bys, and . . . I'll have my phone, and . . ."

Nate nods. "I'll be with her until you come back. We'll be okay."

She pauses, but she doesn't really have a choice. If the detective needs her to go to the station, she has to go. We *are* safe here, too.

"I'm fine," I add. "Promise."

She takes a shuddering breath. "Do you want an officer to stay? I'm sure we could ask Detective Grant to—"

"No," I interrupt. "You can call or text, and the alarm is set. The service monitors it, right? Honestly, I'm *fine.*"

Reluctantly, she leaves.

Once she goes, Nate is silent again. It's not until the outside door closes behind her and we hear the lock engage and the telltale beep of the alarm being armed that he says, "Say that again."

"When people touch me, I see their deaths. One of the nurses has a heart attack. My father dies from some disease in the hospital. You . . . you drown on liquor after the killer finds you along the road." I watch him as I tick off the deaths I've seen, listing them impersonally so I don't think about the details, the feelings, the horrible panic of death.

"And this started after the accident," he half asks, half states.

"Yes."

"But you think it's . . . not from your TBI."

I huff in frustration. "I *know* it sounds crazy, but you're my proof." His brows raise, and he motions for me to continue, so I say, "I knew about Nora and Aaron because of the death vision. When you touched me, I sort of . . . I think of it like *falling* into it. I fell into you, and you were worried about them. You hadn't told me anything about them yet, but I knew their names already."

He's silent again, but this time he's motionless. We sit staring at each other for several tense moments, and then he stands and walks toward me. "How do you think I die?"

I flinch away. "Liquor."

"I stopped drinking." He kneels on the floor in front of me so we're eye-to-eye. "I don't drink *or* drink and drive."

"I know," I whisper. "He forces you off the road, and you don't have your cell phone . . . well, you didn't. The vision changed after I asked you to keep your phone on you. When I saw your death the second time, he broke your phone. It was on Old Salem Road. You were almost home, and it was dark, and—"

"I do drive that way," he interjects. "It's faster."

After a minute pause, he says, "That's why you made me promise to check for my phone."

I nod. "It wasn't enough though. When you got out, you

thought he was going to help. He doesn't help. You need to stay in the truck so he can't touch you."

"Why did I pull over?"

For a moment, I think back, letting myself imagine the two times I've felt Nate die. "You get sick. Ready to throw up. It's like the flu or something."

We exchange a look as I realize how strange that sounds. How would the killer know Nate would have the flu and would be pulling over? That part doesn't make sense. Even if the killer was following him, it wouldn't mean there would be an opportunity—unless there was reason to expect Nate to get sick. I meet his gaze. "He must give you something first. Poison or a drug or something. Don't eat or drink anything that isn't in a sealed container. Until we catch him, you can't risk it. I don't know *when* it happens." I pause. "It was a Friday, I think. You were thinking about visiting Aaron."

"Okay." Nate doesn't look away. "How does it work?"

"It only happens when people touch my bare skin. If I touch *you*, it doesn't happen." I pause. Telling someone feels weird, like speaking it makes it somehow more real. "It has to be bare skin, and it doesn't happen *every* time . . . I don't know why. I didn't even think it was real. I thought I was just hallucinating, but . . . I don't know. . . It *feels* like it's real, some sort of curse or gift."

Nate listens, but instead of telling me I'm crazy, he says, "So I'm going to touch your arm now."

He extends his hand, and I drop my gaze to it. I watch as his fingertips get closer, and then they graze my skin. That's all it takes.

The car swerves toward me, and I have to go off the road to avoid impact. I feel the truck dip and jerk as the front wheel hits the ditch. I'm braking, hoping the brakes don't lock up, praying I don't go into a spin, and regretting the lack of airbags. My brain is racing, rolling into thoughts that seem out of place. I wasn't going fast enough that the accident will be fatal, but I don't have time to be without wheels.

It's dark out, and there are no streetlights on Old Salem Road, but I know the area well enough after driving it every day the past year and a half. It's wooded along the road, but not thick. The front of the truck clips a tree, but it's only a sapling. I start to swerve farther only to jolt to a stop as I smash into a much larger tree.

The truck gives one last shudder as it comes to a stop at the tree, and I shakily cut off the engine. I know there's no real danger of explosion. This isn't a movie, where cars explode constantly.

I unfasten my seat belt and push the door open. It creaks in a new way, and I wonder how much damage there is to the frame.

I wince as I slide out of the truck. I must have hit my knee because there's a sharp pain when I put weight on my left leg. Tentatively, I take another step. Nothing seems to be broken, but I suspect that I'll be limping for a couple days.

After a moment, I pat my jeans pockets and find my phone.

My face feels wet, and I realize that blood is dripping from a gash above my eye.

A car pulls up in front of me, and I wonder if it's the car that ran me off the road or someone who saw the accident. The head-lights shine in my face so I can't see who's inside the car. There aren't a lot of people who drive along Old Salem Road, but there are a few houses and the reservoir.

The lights make the person getting out of the car look like a silhouette. He's not a huge man. I can tell that. I concen-trate on details: size, height, clothes. It's too dark to make out anything about the clothes beyond trousers and a sweatshirt with the hood pulled up. The height makes me think "man." Although he could be a bigger woman. . . . I watch the person walk up to my truck. Something seems wrong. I realize that he's holding his arm straight down, motionless and tight against his body. It seems awkward because his other arm swings as he walks toward me.

He—or she—isn't speaking. I can see the shape of a per-son, and I'm almost certain it's a man, but I still can't see a face. It's there, but I can't focus on any details. His hair that I can see sticking out from under his hood looks brown. The shape of the body, the haircut—short—makes me pretty sure this is a man.

I'm shaking, and I think back to what Eva said. This is the accident she warned me about; this is the person who attacked her. This is the man who killed Amy. I wish I could remember the *details about this attack, the things that she said I did, so I could change them all right now when it's happening.*

I fumble with my phone, tapping the button for my mother, and then look around for some sort of weapon.

He swings his arm out and up, and I realize that he has a crowbar in his hand; that's why he kept his arm close to his body.

I try to dodge him, with some success, but in the next moment, the crowbar hits my shoulder. My phone falls as I duck and grab the Maglite under the seat of the truck. It's not as long as a crowbar, but it's heavy and extends my reach. I just need to get away from him, hopefully knock him down long enough for help to arrive.

The side window shatters as my attacker begins swinging wildly.

I twist my body, putting more of my weight on my uninjured leg. I swing blindly with my flashlight, cursing the lack of street-lights and the blood dripping from my forehead.

"You're not worthy," he says.

I feel bones shatter. He hits my cheek, my nose, and my mouth; the pain is excruciating. I can taste blood.

The added pain from the blow to my face makes me a lot less than steady.

"You're complicating the message," he says.

I hit the ground, and try to struggle to my feet, but I'm trapped between him and the truck. I roll to the side, as he swings again. I try to block it and feel the heavy metal bar hit my forearm, break-ing it. I notice gloves on his hands, covering his skin.

A moment later, I feel it hit my head.

The vision recedes. It's not because I pulled away from Nate, but because he died. *Again.* I know that the killer is a man, that his skin was hidden under gloves, that his hair is brown. I try to concentrate on that instead of the feeling of dying, of *Nate* dying. This time was different from the others. I didn't feel the same sense of being two people at once that I did the first few times. I'm not sure if it's because I chose to do it or the trauma is somewhat lessened by the frequency with which I've been in Nate's death. Either way, I was only-Nate in this one, as opposed to earlier visions where I kept separating myself from the person who was dying.

It's also the first time I'm not shaking and freezing. I'm still cold, and I shiver, but I'm not feeling like I was doused in ice water. Maybe accepting the visions was enough to decrease the side effects—or maybe it just gets easier with practice.

Nate—the real, alive Nate—is still kneeling in front of me, staring at my face, and I don't try to hide the fact that I'm crying again. The brutality of Nate's death was worse this time.

"He's angry at you," I whisper.

In a low voice, I tell him the entirety of what I saw. He remains silent as I talk, not interrupting even as my voice breaks. It's not until I reach the part about him remembering our conversations during the attack that I notice that he's caught my hand in his and is holding on to me tightly. I look at our entwined fingers, and he follows my gaze with his own.

"Why not now? I'm touching you," Nate asks. "Why don't you see my death again?"

I shake my head. "I'm not sure. Maybe if nothing changes I don't see it." I pause, frustration filling me. "I didn't get a rule book or anything. Searching online hasn't revealed any answers, and . . . I don't *know*. It's all guesses right now."

He nods, and I can see by the way his face is scrunched up that he's processing everything. After a few moments, he asks, "So let's test it. If I make a promise, if I decide to change something else, will it change?"

Nate sounds excited as he talks, as if me seeing his death repeatedly is good somehow. He starts to pull his hand away, but I clutch it tightly.

"I need a minute," I admit. It *hurts* to be caught in someone's death. I fill him in on the cold and the shaking, and he hugs me. Then, he nods and sits back on his heels so he's farther away from me.

"He's from here. Maybe not Jessup, but from North Carolina. Maybe South Carolina. He doesn't sound like Grace or anyone from outside the South." I'm still trying to piece together details, doing what people with prosopagnosia do in the real world. It helped me focus when I was inside Nate's death this time, and it's helping me to think about something other than the horror of being beaten to death. "His voice is male, but I couldn't see his skin. Clothes are normal. Hair was brown, I think."

"Were there any words on the hoodie?" Nate asks. His arm

is stretched out so our hands are still clasped. He watches me so intently that I want to run.

"I don't know," I say.

"Did it feel like I knew him?"

"I don't know. I'm not sure I would know that. Maybe?" I shake my head. "I don't know. I'm sorry."

After a moment, Nate leans forward and kisses my cheek. It's sudden and ridiculously exciting—and weird. I could almost believe it didn't happen because he's gone as soon as it happens, and I lift my hand to touch my face as if there will be proof on my skin.

He's still holding my hand and watching me when he says, "I believe you. I just thought you should know."

"Oh."

"I'm sorry that it happened."

"It?" I repeat.

There are so many things that could be "it" that I'm not sure what else to say. The kiss? The accident? The vision?

"I'm sorry that you have these visions, but you're going to save my life." He squeezes my hand this time. "I'll thank you later too, but *thank you.*"

I swallow and look away. I don't want him to thank me. I want him to *like* me . . . and believe in me. At least, I have the second part, and that's more important. I smile. "Why do you believe me?"

He shrugs. "I don't know. Instinct? Trust? I just do."

"Thank you." I release his hand reluctantly. I would rather

keep hold of it, but it feels more intimate than is safe. I shake my head at how awkward this whole crushing on him is, and in a moment more impulsive than my confession of visions, I say, "I like you. I know it's not . . . a good idea, but I do. So after today you can't kiss me or hold me while I sleep if we're going to make it as friends. It confuses thi—"

His lips are suddenly on mine, and his hand rests gently along my cheek. It's not the sort of passionate kiss that leads to losing sense or clothing, but this is *Nate*. Nate is kissing me, and I can't stop myself from leaning in closer. I don't *want* to stop myself. He's kneeling against the edge of the sofa, and I'm tilting forward to reach him. As soon as I curl my hand around the back of his neck, his kiss grows less tentative.

I don't ever want to let him go, but only a few moments later, he pulls away.

His hand still rests carefully on my cheek, and his whispered words are breathy against my lips as he says, "It might not be a good idea, but I've wanted to kiss you for years. If today's the only chance, I'll take it."

I open my mouth to say something, anything, but no words come. He presses his lips to mine for a split second, and then he's pulling back. With the sort of lithe grace that makes him beautiful to watch, he seems to go from kneeling to standing in one fluid movement.

"I'm going to see what's in the fridge for lunch. Your mom said there were a few options, and you didn't eat break—"

"Wait!"

He shakes his head. "No. Give me a few minutes, okay? You told me about my death, and then"—he motions between us—"that's not my area, Eva. I don't do relationships or dating. That doesn't mean I don't want you. It just means I care about you enough to keep my hands to myself."

I blink up at him like he's started speaking a foreign language. It's possible he did because it sounded like he just said he wants me but won't touch me *because* he likes me. It may be the stupidest thing he's ever told me.

Despite his idiocy or maybe because of it, I'm at a complete loss for words. I want to yell at him, but I don't know where to start. He stands there in the middle of the room, looking every bit as uncomfortable as I feel, and we simply stare at each other in silence until I say, "I think there's quinoa-stuffed peppers."

"Keen what?"

"Not keen *what*. It's *keen-wah*." I repeat the word, sounding out the two syllables. "Quinoa is like a grain, kind of like rice, but LeeAnn says it's healthier than gluten foods like pasta." I realize I'm babbling. He's staring at me with somewhat wide eyes now, but I keep talking. "There are peppers stuffed with what looks like something between seeds and sprouts. That's quinoa."

"Right. Peppers full of seeds," he says slowly. "Sounds good. I'll heat them."

He walks away, and I am left alone on my sofa feeling silly for discussing grains when there are so many more important topics to discuss, but he's the one who just banned those subjects. I hear the fridge open and close, then cupboards as he presumably looks for plates, and then I hear the microwave open and close. After a few minutes of listening to him bang around in my kitchen, I decide to follow him.

As quietly as I'm able, I get up on my crutches and hobble toward the kitchen. When I reach the doorway, I see him staring into the microwave the way my father stares at the news ticker on the bottom of the television when he doesn't have his contacts in his eyes—like he can't quite see it, but if he concentrates hard enough, the picture will be less vague.

I know Nate hears my approach. Crutches aren't designed for stealth. He doesn't turn away from the microwave though, so I'm left looking at his back. It's not a bad view, but it is awkward to stand here with only the whir of the microwave in the space where words should be.

"I shouldn't have kissed you." He turns to face me immediately after he says it.

I'm tempted to slap him. When we were kids, I would've hit him for being daft, but we're in a different place now so I simply say, "I disagree, but"—I shrug one shoulder because it's the best I can do while standing on crutches—"you've decided to make this weirder than it has to be, so I'm at a loss."

He tenses. "What's that supposed to mean?"

"We're friends, Nate, and I've crushed on you since middle school." My cheeks burn a little as I say it, but I'm *over* being subtle. Maybe it's the threat of a killer who seems focused on me; maybe it's a fearlessness because of the accident; maybe it's seeing Nate die one too many times. I don't know. All I do know is that I'm not going to ignore the things I think or want anymore. I shake my head. "I may not be your closest friend anymore—"

"You still are," he interjects.

"That's pitiful, you know," I mutter before returning to my point. My voice starts to get louder as I speak, but he's the only one here so it's not like I'm going to attract an audience. "Whether I'm your closest friend or not, we *were* close for years. I almost died, and right now, it looks like someone is out to get you *because of me*. If that doesn't entitle me to say how I feel, then nothing does."

The microwave dings, but he doesn't turn away from me.

"I spent the better part of the past year with Robert. During that time, he wanted Amy, and I wanted you . . . just like the year before when I wasn't dating him. I've never stopped wanting you. Ever. Now, you walk into my life and act like we've never stopped talking. Then you kiss me and tell me you think about me that way, too. I'm not going to ignore that. You can't ask me to either. I'm *sick* of ignoring things, and"—I stomp closer to him and poke him in the chest with my index finger—"I'm sick of being ignored because you have some sort of childhood trauma that makes you shove me away."

I'm all but yelling at him by the time I'm done, but he still doesn't react.

He doesn't speak at all. He simply turns and opens the microwave. Silently, he removes the plate of quinoa-stuffed peppers and, plate in hand, steps around me. He stays mute as he pulls out my chair and pours me a glass of lemonade.

Then, he walks out of the kitchen as if I haven't just laid my heart out in front of him.

DAY 14: "THE PLAN"

Grace

WHEN I ARRIVE AT Eva's house, my mother walks me to the door and waits while Nate opens it and ushers us into the quiet of the Tilling home. They exchange words as if he's an adult, which seems a bit ludicrous considering his reputation around school. The boy might not drink liquor like it's water these days, but he's still slept with more girls than even the best gossips probably know. Back in Philadelphia when I was trying out my rule-breaking persona, he'd have been a temptation. Either my mother trusts me a lot more than I thought or she's clueless about Nate's history. I'm not going to ask her which. Instead, I lean in and kiss her cheek. "It's fine, Mom. We'll be here with the doors locked, police driving by, and a security system. We're *safe* here." I shoot an innocent look at Nate. "Eva did order a case of wine and the strippers, right?"

He opens his mouth, closes it, and scowls at me.

My mother laughs.

"I'm not sure I'm getting paid enough to deal with both of you," Nate mutters.

"I'll be by to pick you up at six," my mom says, and then she tells Nate, "Don't let them out of the house."

He nods, and she leaves. I see her pause on the porch until the door is locked. After a half wave, she walks away—and I slump against the door for a moment. I know she's worried, but I feel like she's overreacting. From the tidbits I overheard and the news reports, it sounds like both Micki Adams and Amy Crowne were out at night or early morning when they were killed. I know the killer seems likely to be Jessupite, but I'm not the sort of girl who spends any time with the locals—at least not alone. Eva is my only close friend, and she's very obviously not the killer.

I'm not as convinced as she is that Robert is innocent. When the detective asked if he could kill Amy to make amends for cheating on Eva, I thought it seemed crazy, but I think a lot of things here seem crazy. And sometimes, I think Robert and his friends are the kings of all that's crazy. Still, I know that Eva understands them in a way I don't, and if she thinks Robert is unable to do these awful things, I mostly trust her. I still wouldn't go anywhere alone with him, but I'm not about to start pursuing him with pitchforks or whatever they use in lynch mobs in Jessup these days.

"She's in the kitchen," Nate says, and then he walks away,

leaving me standing in the foyer. I think he's actually surlier than usual. I wasn't sure such a state was even possible, and after the way that Eva and Nate seemed to be getting along, I'm a little shocked.

When I go into the kitchen, I find Eva staring blankly at a stuffed pepper; she doesn't look any happier than Nate does.

"Eva?"

She looks up and gives me a small smile. "Hey."

"Are you okay?"

"No. Nate and I"—she turns to stare at the empty doorway; Nate hasn't followed me—"had a difference of opinion."

I pull out a chair and sit beside her. "About?"

She looks a little lost for a moment, her gaze drifting to the doorway again. "Apparently, our little man-slut has thought I was worth the time for *years*, but he's decided for *both* of us that nothing can happen."

"I'm sorry." I reach out, but then remember her belief that being touched evokes death visions, so I don't touch her hand. Instead, I let my hand rest near her, so she can take it if she needs.

"He held me while I slept, you know? He listens, and he says all the right things." She huffs and mutters, "Except when he tells me that kissing me was a mistake."

"Kissing you?"

"Today." She gestures toward the living room where, presumably, the kiss happened. The doorway is still empty, but the source of her frustration is somewhere in the house. She shoves her plate away and lowers her head to the table before saying, "I have lousy taste in boys."

She looks past me then, and I follow her gaze to see Nate.

"I'm going upstairs," Eva announces.

At that, she presses her lips together and holds out a hand for her crutches.

"I could carry you," he starts.

"No."

Mutely, Nate hands her crutches to her.

When Eva and I reach her room, she sits on her bed, and after I put her crutches on the floor, I sit next to her.

"I don't want to fight with him," she whispers.

For a moment, she's so tense that I can actually see her muscles clench. Then, she shakes her head and says, "Will you hand me my laptop?"

She pulls up her notes, and she lets me read her thoughts on the flowers and on her death visions. It's creepy to read about my death and about Nate's death alongside details about people who *actually* died. She has a few details about the killer though, and it's the first time I've hoped she really can see deaths.

We start to try to figure who the killer's next victims will be, but I don't know any logical way to narrow in on who's the most vulnerable. "What do the three of you have in common?"

"We're all girls who are finishing our junior year at Jessup," Eva says. "That leaves a lot of possible victims though."

"You and Amy both dated Robert," I add.

"Micki didn't. Neither did Nate." She frowns. "Or you. You were both future victims."

"If Nate is really a victim, the girl part of the similarity is out too," I point out reluctantly.

She grows quiet for a moment, but then, she shakes her head. "Right. So what do we know?"

"That the killer sent *you* a message. I hate to say it, but the one thing everyone has in common is *you*. Somehow everyone is tied to you."

"Micki and I weren't close, though. With you, Nate, and Amy, I see a connection there, but Micki doesn't fit." Eva lets out a small noise of frustration. "If it's girls, Nate doesn't fit. If it's people who . . . get around, you and Micki don't fit."

"Maybe not here, but before I moved here . . ." I leave the words unsaid, but Eva knows about my stupid choices in Philadelphia. "Maybe someone knows that?"

"Micki was a virgin. So that pattern doesn't fit."

"Maybe it's not a pattern," I suggest. "Maybe it's what they 'mean' to you . . . or something entirely different."

We look at the notes again. There's not a lot of information, but we do arrive at a few possible thoughts: the killer is trying to say something about love, fidelity, rebirth, and pride; the killer is tying this to juniors at our school, so has some connection to our class; and he—or she—is focusing on Eva. It's nauseating that someone can be so twisted as to think that murder has anything to do with love. The fidelity part is a little more interesting considering what we now know about Robert's lack of faithfulness.

"So did he kill Amy because Robert slept with her?" Eva wonders aloud. "It's not *her* fault that he was dating me. If it's about being faithful, shouldn't Robert be a target?"

"Maybe?"

Eva and I exchange a look, and she says, "I need to see him then. I need to see how he dies."

"Micki wasn't unfaithful to anyone. Neither were you."

"Nate doesn't date, so that's not it there either," she muses.

After a few more minutes, we are forced to admit that these facts aren't enough to figure out who the future victims are. There are around two hundred people in our grade, so if we look only at the girls, we have maybe a hundred or so potential victims. That's a lot of people. If we narrow it down to people who are faithful or have pride issues, that's . . . impossible to figure out.

"They might not all be girls if your visions are real, but they *are* all people you spend time with. That's the only thing in common between the victims and me and Nate, too. It seems pretty simple, but it's all we have."

"So I need to start looking at my friends' deaths," she says softly. "If I'm all that everyone has in common, we need to start looking at their deaths to see who the next victim is."

We decide to start with the people most likely to visit her. Rather than text them all, she simply sends a message to Piper, who was to visit soon anyhow. "Bored and trapped in the house. Invite the usuals to come over for lunch."

A few moments later, she reads Piper's reply: "On it."

I'm not sure who all will be around, but I suspect that Piper will just send a group message to some combination of their core group: Laurel, Jess, CeCe, Bailey, Madison, Robert, Reid, Grayson, Carter, and Jamie. To be sure that Robert comes, Eva sends another text to him.

Quietly, Eva tells me, "The idea of having most of them in the house with Nate makes me want to cringe, but I need to start looking for more clues."

"You *do* know Nate slept with Jess . . . and possibly with Piper."

"I know what he's done the past two years, Grace," she says. "It didn't cure my crush when he was doing it, and it's not curing it now."

At the sound of a throat being cleared, Eva glances at her doorway. Nate stands in the hall awkwardly, hands shoved in his pockets and lips pressed together as if he's disapproving of something—quite possibly the words he just overheard.

Eva tilts her head, her chin jutting out as if she's about to challenge him. "Did you need something?"

He shakes his head. "I'm not going to even try to answer that one, Eva."

He stays outside of her room, like there's a line he can't cross, and I have the overwhelming urge to yank him inside, run out, and close the door on them. He needs to get past whatever this is, but I'm not so heartless as to put Eva in that situation—at least not today.

"The social elite are stopping by," I tell him.

"What?" He looks from Eva to me and back at her. "What did you do?"

"Texted Piper and Robert." She folds her arms over her chest. "I'm investigating. All the victims are tied to me, so I'll look and see if we can figure out who's next."

"You let her do this?" He glares at me.

"Check the attitude, Bouchet." I stand and step between them. "Crazy killer is obsessing on her. What do you think she's going to do? Sit around and wait for him to kill another girl?"

Nate folds his arms over his chest and says, "If the victims are all tied to you, don't you think the *killer* might be too?"

"They're my friends, Nate. They might be jerks sometimes, but no more so than you."

He doesn't look convinced, but I'm with Eva on this one. I don't know what a killer is supposed to look like, but I'm having a hard time picturing anyone I know as a murderer. They're potential victims, though, and I really hope that Eva *can* see deaths because I don't want anyone else to die for real.

DAY 14: "THE ADULTERER"

Judge

I KNOW HE'S THERE, close to her, touching her like she's his. She's not. She's always been mine—and she always will be.

Her mother hired him, invited him into her home, and I am confused by it. I don't understand why she picked *him*. Why didn't Mrs. Tilling place an ad? Why didn't she ask Eva's friends? I could have been there every day. She'd see how life should be then. She'd understand my love for her, my need for her. I could touch the cuts on her skin, marks that no one else has put on her, like symbols of our connection. If I study them, I wonder what they'll say. What messages are written on her skin for me to read?

The Lord is mysterious, and I don't even begin to understand his ways. When the glass carved her face, I didn't think to wipe away the blood to find the messages that the Lord might have left there. He carved the commandments in stone tablets. He spoke through a burning bush. Perhaps, Eva's skin is the parchment on which he wrote our own private commandments.

I can't let Nathaniel Bouchet taint her. I can't let him study the messages the Lord has left for me on Eva's skin. The more I think about him being alone with her, the angrier I become. I'd hoped that she'd be only mine by now, but she hasn't come to me or called me. I was very clear. I sent her the flowers, the cicada, the words etched into Amy's skin.

And that was all after I *gave up* Amy. I sacrificed her. I left so many clear messages for Eva, and yet . . . here I am without her. I don't understand. I lower my head to my hands and listen for instructions. I don't know whether Eva is testing me or not. I don't know what to do.

I flip through the pages of my photo albums. One of these girls will be the next choice. I study them, look at their faces as they were captured, and I wait for inspiration. I need this next message to be the one that makes Eva come to me.

Carefully, I touch each face, waiting to feel something, hoping for clarity. Beside me, on the dresser beside my bed, Eva watches from a picture frame my grandmother gave me. It's one of those heavy Waterford crystal ones. She likes those. She told me that someday I could use it for my wedding picture, but for now, it holds a picture of my bride-to-be. I keep it in a drawer when I'm not home, but every day, I open the drawer, take the picture out from between the pairs of folded and pressed boxers, and position it so I can see Eva while I study. She inspires me. Sometimes, I confess to her when we are alone in the dark. I tell her the things I've done that shame me, and I know that in her own bed she is forgiving me. When she meets my eyes and smiles as she passes me in the halls of our school, I know she has forgiven me.

And I forgive her.

I forgive every time she lets someone else too near her; I forgive her weakness for not coming to me after the first time I knew she loved me too. I forgive everything. I always have.

Bouchet, though, is not something I can forgive. I saw her face when she offered herself to him at Piper's party. Like a virgin to an altar, she walked up to him, and he cast her away. I thought it meant that he knew that she was not for him. Now, though, he stands at her side like a lover or a servant. He doesn't have the right to be either one. I can accept Grace walking at Eva's side. She is no threat to me. She could even be a part of our new life. He cannot.

He's trying to break the seventh commandment, and he *is* breaking the tenth. The Bible is clear that "Thou shalt not commit adultery" and "Thou shalt not covet thy neighbor's wife." Eva might not be my wife in law, but in my soul she is. It is my duty and my right to protect her.

DAY 14: "THE TESTING"

Eva

I look around the room at the people who've come. Aside from Grace and Nate, Piper, Laurel, Jess, CeCe, Madison, and Bailey are all here. According to Piper, the guys—Robert, Reid, Grayson, and Jamie—are on their way. Carter can't come. They're my closest friends and classmates, people I've known since elementary school, and I've invited them here so I can see them die. If I had a better plan, I'd try it, but this is the only idea I have.

I still feel frightened and guilty for what I'm about to do.

"Piper?" I call her nearer. I might as well start with the girl who's been closest to me for the longest. Grace is my best friend, but Piper has been in my life as a confidante forever.

She smiles as she walks toward me. "What's up?"

"I'm still a little unsteady. Can you help me up?"

I hold out my hand, and she reaches hers out automatically. Getting her to touch me is easy.

He's straddling me. He grabs my arm and jerks it down, pinning it under his knee.

He stares at his own hand. "You tore my glove."

"I'm sorry," I whisper.

He reaches out for something. I look at the gloved hand as it grabs a bright red bottle that's rolled across the rug. In a moment, the bottle is at my lips.

"Here," he says. "Take a sip."

I stare up at him, but my mouth doesn't open. I try to stare at his face, his clothes, to see anything that will help. His face is a blur.

"There's blood in your mouth, Piper. I'm going to give you some water." He opens the bottle with his teeth, biting it and tugging up. "Open your mouth."

"Please, let me go. I'm sorry. I don't want to die."

He puts the bottle in my mouth. "Swallow."

The water streams in so fast that it's choking me, and I know it's not just water. He wouldn't force me to drink if it was just water. I'm being drugged.

"In a few minutes, we're going to get up and go to the car, so we can give Eva her message," he explains. "I'll help you out to the car so you don't fall."

"Please! I'll do . . . anything. Whatever you want. Please?"

He shakes his head. "I just need you to help me with a message."

"Eva!" Nate is pulling my hand from Piper's, rescuing me from being inside her death.

The rug . . . that's the rug in the foyer of her house. The killer is in her house. She is murdered in her own home.

Piper, the real Piper who is in *my* house, stares at me with an expression somewhere between discomfort and intrigue. She rubs the hand I just released as if I held it too tightly, but she says nothing. Then her gaze darts to Nate as he puts an arm around my waist.

"Something you forgot to tell me?" Piper says in a low voice. She arches a brow and looks pointedly at Nate's arm.

I shake my head. I don't even know how to speak right now. I want to believe that everything's okay. It's not.

I realize belatedly that everyone in the room is watching us, and I don't know what to say. Piper is going to be a victim. Judge—whoever he is—is going to kill her.

"You should sit back down," Nate orders. "Chair or sofa?"

"Sofa." I glance at Piper and answer the question she'd ask if we were alone. "I'm not sleeping with him. We are friends though."

I hear several other muffled gasps and laughs throughout the room. Nate turns around and looks at me like I've just lost my ever-loving mind—and I may very well have lost it. I don't know what to do. How do I save Piper? She grins at me and walks away.

"Don't leave, okay?" I call out to her. I don't know what to do yet, but I can't let her go home . . . which is absurd. What am I to do? I can't insist she never go home. I muffle a cry of frustration against Nate's shoulder.

"Come on," he urges.

I want to tell him, tell *Piper*, but she's walked away. Quietly, I ask, "Keep an eye on her for me?"

He freezes, lips open on a question he can't ask in front of everyone.

I nod.

"Okay," he says. I know then that he believes in my visions completely. He just agreed to watch Piper—a girl he can't stand—because of my vision.

I turn my back to him and make my way to the sofa. When I reach it, CeCe is there ready to help me sit. I smile and say, "Thanks."

"You have some brass balls on you," she says in a low voice. "I thought you left those back in middle school."

"I found them again," I say.

"I see that. The way you're acting is all but admitting there's something going on with Nate. *No one* has had the nerve to do that."

CeCe reaches out for my crutches.

I tense. This is what I need: to see their deaths and look for clues. I still tense as I wait for her hand to brush mine. After my vision of Piper, I'm not ready to do this, but I need to try. I don't release my crutches until CeCe touches me. Her knuckles graze my hands—and nothing happens.

"Eva?" CeCe prompts.

"Sorry." I release my crutches and balance on my one foot. "I guess I'm a little out of it today."

"We all are."

Why didn't it work? I stare at her and resolve to try again.

She sets my crutches to the side and reaches out one arm so I can use it to steady myself. I wait until her arm bumps my hand.

Again, nothing happens.

I want to understand why it didn't work, but I don't know how to figure that out. It's not the most pressing issue either. I need to figure out how to keep Piper safe and, hopefully, be sure none of my other friends here are victims-to-be.

I'm quiet as CeCe helps me to settle on the sofa. Holding on to her arm is almost like holding Robert's or Nate's. I feel corded muscles under her skin, and I'm astounded at how strong she is. Grace is strong, but her biggest strengths are in her legs—which I'm sure help her plenty but wouldn't be very useful in the same ways. CeCe clearly works out differently. If the killer attacked her, maybe she'd be able to fight. Is that a factor? Is he only picking people he can overpower?

"You're strong," I say stupidly.

"Swim team, tennis, and weight training." Her expression grows serious then and she adds, "Once you're healed, I'd be happy to help you with your PT."

"My . . . ?"

"Your physical therapy." She motions to the leg that I have stretched out on the sofa. "I figure Grace will help with it, but if you need another person, I'm here. It's one of the careers I'm considering."

"Thanks. That would be great, actually." I'm oddly relieved that she was thinking in terms of my recovery, not in terms of the killer out there.

The sudden peal of the doorbell startles me, but before I can get back to my feet, I hear Grace call out, "It's Grayson and them."

A few moments later, the familiar sounds of Robert's closest friends comfort me. This is normal. This is my real life. Even when I hear Robert's voice, I stay mostly calm. I know the detective questioned him, but I can't believe for even a moment that he's capable of the kind of violence that the killer has used already—and will use against Nate and Piper if we don't stop him.

I listen as they talk softly. I can't tell what they're discussing at first, but then I hear the words "fireball" and "better if the speakers were moved." I'm glad they came. Even with everything going on, they sound normal.

But when my eyes meet Robert's for a moment, I realize that he's simply pretending that everything's normal. He looks terrible. I'm not surprised though. It can't be easy to deal with visits from the police, Amy's death, my accident, and his secrets coming to light in such a terrible way.

I offer him a small smile.

"Yeung said you were tired." Reid's voice pulls my attention to him as he flops in the chair across from me. "I'm sorry you were hurt."

Maybe guys just have a different way of seeing things.

Someone attempted to kill me, broke my leg, damaged my brain, and scarred my face. Reid stares at me like it's okay to gawk.

"What?" I don't mean to snap, but my voice is harsh.

"Nothing." He shrugs. "I said something. You say something in reply. That's how people have a conversation. You know this. We've done it a million times. So let's start again." He takes an exaggerated breath. "Yeung says you're tired. I'm sorry you got hurt. Now, you say . . ."

"She says, 'Why don't you be a little more considerate?' " CeCe answers. "You're staring at her."

"Hmm, you don't *sound* like Eva," Reid says. His smile is so slow to follow his words that for a moment I think that he's genuinely angry with CeCe, but then he shakes his head and adds, "Don't treat her like she's going to break if we mention it. She's strong. She was in the hospital, but it's not the end of the world. She's still *Eva*." He bends over the arm of the chair, twisting his body and glancing toward the door. "Rob! Hey, Rob!"

Robert comes to the door of the room. "What?"

"Do you mind if I go out with Eva now that she dumped you?"

"Screw you." Robert's face flushes in anger.

Reid has already moved on. He calls, "Jamie, what about you? Want to flip a coin to see who gets to ask her out?"

Before Jamie can answer, Nate strides into the room. "Mind your manners around Eva."

Reid laughs and turns back to me. "See? You have a few cuts, but every guy here still wants you." He lowers his voice until it's barely a whisper and adds, "I think you're even *more* beautiful now."

Before I can figure out what to say to that, I see Robert coming to join us.

Reid glances at him, and then turns his attention back to me. His voice is at a regular volume again when he says, "You're still *you*, Eva, and I'm not going to pussyfoot around you."

I shake my head. I appreciate the sentiment, I suppose.

"Someday you're going to say something stupid to the wrong person," I tell him.

"Inevitably." Reid swings his legs off the chair. "I'll leave you to your guard dogs."

As if he's unaware of the at least half-dozen pairs of eyes fixed on us, Robert sits in the chair Reid just vacated. Unlike Reid, Robert isn't slouching or throwing his legs over the arm of the chair. He sits like my father would, the picture of a stiff spine and correct angles.

"Are you okay?"

Robert shakes his head. In a near-whisper, he says, "No. Not really."

"Me either," I say just as quietly. "I'm so sorry that Amy—"

"Please don't." He pulls the chair right up to the sofa so we have some semblance of privacy. "I cared about her. You have to believe me, Eva. I won't ever get to tell her how much, but

I did. I just"—he shakes his head—"it seems stupid now. I lied to myself and to you. It was stupid, but I was so afraid of what my parents would say. Instead, I have to listen to them yell at each other, blaming each other and me, for the police, for what people will think, for what *your* parents will think."

He reaches out and grabs my hand. I vaguely notice how clammy his skin is before I fall.

I open the medicine cabinet. My mother's "nerve pills" sit there so innocently. My nerves are a mess, so it makes a strange sort of sense to me. I open the bottle, tap some of them into my hand, and then clap my hand to my now open mouth.

Carefully, I set the bottle on the edge of her sink. It's one of those pedestal sinks. It's a term I only know because of her. I also know that it only took one tab of the Vicodin she had for her pain after her face-lift and "tummy nip," and she was knocked out. I weigh more, but I also took the other pills, so I'm not sure how many I should take. There are only five pills left, so I take four of them. I don't want to use all her medicine in case she needs it.

I'm not trying to overdose. I just want to be calm enough to do this. I'm not sure how many pills that will take or how long they take to work. To be safe, I take another handful of the Xanax.

I already left a note, several of them, in fact. I labeled each envelope, and then I dropped them in the mail on the way home. Sending it by email wouldn't give me enough time, and leaving the letters at home would probably mean the police would get them instead of the people who should get them.

Amy can't get hers. I buried it at her grave though. Maybe that's stupid, but I don't know how the whole afterlife thing works. Maybe it's the thought that counts or maybe the dead really do stay here on earth like ghosts. Better to be safe.

My hand wraps around the grip of my father's snub-nosed gun. I don't know what caliber it is. I'm sure he's told me repeatedly, but I don't like guns. They make me nervous. That's why I needed my mother's pills. They work, too. My hand is hardly shaking at all as I put the barrel between my lips. It's cold, and it feels strange on my tongue. I squeeze the trigger.

I jolt out of Robert's death, jerking my hand away, and whisper, "Don't."

"I would never hurt you or her," Robert is saying, possibly repeating. "You believe me, don't you? I couldn't. Not you, or Amy, or Micki. God, Eva, you have to be—"

"Stop. Robert, just *stop* a minute."

He looks like he's going to cry, and I snatch his hand back and squeeze it so tightly that he winces. My earlier intentions about not seeming crazy have all vanished. I tug so he's half falling into my lap and tell him, "You listen to me, Robert Anthony Baucom. I *know* you. You're weak sometimes, and you shouldn't have been unfaithful to me *or* Amy. But, so help me God, if you even think about hurting yourself, I'll march myself right into Hell and drag you back. Despite what you did, you're my *friend*, and I believe you. Your parents are being . . . well, being *them*, but you're going to ignore their anger just like you have a dozen times before."

He's nodding, and he's staring at me like he's seen something horrible and wonderful all at once. "How did you know I was going to—"

"Doesn't matter. I *do* know, and you better promise me that you won't do it." I squeeze his hand harder. "They'll catch him, and I want you to promise that you're going to be sitting in the courtroom with me. For me *and* for Amy. You have to be there at my side for her. I need you to be here. We'll be friends again, but you can't . . . you *may not* try to kill yourself."

He swallows. "The detective asked questions that made it seem like she thinks that if it wasn't me doing it maybe it was my fault. If you both got hurt because of—"

"They have to look at every possibility." I wish there were reassuring things I knew to say, but there aren't words that make this any better. I'm not even sure I can tell him that it's fairly obvious that the killings are connected to *me*. All I can think to say is: "They'll figure it out, though, and they'll catch him. You promise me you won't hurt yourself."

"I promise," he says.

For a moment, I stare at him, trying to see if he's lying. I'm not comforted by the fact that he apparently lied to me successfully for almost a year, but I can't do anything else right now. I add, "We're friends, Robert. That's what you asked me to be. I'm willing to do it, but friends are honest, okay?"

He nods, and we sit quietly for a few seconds. Then he says, "Thank you. I don't know how you knew I was going to . . . but thank you."

"You gave me your word," I remind him. "Don't break it this time. Swear it. You call me or come here or something if you need to, but if you kill yourself . . . I won't forgive you."

"I swear I won't do it," he says. He leans closer and kisses my cheek, and I don't see his death. I wouldn't this time though: I still have his hand held tightly in mine.

I let go, and he stands and walks away. Any doubts I still had about my ability are gone. Robert confirmed that he was suicidal *after* I saw him in my vision. I don't know why or how I can do this; I don't know if it'll fade as I finish healing. All I know for sure is that I have a way to help save my friends. I just need to make sense of it.

I think I stopped Robert's death. Now, though, I need to figure out how to save Piper. Even though I can't see faces in the visions, I can see enough details to make a difference. I need to use them to figure out who the killer is—and I need to do it *now*.

DAY 14: "THE PROOF"

Eva

I LOOK AROUND THE room for Nate. Not surprisingly, he's watching me. All it takes to beckon Nate over is a slight incline of my head. Once he's at my side, I share my new idea: "I need you to stop hovering. It makes some of them nervous. Help me find excuses to have them touch me. Tell people to check on me to see if I need help or to come over and hold my hand to let me know that they're not freaked out by my slasher-chic look."

"Don't say shit like that." He brushes my hair back from where it had fallen on my cheek, exposing the worst of my scars in the process. "If any of them are making you feel like—"

"It's not them," I interrupt. "*I* know what I look like."

Quietly, Nate says, "Obviously, you don't. You're the most beautiful girl in the room."

Part of me wants to yell at him; the rest of me wants to kiss him until he admits that he's an idiot for thinking we can't date. I can't do either right now, so I settle on telling him, "This is that boundary thing I was talking about. You can't say things like that and then push me away."

He stares at me, but instead of arguing, he nods. "Piper says she'll stay until everyone else goes home. I tried to talk to her—not about *that*, but just talk. We were . . . civil."

"Thank you." I glance around the room, noticing more than a few gazes on us. I don't want to say anything that can be overheard. "I saw her."

"With him?"

I nod. Tears threaten to fill my eyes. The visions have been awful from the beginning, but now that I know without a doubt that they are real, they seem more horrific. The murderer will kill Piper. I don't see any details I can ask her to change to try to prevent it—other than the fact that she was at home.

"We'll figure it out," Nate promises.

He waits until I give him a small smile and a nod, and then he calls out, "Hey, Madison, hold up a sec."

Once he walks away, I fix a smile on my face and look around the room. Bailey sees me and comes to join me on the sofa. A few minutes later, I discover that she'll die of breast cancer decades from now. It's not a subject I can figure out how to mention casually. "Never too young for self-exams?" or "Did you know that one in eight women will be diagnosed with breast cancer?" aren't sentences that fit neatly into a conversation about whether lowlights would be too daring for her personal style. I like Bailey, but she's determined to only talk about surface subjects right now. I think it's her way of avoiding the things we don't want to think about: classmates' murders, my giant facial scars, and how terrifying it is that our friends are dying.

The next hour is a mix of conversations and deaths. I discover that Laurel dies of something heart related, and Grayson dies in a car. I'm not sure if that means he's a potential victim or not. Micki died in a car crash, but drunk driving is a more likely possibility with Grayson. He moved away too quickly for me to see much. I try a second time to get back to his death, but just when I finally convince him to rub a knot in my shoulder, Piper swats him away. She's watching me curiously. I'm tempted to point out that grief and TBIs both make people act out of character; instead my attention drifts to Nate, who is talking to Madison again. It reminds me of parties when I watched him flirt with girl after girl. This time, though, Piper isn't gossiping at my side.

I wave at Jamie. Unlike Reid and Grayson, he's always been a bit standoffish. It's not that he does anything rude. He just doesn't seem to know what to say or do around me. His father has worked at the winery for our whole lives, just like Reid's grandmother, but I think that detail makes Jamie nervous around me.

"Are you . . . did you need something?" Jamie asks as he comes toward me. He doesn't sit, and I wonder how to convince him to touch me. It's frustrating that they have to initiate the touch for me to get the visions.

"I'm just bored." I try a flirtatious smile.

Jamie nods. "Because you're on crutches."

"Yes," I say patiently. "And because I'm here by myself."

He frowns. "Everyone's here. You're not alone."

"Here on the *sofa* alone," I clarify.

At that, he nods again, but he doesn't join me. He stands staring at me silently until I'm ready to throw something at him. "Do you want to sit down with me?"

He shakes his head. "I'll go find Grace or Piper for you." Then he walks away.

So far I've only eliminated CeCe, Laurel, Robert, and Bailey as victims. That leaves Madison, Jamie, Jess, Reid, and possibly Grayson as potential victims. The boys are less likely, I think, but I still need to be sure.

Piper comes over as soon as Jamie leaves me.

"Hey," she says as she flops down next to me.

This is it, my chance to talk to her, to try to figure out how to keep her safe. I smile at her and decide to go for as close to honest as I can be without telling her about the visions. She's my friend, and I trust her in a lot of ways. I also know her well enough to know that this isn't something I should share with her. She's melodramatic on her best days.

"The killer is fixated on me," I say bluntly.

Her mouth gapes open, and she blinks rapidly.

I barrel on, "He tried to kill me. He *did* kill the girl who was sleeping with my boyfriend. I think that means that he's more likely to attack people closest to me, and Piper, you've been one of my closest friends since before we were even in school."

"Jesus, Eva . . ." Her voice is breathy.

I grab her hand and squeeze. "I'm scared, Piper. I'm scared for all of us." I look past her to the room full of our closest friends. "You and Grace, you're the ones closest to me. Everyone at school knows that." I look back at her. "Ask your parents to let you go stay with your grandmother down in Charleston. Stay at Bailey's or somewhere else tonight. *Explain* it to them. They'll listen to you."

She squeezes my hand so tightly that it hurts. "And what about you?"

"Between the police passing by the house constantly, Nate at my side like a bodyguard, and the monitored alarm system, I'm safe here." I meet her gaze and add, "The police can't watch all of our houses constantly. I know they're trying, but—please—leave right away. Tonight. Go see Grandmother Eliza for a few weeks."

She stares at me for a moment before agreeing. "I'll call my mom. She'll let me go if I tell her I'm scared." Quickly, my hand still in hers, she leans forward and wraps her other arm around me. "It will be okay."

In another moment, she's released me and is walking out of the room, her phone already in hand. I hope that's enough. I *hope* she goes away tonight. Maybe I should tell everyone to get out of town.

I start to feel a little panic-stricken as I look around the room. I don't want anyone to die. How many of them are at risk? So far, Robert and Piper were at risk in different ways. Who else here is? I need to know. I need to be sure they're all safe. I start ticking names off my list and seeing who's nearby.

Reid is standing to the side watching Nate and Madison talk. I need to check both Reid and Madison. She's not even looking my way, so I catch Reid's eye and call out, "Reid?"

He pulls his attention away from them and looks at me in what I think is gratitude. I didn't ever notice him having an interest in Madison, but with the way he's staring at her and Nate, I think I must've missed it. He looks left out. Maybe he can help me keep watch over her. Maybe that's the key: I can ask friends to start sticking close to other friends. Not everyone can leave town. I know Reid can't. He's lived with his grandmother most of his life. His parents passed away when he was pretty young.

"What do you need?" Reid asks.

"Company?"

His dark expression fades completely. "As you wish."

I can't help laughing. Robert's friends are all so different from one another. Where Jamie is aloof, Reid is impulsive, and Grayson is simply . . . nice. He's friendly, but not particularly memorable. Sometimes I think they're friends for the same reason Piper and CeCe are: a lifetime of habit and parental influence.

Reid drops down to the floor in front of me, and apparently

decides that the most natural position is stretched out flat with his head aligned with my feet. "Sometimes I wish we had a joker hat to pass around," he announces.

"Because I'm bored?"

"No. Because *I'm* bored. If we had a joker hat, we could pick someone to entertain us. I've spent half the parties this year talking to"—he waves his hand loosely from side to side, taking in the whole of our friends—"them. Sometimes, I find it all very depressing."

I think about the nights Robert and I talked about feeling trapped by our families, confused by sorting out what we want from what we know we're expected to do, and how stifling life in Jessup can feel. I can't say I'm surprised that Reid feels the same way. I'm only surprised that he's admitting it. We're friends, but not of the let-me-confess-my-fears-and-doubts sort.

As much as I suddenly want to just talk to Reid, I need to finish what I set out to do. I failed with Jamie. I won't fail here, too. I dangle my foot over the edge of the sofa in the hopes that Reid will brush up against it. Instead, he slides farther away. I can't think of any other way to subtly get him to touch me. That's when I realize that I'm being foolish: of all the people in the room, he's the one least likely to look at me oddly for anything I do or say.

I reach down, extending my hand toward him, and say, "Put your hand on my pulse for a few seconds."

He stares at me for an extra moment, but then he sits up and does as I asked.

A girl is screaming; another girl is yelling, "Stop it!"

I can't believe that this is happening to me. I did everything right.

I hear a car coming toward us. The road is dirt and gravel, and I hear the wheels crunch over it.

Someone is hitting me, trying to hurt me. I turn to try to look at her though. I'd die to protect her, to keep her safe. I step backward, but before I can turn to see her, I feel a sharp burning pain in my chest. There's a moment between the feeling and the realization, but I know then: it's a bullet. I've been shot.

I fall to the ground. I want to go to her, tell her that I love her, but I can't move.

I gasp as I return to the now. Reid is on the floor, his hand on my wrist. "It's fast," he says, and I realize that he's talking about my pulse. "Are you feeling sick . . . or something?"

I shiver. "No."

He's watching me intently, but all I can do is offer him a weak smile and an even weaker explanation. "There's just so much going on lately, you know?"

"You're safe now, Eva," Reid says. He's still holding my wrist and staring at me. "I don't think you have anything to fear."

I pull away. "I'm sorry. It's just . . ." My words fade as I try to figure out what to say. Sorry I just saw you become another victim? I swallow as I stare at him. How do I save him? There has to be *something* I can do. I think about the details of the vision, but I don't have any immediate solutions.

"It's fine." He folds his hands together under his head. "You never need to tell me you're sorry. For anything. I like that you don't act like *them* all the time. I like that we can be honest, instead of pretending all the time."

I'm so not honest right now. I don't know what to do or say. Why *Reid*? Why would the killer shoot Reid? Who was he trying to reach? I know it's not Piper. Who does Reid love so much that he got killed trying to save her? I'm terribly awkward as I blurt, "Do you like Madison?"

He stares up at me in apparent shock.

"I saw you watching her."

Reid nods, but says nothing.

"You deserve to be happy. We all do," I say. "If she'll make you happy, do something about it."

"Really? I don't know if I should. It's hard to know sometimes."

"You can always talk to me if you need." I smile at him. "I'm here for you, you know? I think . . . I think maybe we should spend more time together. Maybe you could visit me more."

If I can keep him close, I reason, maybe I can keep him safer. He can't leave town like Piper can, so I need another answer.

I'm not sure I've seen him so excited. "Really? You mean that?"

"Sure," I say, more confidently now. I don't want him to get the wrong idea, though, so I add, "Maybe we can talk about Madison, too. I saw you watching her, and I want you to be happy, you know?"

"Madison? You think so?"

"Definitely! Just be yourself, Reid. Talk to her like she was me." I pause, feeling a little awkward, knowing it's going to sound insane no matter how I say it, but I flash back to him standing outside, trying to reach the girl he loves, and getting shot. Quickly, I add, "But inside. Do it *inside*."

"Okay." He reaches up and touches my calf. "Thank you."

I think about the killer, the recently dead, and I murmur, "I hope it helps."

I'm still trying to figure out if there's anything else I can say or do to keep Reid safe when Grace comes over and says, "Madison and Bailey left. They said to tell you good-bye."

"Yeung," Reid greets Grace.

She ignores him, instead looking back at me and adding, "I think everyone's going to head out. Nate says you need a nap."

"He wha—"

"And I agree," Grace continues as if I hadn't interrupted her. "So I'm going to get a ride home. I texted the General, and she said it's okay as long as I'm in a group."

"Robert can give you a ride," I suggest.

She meets my eyes, and I see hesitation there. I'm certain that Robert's not the killer, but I can't tell Grace I have proof. I'm about to suggest she ask Piper when Reid speaks up.

"Do you want me to give you a ride, Yeung?" Reid offers.

"Rob's going the other way because Jamie is riding with him."

I think about the vision. Could it have been Grace scream-ing? It was afternoon from the look of the light, although it was hard to tell because of the trees. It could've been evening. "Straight home, right? You'll take her straight there."

Reid gives me a wide smile. "Promise."

"Text me when you get there," I instruct.

CeCe walks over to join us, obviously having heard the discussion, and asks, "Can you take me too? I may be forced to scream if I have to listen to Jess go on about her new diet any longer."

"Hmm. Make CeCe scream or not? That's a hard ques-tion." Reid crosses his arms and stares at her.

"Reid?" I say gently.

He looks at me, but doesn't offer any smart remark. "Eva."

"Would you *please* give CeCe a ride too? For me? Grace's mother would feel better if she was with two people, and then I'd feel better because she wouldn't be so worried that she'd deny me Grace's company."

Another wide smile comes over him, and he kisses my cheek again. "At your service as always." Then he turns his attention to Grace and CeCe and announces, "Yeung gets shotgun."

I think again about telling Reid more than I have, but I don't know how. I quickly replay the details of my vision and then ask, "Are you going to talk to *her* tonight?"

"Should I?"

All I need to do right now is get Reid through tonight. I suggest, "Maybe go straight home. Stay in. Think about it tonight, plan it out, and then you can go see her in the morning. Afterwards, come see me, so I can hear how it goes."

"Tomorrow," he says softly. "You think I should do it tomorrow morning." He shakes his head. "Are you sure?"

"Yes," I assure him. I lean in and kiss his cheek. "Good luck."

CeCe and Grace are watching us with blatant curiosity, but I'm not going to embarrass Reid by letting them know who he's crushing on—or according to my vision, in love with. Hopefully, he'll tell Madison how he feels, and then I have to tell him that he's a potential murder victim before evening falls again.

"Let me get Eva settled and then we can go," Grace interjects. "My purse is up there anyhow."

Grace and I head to the stairs, but I refuse to go up on my butt this time. I tell her, "Just walk behind me so if I fall you can help steady me—not that I'm *going* to fall."

She grumbles, but agrees.

We're halfway up when Grace says, "Thanks for stepping in with Reid. I'm not up for twenty minutes of the 'why sex is just like saying hello but naked' conversation. He needs a girlfriend—or a hobby."

I pause on the landing. Steps are harder than they look when you're on crutches. When I reach my room, I go to sit at the edge of my bed. I'm tired from the death visions and the

trip upstairs and from trying to pretend like I'm not five minutes from crying.

"Reid's going to get shot," I blurt now that we're alone. "I
saw it. He's trying to tell some girl—I think Madison—that he
loves her, and he gets shot."

"Wow." She lowers herself to the edge of my bed.

"And Piper. The killer was in her house. He drugs her." I
shudder at the memory of that vision. "She's going to stay with
her grandmother."

"You told her?" Grace sounds shocked.

"No!" I smile slightly. "I just pointed out that she's been
my best friend forever, so she's in greater risk."

"Like me," she whispers.

I grab her and hug her. "I won't let anything happen to
you. You're here inside Fortress Tilling, and then you avoid the
library. I *saw* it, Grace. That was where you were. You cannot
go there."

"If your visions are real," she adds.

Quickly, I fill her in on what I saw in Robert's death. I
finish with "Robert admitted that he was suicidal. He was
shocked that I knew, but he *admitted* it."

Grace sighs. "So it *is* real . . . which means if Piper leaves
Reid is the next victim."

"And that we know where your risk is," I add. "We can
keep you safe, and hopefully all of them. Piper will get out of
town. Reid's death was outside, in the late afternoon or early
evening, with a girl there, and by a bullet." I pause, thinking

over the visions I had. "I told Reid to go right home and stay there. If he listens, he should be safe—for now."

It's not a great plan, but it's the best I have right now. Maybe we can keep everyone safe until the police catch the killer.

"Yeung! Let's go," Reid calls up, forestalling any more plotting.

"Coming!" She turns back to me. "Tell Nate everything. I'll call you later."

Once she grabs her bag, Grace heads downstairs and joins the stragglers who, from the sounds of it, are waiting at the door for her. A few minutes later, I hear the door close behind them, and then it's only Nate still in the house with me.

I pick up my laptop and go to my file of death visions. Then I start adding the ones I just saw before I forget too many details.

I'm sitting with my back against my headboard. My leg is stretched out, raised slightly on a pillow, and it occurs to me that this is a lot like being in the hospital—just more comfortable. It's quieter too, so much so that I could almost miss the sound of Nate coming up the stairs. I don't though because I'm sitting here waiting for him, nervous that we'll fight and hopeful that he'll hold me so I can feel a little less awful. Seeing so many deaths was horrifying. These are my friends, and I just watched most of them die.

Nate stops in the hall and leans against the doorframe, not quite inside my room. "We should talk."

"Robert's not the killer," I start.

"I meant talk about what happened in the kitchen," Nate says quietly.

"No." I shake my head and continue to focus on the killer. I skim my sketchy notes and tell him, "Reid gets shot. I think he might be the next victim—or maybe Piper. She's drugged and killed in her house. I talked her into leaving town, so I hope that her family lets her. CeCe didn't have a death vision. I don't know why." I think back over the snippets of deaths I saw and felt, and I shudder. I have to look at Nate when I tell him, "I saw Robert's death. Suicide. Over all of *this*."

I feel a little guilty for violating Robert's privacy this time. It was different with Grace, but I need Nate to know, too. I want him to be nicer to Robert because I'm not convinced that the danger of Robert committing suicide has passed. I hope Robert will keep his word, but knowing both of his girl-friends—because that's what Amy and I both were—have been attacked by a murderer has to be devastating.

I realize that Nate is staring at me. Maybe it's my deluge of words, or maybe it's because this is far from what he said he wanted to discuss. I don't know. I meet his gaze and wait though. I need him on my side. I'm scared, and tired, and still recovering from the accident. I need him to help me—and to be someone I can trust.

"Eva," he starts, but he says nothing more. He's still in the doorway to my room, but the way he watches me makes him feel closer.

"I'm tired, Nate, and I don't want to think about it, but"—I look back down at my laptop—"I'm guessing that the killer isn't waiting around forever. Reid dies in the afternoon or early evening, and he's with a girl he loves. Since he isn't going to be with her tonight, I need to figure this out before tomorrow. I'm going to talk to him tomorrow."

"He's safe tonight?" Nate asks.

"Yeah. I'm pretty sure. I got him to agree to stay home tonight. He's going to tell her how he feels tomorrow morning."

Nate walks farther into my room and says, "If everyone's safe for now, can we *please* talk about what happened with us? I want to ta—"

"I already told you how I feel," I interrupt without looking up at Nate. "You don't want a relationship. I didn't ask for one. We're either friends with rules or friends with benefits. It's up to you which it is."

"You're not the sort of girl who—"

"*Don't* tell me what sort of girl I am, Nate." I flip the laptop closed with more force than I should. "I'm the sort of girl a killer is sending messages to, the sort of girl who was attacked and left for dead, and the sort of girl who, oh yeah, sees deaths and is trying to figure out how to save her friends. Trust me when I say that a night with the Jessup man-slut isn't the worst thing possible. It's insulting that you think it's okay for you to sleep with half our class, but I'm supposed to be . . . What? A blushing virgin? I'm *not*."

He watches me in silence again, and I think he might do a repeat of the exiting act from earlier. Instead, he sits on the very edge of my bed beside my uninjured hip. He takes my computer and sets it on the nightstand. He doesn't look at me, choosing instead to stare at his shoes, as he admits, "I don't know what to do about you. I've never known what to do with you, not once I noticed that you were a girl."

"Are you looking for suggestions other than the two I already offered?"

"Maybe."

I scoot over so we're shoulder to shoulder. He still faces the door and wall beside me, so we're sort of perpendicular to each other. Cautiously, I touch his arm, and when he glances at me, I say, "If friends or friends with benefits is out, then I say you ask me on a date."

"And then?" He turns to face me finally, bending one leg and moving a little farther onto the bed, and I realize that he's afraid. "I'm not the sort of guy your family would approve of, not like that."

"Really?" I say gently. "You can't honestly think my mother is blind. She *hired* you."

"Being the help is diff—"

"She hired you because she knows I like you"—I lean closer and kiss his jaw—"and that you like me."

"If we date and I fuck up, we won't be friends. I don't want that."

"So we don't fuck up." I kiss him then, cautiously at first. I'm not used to being the aggressor. There's never been anyone I've wanted to kiss as much as I want to kiss Nate. I feel like I've been waiting for this kiss, this conversation, this *boy* since

I first noticed boys. He's the one. He's *always* been the one.

I stop being tentative. I reach up to hold on to the back of his neck, and I press closer to him. It's awkward because my leg limits my ability to move, but after he kisses me back with the same urgency, I stop noticing my leg and everything else.

DAY 14: "THE TASK"

Judge

BARELY A MONTH AGO, I'd entered into my darkest time, my doubtful wandering through the desert. In my doubt, I nearly killed the one who was meant to be my helpmate. Today, Eva invited me into her home and told me what to do.

The journey to this day has been so long. It took me years to comprehend that it was Eva I needed. For years, my grandmother told me that the Lord had made a woman just for me. She promised that I had only to wait and watch; His ways are sometimes hard to know but if we are open to His messages, if we listen for His orders, we'll know.

I waited. I watched. I studied them all.

Then I realized that Eva was the only one who could truly understand me, so I waited for her to heed the Lord's message, too. I knew Eva had heard His voice when she told me that there was a girl out there for me, and if I would be less crude, I'd find her.

I made sure she saw me be kind and good. I thought that it would be enough, but then she didn't come to me. I still wasn't good enough. She punished me by sleeping with Robert.

But I forgave her. I kept trying—until I saw her turn her gaze so often to Bouchet. I drove the car into her body, even though it hurt *my* heart and lungs to do it. When God spared her life, I knew that we still had a chance, so I left her messages. I even sacrificed Amy. I did everything right.

And now . . . and now . . . she rewarded me. She asked me to touch her. It was only for a moment, but it was pure and good. Soon, she'll ask me to touch her all the time.

First, I must complete the mission Eva gave me today. I know this is the final challenge. I'll do a good job, and then I'll go to Eva's house, just as she said I should.

As I drive, I think about how to do it. Madison is difficult. She's a challenge.

"Reid?"

CeCe is talking. I'd considered her. I still want to, but *Madison* is the one Eva chose for us. I see now that CeCe would be too easy for the trial Eva wants me to complete. Like a knight of old, or a soldier fighting for the South, I wish I had a token of Eva's regard to carry with me on the battlefield. Maybe I'll ask for one next time.

"Reid," CeCe snaps. "You missed the turn."

"Maybe I just wanted to keep you with me longer."

"Funny. Turn around."

Beside me, Grace is silent, and I remember that Eva didn't want Grace left alone with anyone. Eva *told me that*. I'm not going to risk upsetting Eva when we're so close to our future. "Sorry but Yeung needs to get home first. Right, Yeung?"

"She's past my house though," CeCe objects.

I shrug. It's hard to talk to girls who don't matter as much as my Eva does, but I have to do as Eva wants. I'll spend the rest of our lives doing as she wants. I've been waiting so long, but today, she let me know that she's almost ready for our union. I felt her hesitation when she asked me to touch her, but she did it. There, surrounded by all of Them, and even with Grace and Bouchet in the room, she asked me to touch her.

I ignore CeCe and Grace as I think about Eva's skin. She was as excited as I was. Her pulse felt like a small hammer under my fingertips. I knew when I touched her that she has been receiving my messages. She has heard me, and she is glad. She told me that she saw me, but no one else did. That's why she gave me a task: it's to show her my love and loyalty.

Together, we chose the next message. I'd hoped that she'd seen the rightness of my choices, but I'm excited that she made the choice for me—for *us*—this time. Eva let me know that she's a part of the mission. After I do as Eva directed, we'll be together. She told me that today. She *knew* I needed to give her one more lesson. She told me, "If she'll make you happy, do something about it."

"Left here," Grace says.

Silently, I pull into her drive and wave as she gets out of the car. Then, I pat the passenger seat. "Come up here, CeCe. I'm not going to play chauffeur."

CeCe mutters something I can't make out, but she obeys. We watch as Grace walks to the door. Once she's inside, I smile at CeCe and suggest, "No witnesses now, Watkins. Call your mother, and tell her you're staying over with Piper for a while."

"Why would I do that?" She has her phone out already though.

"Let me take you on a date. No one has to know." I take her hand in mine and pretend she's Eva. I give her the comforting look I want to give to Eva. "Just a date, Cees. We'll get some picnic stuff and go down to the lake."

"I'm not like . . ." Her words fade, and I know she was going to say "Amy," but caught herself. Instead, she says, "I'm not sleeping with you."

"I didn't ask you to," I point out calmly. I miss Amy, and I need someone to ease the excitement I feel right now. CeCe is here. Maybe she'll help me out a little. I smile at her and add, "I suggested you go on a picnic with someone who thinks you're worth spending a little time with. Is that such a bad thing?"

For a moment, she's silent. She stays that way as I put the car in reverse and back out of the Yeungs' driveway. We're several blocks away when she says, "All right."

DAY 14: "THE KISS"

Eva

It feels like only a few minutes, but it was almost an hour ago that I started kissing Nate. He's the one to pull away, but instead of telling me again that this is a mistake, he says, "If we're dating, we're *dating*. Going out places, and doing this right."

"Right." I've never been kiss-addled before, but I feel like I have a buzz from him. I wonder if he does too because I'm fairly sure his words don't make any sense.

He moves so he's beside me on my bed, instead of half on top of me, and kisses my temple. When I try to slip my hand back under his shirt where it was before he pulled away, he catches my wrist and says, "No."

"No what?"

"If we're dating, we have to go slower than this." He has an arm around me, and he kisses my head again. "We need to be like . . . normal about it."

I want to laugh, but it would be rude. "You realize that it's not like there's a normal time between dating and sex, right? It's about the two people. If we wanted to have sex today—"

"Today?" He sounds nervous.

"So you're saying we can date, but we should just kiss . . . and not 'like that'?" I turn my head and kiss his chest.

He puts his hand on my cheek and tilts my head so I'm looking at him before he continues. "I don't want to fuck this up by going too fast."

I put my hand on his and say, "How about you trust me to decide how fast is too fast for me, and I'll trust you to decide how fast is too fast for you, and if we end up on the same page at some point, *that's* when we go further?"

"Fine, but I'm not ready. Not with you." He swallows. "This is going to sound stupid, but I want to wait until it's not *just* sex."

I almost tell him that it wouldn't be, not even today. "So we wait till it's making love."

He looks even more uncomfortable when I use that phrase, but he doesn't try to suggest that he meant something else. He studies my face like he's expecting a rejection before asking, "That's okay?"

I stretch up to kiss him before saying, "Very, and it's not stupid."

We're still cuddled up together talking and sometimes

kissing when my parents get home a little while later. Nate doesn't quite leap out of bed when he hears the door open, but it's close.

"Relax, Nate."

"I don't want them to think—"

"That we're dating?"

"I don't know. Maybe? I don't want them to hate me." He rubs his head. "I didn't know if you wanted them to know."

"Don't be an idiot." I shake my head and call out, "Mom? Could you come up here?"

In a matter of moments, she walks into my room. Her eyes are a little wide, and she's studying me not-so-subtly. "Is everything okay? Are *you* okay?"

"I'm fine," I assure her. "Everything's fine."

I can see the tension flee as her shoulders visibly relax. In a split second, she goes from worried to the seemingly emotionless woman I've seen most of my life. I know now that it's a mask, but it's a convincing one. Then she glances at Nate, who is standing awkwardly beside my bed, and then at my bed. The pillow and comforter are still compressed from where he was lying beside me.

"Do you mind if I see Nate? Go out with him?"

Her expression doesn't change, but Nate's does. He looks at me like I've lost my mind.

My mother scowls at me and then turns her scowl on Nate. "There's a killer out there, Nathaniel. You can't take her *out* until he's caught."

"Can we date *here?*" I clarify.

My mother frowns. "Why would you ask that? I've never had to approve your dates before."

I watch Nate's expression switch from nervous to pole-axed.

"Because you hired Nate."

"But you were friends first." She looks at Nate and asks, "Are you still going to do the job I hired you to do?"

"Yes," Nate says.

"Well, then, I see no reason you can't ask my daughter out." My mother reaches out and pats my leg. "It's sweet that you asked, but I think you scared Nate a bit. I'm going to go fix dinner. Are you staying?"

"Not tonight, ma'am," he says. "I'm heading out in a minute."

She nods and sails out of the room with the same calm expression that she usually has. I like it much better than the alarm I saw when she walked into my room. Nate watches the empty doorway, and I hold in my laughter at Nate's stunned expression until I figure my mother is downstairs. I wouldn't want her to think I'm laughing at her.

Nate shakes his head. Then he walks over to the bed again, and I reach up and take his hand. I tug, and he bends so I can kiss him.

"Text me so I know you're home safe?"

"I'm going to Durham to see Aaron. I'll have my phone, and I'll be safe."

He's still bent down so our lips are close together, so I kiss him one more time before I say, "Will you still text me when you get to Durham?"

"Okay." He kisses me this time, and I want to pull him back down to the bed. I wonder if I'll ever stop feeling like I could spend forever just kissing him.

Nate steps backward and shakes his head. It seems surreal that he feels as overwhelmed as I do, but when I look at him, there's no denying how affected he obviously is. I feel different, powerful, maybe more so because *he* wants to wait.

He walks out, and a few moments later my mother comes in and asks, "Are you eating up here or do you need help coming down?"

"Up here if it's okay."

She nods and goes to the hallway. "Up here."

A few moments later, I'm stunned to see my father walk in with a tray of food. It's not the tray, or my father, but the fact that he's brought plates for three people. "I told you," he says to my mother.

"You were right." She laughs and walks out of the room again.

"Mom?"

"Be right back," she calls back. Dad follows her.

When they return, he's carrying a card table and two folding chairs, and she has a second tray with drinks and condiments. I watch speechlessly as they set up a makeshift dining room beside my bed. Once the second, smaller tray is empty, my mother sets it on my lap and puts my plate and drink on it.

"So, what's this about you and the Bouchet boy?" my father asks.

I blink at him. I'm not sure he's ever asked me about a boy in my entire life. I open my mouth, realize I'm not sure what to say, and then close it.

"I told your father about my new parenting plan," my mother offers with a small smile. "I read an article at lunch today that says talking about the day's events is critical. You weren't dating Nate yesterday, correct?"

"Correct."

"So it's today's events." She nods once and takes a sip of her lemonade.

Both of my parents are watching me, and I think they look a little nervous. This is new territory for all of us. My father obviously follows her lead on parenting, although I never realized how much until now. I take a deep breath, and then I start to tell them a slightly modified version of the day, of my feelings for Nate, of how he thinks I'm beautiful even with all these fresh scars, of how he's never had a girlfriend. They listen. They don't ask awkward questions, even though I know my mother saw the proof that he was next to me in my bed. I don't tell them the death visions part or the fact that I have a newly discovered sex drive. I'm not sure either of those details are things I'll be telling them ever, but it's sort of awesome to talk about all the rest.

For a day that started pretty awfully, I think, perhaps, there is a little bit of light in the darkness. I'm dating the boy I've been dreaming of for years, and I feel certain I have stopped the killer, at least for tonight.

Yes, perhaps there is some light in all of this. And I am thankful for it. Without it I fear I might lose my mind. My parents are chatting about Nate and their workday with me. I don't completely stop worrying about the killer, but I push the worries to the back of my mind to deal with tomorrow.

DAY 14: "THE CHALLENGE"

Judge

I TRIED TO PRETEND that CeCe was Eva, but that didn't work. Eva's skin feels softer. I tried to pretend she's Amy, but that wasn't quite right either. I kissed CeCe, and she let me put a hand under her shirt, but she wouldn't let me take it off or even unhook her bra. I even tried to listen to her talk about some marathon thing she's doing in Raleigh. I nodded, and I smiled, and I tried to listen. My big reward? Kissing.

I miss Amy.

After it's pretty obvious that CeCe isn't going to budge, I drive her home.

When I pull into her drive, she leans over to kiss my cheek. "Call me," CeCe says as she closes the car door.

I drive back out to the lake, thinking about Amy. I miss her. She looked so content before she died. I think that the secret is the water. It made her pure, washed away her sins like a baptism.

When I reach the lake, I park in an area a bit away from where Amy and I spent our last night together. It's not night yet, so there are a few people out walking along the trails—but not as many as there usually are. I noticed that earlier. I think that's why CeCe only let me get as far as I did. Maybe if it were darker, she'd go further.

I feel different here. I've driven out to the spot where Micki died, but it doesn't excite me like this does. Micki's death simply wasn't as personal. Amy was special.

Being with Amy was the Lord's will. The signs were there. She was the inversion of Eva: the whore to Eva's virgin. Robert touched her because Eva was too pure. It only makes sense that I would too; after all, Eva's mine. Robert was my stand-in, like Amy was Eva's.

I wonder if I have to kill Robert so the good in him comes back to me. Amy had parts of Eva, and now that she's dead, Eva reached out and touched me. It's like the parts that were trapped inside Amy joined Eva.

Because Amy died, Eva asked me to touch her. She gave me a mission.

I think about Robert. We've been friends our whole lives, but I'm not sure I want his traits in me. I like who I am. I'm not sure what to do about him.

The sound of the waves makes me think about Amy-Eva. Now that Amy's gone, I see that she was a *part* of Eva.

That's why being with her mattered. That's why she had to be sacrificed. The Lord works in mysterious ways. I didn't quite understand how complex Eva was until today when she touched me.

I pull off my shirt, shoes, and socks. I set the shoes side by side on the passenger seat, roll my socks together, and fold my shirt the way I always do. A quick glance outside lets me know no one is nearby right now. Barefoot in only my trousers, I get out of the car and walk toward the water. I can almost see her there on the ground. Amy-Eva looking up at me, satisfied with how happy I made her. I unbutton my trousers, fold them neatly, and drop them on the ground.

Once I wade naked into the water, I sigh. I wonder how long it will be until Eva looks at me like Amy-Eva did. Soon, I expect, especially if I do a good job with Madison.

DAY 15: "THE TALK"

Eva

THE NEXT MORNING, I'm awake before Nate arrives. After my mother shows him into the kitchen, where I'm having a far healthier breakfast than I want, she announces that she's going to work at home for a couple hours, and then she gives us a strange look and asks, "Are you dating in the house today?"

For a moment, Nate stares at her with the sort of expression on his face that makes it hard not to laugh. He recovers quickly though. "We hadn't made any plans."

"LeeAnn is coming by to cook, so if you want, you could have a faux restaurant date," Mom offers.

I make a shooing gesture at her. "Go work on . . . whatever it is you do."

She laughs. "Organizing my schedule and your father's next month, so we can maximize our time at home to actively parent."

I groan and lower my head to the table. "You're going to kill Dad and me too, Mom. Relax."

"Eva Elizabeth Tilling, you do not get to say that!"

At the sound of her voice, I look back up at her.

"You could have died. I'm allowed to be overinvolved for a while. The article I read about parenting after traumatic events is very clear." She folds her arms over her chest. "We need to be here for you. You could have nightmares, stomachaches, depression, or a plethora of other things. We have to be attentive to you so we notice changes. Shared meals and a healthy diet are important, but listening is *crucial*."

My mother looks like she might start crying, and I realize that I'm staring at her open-mouthed. I'm not sure how to deal with this new version of my mother. I know my accident scared her; it scared me too. We're staring at each other, but not speaking.

After a few moments, Nate's voice interrupts the tense silence. "I'm going to go look for a movie on demand. Maybe we can have a movie date."

"Check the collection in the media room first," Mom suggests.

Once he leaves, my mother flops into a chair. "I'm sorry. I'm not trying to embarrass you."

"You didn't," I promise. "I'm scared too, you know? The murderer is killing my friends, and he sent flowers to *me*. He carved *my name* on Amy. I get being scared. Really, I do."

My mother folds her hands together on the table in front of her, and I reach over and put my hand on top of hers. We sit in silence for a few moments before she says, "Jessup is supposed to be a safe town. Your grandfather is coming home in two days, and I know it's silly, but I want to be able to tell him we're doing everything right. I want him to know we're keeping you safe."

"You are."

My mother nods. "You're not suicidal, are you?"

"No."

"Stomachaches?"

"No."

"Nightmares?"

"No." I smile at her. "I'm okay. I'm scared, and I wish I hadn't seen those pictures of Amy. I wish I knew why the killer is targeting my friends . . . and me. I'm safe here though. I'm coping fine with this and with the accident. Grandfather Cooper has nothing to complain about. He's probably worried about you as much as me."

"I know. He's just hard to please." She looks a little guilty as she adds, "One of the things I love about your father is that he doesn't doubt me when I say I can handle something, and he's always thought you were capable—more so than your grandfather thinks I am even *now*."

"You knew what to do yesterday when the sicko sent a package to me. You knew to have someone here with me, and you're trying to make sure I'm safe without being totally trapped at home bored. I know it's not just my crutches that made you hire Nate."

My mother nods. "They'll catch the killer. Detective Grant is good at her job."

Neither of us mention how long it could be until they *do* catch him or how many people might die before then.

"I'm going to work in the den for a while. Why don't you go visit with Nate?" She pauses awkwardly and then in a whisper, she asks, "Do I need to worry about what you're doing with him when we're not home?"

"Mom!"

"Parents talk, Eva. I've heard enough to know that Nate has run wild since his father left."

My face feels like it's on fire, but I don't look away from her.

"Are you still taking your birth control pills?" she asks.

"I am."

"Good." She nods. "I've never regretted being a mother, but it's not something to do young. Nathaniel should see his doctor, too. There are a lot more diseases than I knew about when I was your age."

She leans in and kisses the top of my head. "I'm going to get a bit of work done in the den then. Do you need help into the room?"

I shake my head. I'm perfectly capable on my crutches now, and even if I wasn't, I don't know that I could bear walking into the room with my mother and seeing Nate just now. She's always been very practical about sex. Maybe it's because she became a mother so young, but she made sure I was on birth control when I started dating Robert seriously, and she gave me such a frank sex talk that I'm surprised I'm not still blushing several years later.

After she leaves the kitchen, I stand and tuck my crutches under my arms. Life after my accident is weirder than I could've ever expected. In only a few weeks, everything I thought I knew has changed. When I woke up and saw my face, I thought that my scars would be the biggest challenge. I thought I would have to be okay with Robert ignoring me because no one else would want me. I thought I would have to handle everything on my own because my parents didn't want to be bothered. I was wrong about so much.

I look at Nate as I thump my way into the media room. It's comfortable here, all dark wood, black walls and ceiling, and three rows of deep red reclining chairs.

Nate's sitting on the floor reading the back of a movie. He looks up and grins at me, and then he gestures at the stack of movies on the floor beside him. "Did you want to watch something? We can, but I just wanted an excuse to give you privacy."

"Sure." I sit in one of the chairs and prop my foot up. I figure I might as well say something about the conversation with my mother. If not, it'll bother me until I do, so I blurt, "Mom thinks you should get tested for STDs before we have sex."

He lowers the movie in his hand. "Say again?"

"Tests," I repeat, my gaze on the floor, not on him.

When I look up, he's coming across the room to me. He

sits beside me and takes my hand. I don't see his death when he does. What I do see is the look in his eyes. He's worried.

"I swear that I won't ever do anything to hurt you. No lies. No cheating. I can go to the doctor weekly if you want."

"No," I say. "I trust you." I realize as I say it that I *do* trust him. That moment of doubt isn't about him. It's about me. I gaze at Nate as he is cueing up the movie. He is beautiful and experienced, and I'm a maze of scars who couldn't keep her boyfriend *before* these cuts were all over me.

"Nate, just . . . if you decide you don't want to be with me, you'll tell me before you go out with anyone else, right? If you decide that the way I look is too—"

"Not going to happen." He kisses me briefly before continuing, "If I lose my mind and think there could be anyone I like more, I'll tell you, but it's not going to happen."

"Thank you." I lean my head against his shoulder. "I need to try again. I need to see the people I missed, get them to touch me so I can see their deaths, *and* we need to talk to Reid," I start.

"After your mom leaves," Nate finishes. "Let's just relax for an hour or two. Most of them are probably still in bed."

He's right. I *know* he's right. "Let me text Grace."

My fingers race as I let her know my tentative plan so far: watch movie with Nate, then see her, then talk to Reid, and then we'll figure out how to check on the people I missed yesterday. Once that's sorted out, and I express sympathy to her for the General's insistence that running is temporarily forbidden, I sit in the dark with my new boyfriend. The movie hasn't even started when I begin laughing. He's picked *American Pie* to watch.

"It seemed fitting," he whispers.

I roll my eyes, but I nestle as close to him as I can in the chairs. That's the other limitation with this room: I'd rather not have a chair arm between us. We lace our fingers together, and for the moment, it'll have to be enough.

DAY 15: "THE EPIPHANY"

Judge

MADISON REFUSED TO GO out with me. I called her last night, and she laughed. If she hadn't done that, I wouldn't be sitting here watching and waiting for her parents to go to work. That's the challenge, though. I've only ever left a message in the dark. Eva knew. She knew this—the daylight and with no time to plan—would be a test of my resolve. I won't fail her. I have roses—red and white tied together for unity—next to me on the passenger seat.

After the Tremonts leave, I walk up to the door and ring the bell. I stand with my hands behind my back so she doesn't see my gloves or my water bottle. It's a refillable one that I can squirt in her mouth so she doesn't leave her DNA on it. There's no graceful way to get her to drink the water with GHB, so I'm going to have to force her. A few weeks ago, I practiced holding down a dog and pouring water in its mouth in case I needed to do it. I think the key is keeping the front feet trapped—or in Madison's case, her arms. I just need to get her in the house first. I can't do it on the porch.

"What do you want?" Madison folds her arms over her chest.

"Eva," I admit. It feels good to say it. "I want Eva to be happy, and you want Bouchet, so we can work together."

She stares at me for a moment before saying, "What makes you think I want Nate?"

"Don't." I shake my head. "Just let me in so we can talk, or come with me."

For a moment, I think she's going to cooperate. I hope she will, but this is a test that the Lord set. I would have preferred Piper. She would have been easier, but Eva picked Madison as a challenge.

"I can't, Reid. My parents would lose it if I went out without telling them." Madison steps back and starts to close the door.

I shove my foot forward and push her back into the house. "I understand."

Her eyes widen, and she opens her mouth to scream. I slam the palm of my hand into her mouth to keep her quiet and step inside her house. She starts to fall, but I grab her arm—dropping my bottle in the process.

I shove the door closed behind us.

There are tears in her eyes now. It reminds me a little of

Amy. "Shhh, come on now. You need to be quiet."

She's shaking, and I sweep her feet from under her and push her to the floor. I still have my palm shoved into her mouth, and she's trying to bite me.

"I don't want to hurt you," I tell her. "Stop! Maddy, *stop!*"

There's a wash of guilt as I realize how we're lying on the floor. My hips are up against hers, and she looks afraid. I realize why, and it makes me feel horrible. "I'm not going to do *that*. Shh!" I push my hand tighter to her mouth. "I told you I want to talk to you. I need you to give Eva a message."

Madison nods.

"If I pull my hand away and let you up, will you help me?"

She nods again, so I remove my hand slowly. She stares up at me with tears rolling down her cheek and blood on her lips from where I had to shove my hand against her mouth to keep her quiet.

"You're bleeding." I lean in and kiss her blood away. "Shhh. I just need your help. Everything will be okay then. I didn't want to hit you. You shouldn't have closed the door like that."

"I'm sorry." She's shaking, and her voice sounds rough. She swallows before she asks, "What do you need?"

"I need you to come with me to give Eva a message."

"I could call her," Madison offers.

It's cute how she thinks she can come up with a better plan. I laugh and kiss her nose. "No. I know what I'm doing." I straighten up so I'm straddling her rather than pressed against her whole body. I grab her right arm and pull it down so it's pinned under my knee. That's when I notice my hand. "You tore my glove."

"I'm sorry." She starts shaking again. "I didn't mean to."

I reach over and grab the water bottle that I dropped. "Here. Take a sip."

She stares up at me, but her mouth doesn't open. Her lips stay tightly closed.

"There's blood in your mouth, Madison. I'm going to give you some water." I open the bottle with my teeth, biting it and tugging up. "Open your mouth."

Her hips buck as she tries to shake me off, and her left hand comes up to try to scratch me. She scores her fingernails across the bottom of my throat, and I drop the bottle to grab her wrist.

"Amy was very happy at the end," I tell Madison. "We'd been together for months. Robert never knew. That's why she went to him the night Eva got hurt. I told her to tell him that he should break up with Eva. I knew he wouldn't though. Then Eva would be alone. I thought she'd die when I hit her. I thought I killed her, but the Lord spared her. That's how I knew that what I was meant to do was work harder to *teach* her."

Madison sobs, but she stops trying to throw me off her. "Please, let me go. I'm sorry. I don't want to die."

"Would you touch me like Amy used to?" I stare down at her. I feel ashamed that I feel excited by the movement of her hips under me, but the only time anyone has ever arched up like that was when we were naked. I think it's probably normal to be excited. "If I asked you, would you?"

She doesn't answer. "Would you let me go if I did?"

It's not a no, but she doesn't want me. That much is clear. I hoped, but she doesn't want me. Eva will. Once she knows I did what she asked, she'll want me. I pick the bottle up and put it on Madison's mouth.

"Drink the water," I tell her.

She tries to turn away, so I grab her chin to hold her still. She bucks up again.

"Stop that. You don't really want to, so *stop*."

The water is a stream, not so fast that it'll choke her. It was easier with Amy. She trusted me. Madison doesn't seem to want to help me. It'll be okay though. All I need is about fifteen minutes. The GHB is quick acting, and then she won't resist.

"In a few minutes, we're going to get up and go to the car, so we can give Eva her message," I explain. "I'll help you out to the car so you don't fall."

"Please!" Madison smiles up at me. "You're not a bad guy. I won't tell anyone you were here. Just go. Leave me here, *please*. I'll make it up to you. Do . . . do what Amy used to for you." She sniffles. "I could. Just don't kill me. Please?"

If she hadn't waited until she had the medicine, I could've let her, but she'll be unconscious soon. I don't want that. I shake my head. "I just need you to help me with a message."

For about twenty minutes, she keeps making offers,

promises, but it's too late. I do kiss her when she asks because she sounds so honest. That's all. I suspect this was a test, to see if I was worthy of Eva. I wonder if she even told Madison to offer herself to me. Later, I'll explain to Eva that I was faithful to her. All I did was kiss Madison. It's probably a little frightening to know you're going to die but not understand that it's for a greater cause.

Finally, the medicine kicks in enough that she can't fight me, so I help Madison to the car and fasten her seat belt. I'm a little nervous that my car was outside so long, but I still take a moment to tuck red and white roses inside the top of her shirt. I'd already cut the thorns off before I came here, so I don't hurt her.

I don't like the extra time, but I want the message to be perfect, and it's not like I ever keep the same car anyway. I get them for a little while, and after each message, I get new ones from my uncle in Durham. He buys junkers, and if I run a few errands for him, he lets me borrow cars. I don't tell people— mostly because I know that the packages I pick up are drugs, but also because he's one of the relatives we don't mention.

I have to drive past the lake the first time because there's a mom and her kids, but when I loop back, they've gone. After I park, I put duct tape over Madison's mouth. I'm not sure if she'll scream. Then I gather up the knife I had under my seat and carry it and Madison to the edge of the water. After I lower her to the ground, I use my knife to write: To Eva. Forever. Then, I pull out my phone and take a picture. I don't send it yet. I want to be with Eva when she sees it.

I leave my phone on the ground, but I keep all of my clothes on as I wade out with Madison.

"Shhh," I whisper. I kiss the top of her head as I hold her body under the water. She thrashes a little more than Amy did. It makes me a little sad that the only times Madison thrashed in my arms were when she was sad on the floor of her house and now that she's drowning. I'll have to talk to Eva about a better plan so I can make the next girl happy before she has to die.

I remind myself that today is about Eva though. We'll finally be together like husband and wife. I wonder if I should've written vows or if she'll want more traditional ones. We can't legally marry yet, so maybe we'll just speak from our hearts tonight.

We'll need to stop at my house for my suitcase first. I think about the busy day ahead of me as Madison stops moving, and I let her go. I set her free in the water.

I've done it. I did what Eva said to do, so now she'll be mine. This was it: my test. I passed, too. I know it. My heart-beat feels like I just finished a workout, and I worry that I'm too dirty and wet. I can't stop though. She'll forgive me for not looking my best. She's probably there waiting, as excited as I am.

I wipe my face on my shirt, and then I get in the car to go to Eva's house. Today is the day we'll finally be together. My Eva will be in my arms where she belongs.

I obey all the traffic rules as I drive.

When I arrive at her house, I see that her mother is still home, and Bouchet's truck is in the drive. I'm glad I came straight over; I don't like him being around her. I put a button-up shirt on over my T-shirt, so I can hide the scratches on my throat. I don't think Mrs. Tilling would understand. It's better to be presentable anyhow. I button my shirt, which is already wet from my soaked T-shirt under it.

My hands are damp when I walk up to the door, so I wipe them on my trousers before I ring the bell. It doesn't really help. My trousers are soaked.

"Mrs. Tilling," I say. "I'm here to see Eva."

My future mother-in-law seems startled, and I bet it's because I'm still wet and muddy. It's foolish, but I couldn't wait. Eva is probably sitting inside wondering when I'll get here. I didn't tell her *when* this morning I'd talk to Madison, and she didn't pick a time. She might even be surprised at how fast I was. I smile at Mrs. Tilling and tell her, "I got stuck, and I had nothing in the trunk. I usually have a gym bag. My house was rekeyed, so I came here to see if I could clean up and check on Eva."

"Eva's in the media room with Nate. Why don't I get you a towel and something of Mr. Tilling's?"

I don't want to stand in the foyer. I want to see Eva. "Not to be indelicate, but I'd really like to use your bathroom. I'll use the towel in there if it's okay." I give her a reassuring smile and add, "Please?"

She shakes her head, but says, "Of course, Reid."

I keep my smile in place and slip out of my shoes. I don't run to the media room even though I want to. I walk, maybe a bit faster than normal, but it's not a run.

As I pass the doorway to the media room, I see Eva. Nate Bouchet is in there too, but he's not helping her. He's not doing his job. He's *kissing* her. He's touching *Eva*.

"What are you doing?" I watch them as he stands up and puts himself between us. She doesn't tell him to move, doesn't apologize to me. Nothing.

"How *could* you?"

"Reid?" Eva frowns as she stares back at me. There's no guilt in her expression, and I realize that she's become too much like Amy.

"I won't share you the way I did with Amy," I tell her, hoping she'll understand. "I can't. I love you."

"What?"

"It was one thing for her to be with Robert and me, but you? You're special. I did everything right. I did what you said." I realize that this might be the last chance I have to explain. I pull out my phone and hit send. "Look! I did what you asked."

She looks at Nate and then at me. "What do you mean?"

Her phone chimes, and she pulls it out.

I realize that her mother is standing behind me now. "Reid, I think you should leave."

Eva is staring at her phone. Her mouth is open, but she isn't speaking. As I watch, her phone drops to the ground.

This is wrong. All wrong.

I turn and shove Mrs. Tilling aside. She hits something and stumbles, but doesn't fall. I don't stop. I run. I leave the door open behind me, and I jump in the car. I'm not sure if Mrs. Tilling called the police while I was yelling at Eva, but I need to get out of here just in case.

I feel like my heart was just shredded. I did *everything* for her. How could Eva do this to me, especially now?

I need to get help.

DAY 15: "THE CABIN"

Grace

WHEN I LOOK THROUGH the peephole and see Reid standing on my porch with tears in his eyes, I know that something bad has happened.

"Grace!" He pounds on the door. "I need your help. *Please*, Yeung. It's Eva."

I yank the door open. He's muddy and wet. I've never seen him this emotional.

"What happened?"

"Eva," he says. "It's Eva. She's hurt."

"What? Where? Is she okay?"

"You need to come with me." He looks frantic, and I suddenly feel like I'm back in the hospital watching her lying there motionless in her bed. "Now. We need to go *now* before it's too late!"

I grab my phone and my shoes, not bothering to put them on, and follow him to the car. "She just texted me a little while ago." I glance at my phone as I reach the car; it's not working. "There are no new texts."

"Hold on." He stops at the trunk and pops it open. "The seat's all wet."

When I try the car door, it won't open. "It's locked."

"I know," he says, and then I feel something hit me. I start to fall, and that's the last thing I know.

WHEN I OPEN MY eyes, I am in the dark. I try to sit up and thunk my head. I feel around, hoping I'm wrong, but between the low barrier over my head and the sense of movement, I realize that I am in a car trunk. Worse yet, I am in Reid's trunk.

Reid.

Reid is the killer.

I'm trapped in the *killer's* trunk.

I think back to Eva's death visions, and I remember her saying that I was at the library and then shoved in a trunk. Obviously, something changed, but I was still shoved in a trunk.

Does that mean that I'm going to die? Was part of the vision—the trunk part—accurate, but not the rest? I don't know how much stock I put in her visions. I cannot believe that this is the start of my death. I *won't* believe that. I can't.

I search the darkness around me for a weapon. I'll fight him with whatever I can. I don't find anything at first and then I feel my phone.

"Thank you. Thank you."

I try to dial 911, but nothing happens. The phone works; the battery is good. There's no signal, though.

I keep trying, hoping we were just passing through a dead zone, but nothing changes. I can't make a call or send a text or email.

I have no cell signal, no weapon, and I'm trapped in a sweltering car trunk. Air conditioning apparently doesn't blow into the trunk, and the mix of fear, heat, and motion makes me wonder if I'm going to throw up.

I hear the change and feel the thump as the car leaves the road. I'm jostled around as we go over what is either a dirt road, or no road at all. The realization that we're leaving the road terrifies me. North Carolina is a state full of thick growth. Kudzu—a seemingly beautiful but incredibly destructive ivy-like vine—covers whole trees and buildings, drapes from utility poles, and it's far from the only plant gone wild in this state. Whatever fate awaits me at the end of a dirt road isn't one I want.

When the car stops, I still haven't found anything to use as a weapon, and I feel increasingly horrible. The dizziness and headache are the least of my problems though. I opened the door to a killer, one who is now opening the trunk and looking at me.

I try to kick him, but he grabs my leg and says, "Don't make me hurt you."

"You . . . you're him." I know it's true, but I need him to confirm it. "You killed them."

"I *sacrificed* Amy, but yeah, I killed Micki and Madison." Reid motions me out of the trunk.

I thought I couldn't get any more afraid, but I was wrong. His words make me unable to breathe. I didn't know Madison was dead. She was alive yesterday. I *saw* her yesterday. That means he killed someone today, someone I *knew*, someone he's known his whole life. Sometime between driving me home yesterday afternoon and kidnapping me this morning, Reid killed Madison.

"Come on, Yeung. I haven't got all day."

As soon as my feet touch the ground, I start to run. My odds aren't great, but they're better than they will be if he locks me up somewhere. I *have* to try. I don't get very far before he tackles me from behind. I'm pinned facedown in the dirt under him.

"Please don't do that," he says, his mouth next to my ear.

I fill with the same fear that I'm sure every girl has felt trapped under a boy. This sense of helplessness makes me start to twist and squirm to get away. I don't scream at first, trying to save my breath for fighting, but when I can't get him off my back, I open my mouth to scream, too.

Reid clamps a hand over my mouth. "Don't do *that* either."

I remember the detective—and the picture she showed us. Amy had words carved into her skin. She was killed. I try to scream again, even though his hand is on my mouth.

"No!" Reid's hand tightens over my mouth. He shoves his other arm under me, wrapping it around my waist. He hauls me to my feet. I try to go limp, to use my body weight to throw him off balance and get free.

It doesn't work. He pulls me tighter up against him. I try to squirm out of his hold, to kick my legs back at him, but it makes no difference.

I'm not sure what he's going to do, but I'm certain it's not something I want to find out either. I'm tired, and my head hurts, and I don't know how to escape.

Then he drags me back toward the car, and I realize that he's parked outside a falling-down building that was hidden by trees and plants. It's a cabin, the sort that I've been to for a few parties. It doesn't look big; the size of the whole thing is more like a one-car garage than a house. The windows are covered with plywood, and the outside looks like no one has been here in years. Kudzu covers the whole of it so densely that I'm not sure how we'll get inside.

"Now, if you don't try to run again, I won't hurt you," Reid says. "If you do, I *will* hurt you. Eva wouldn't like that, so I'm trying not to do it. Do you understand?"

I can feel his breath on my ear, and I whimper despite myself.

"Nod if you understand."

I'm not sure I could get free to run, and I realize that no one is near to hear my screams. I nod. I don't know what else to do.

Reid uncovers my mouth, but he doesn't release me.

He pushes aside the thick vines and reveals a metal door.

With one arm still wrapped around my waist, he holds me against him as he fishes a key out of his trouser pocket. Then he unlocks a padlock that's been shoved through a makeshift hinge someone—possibly Reid—welded onto the door.

When he opens the door, I gasp. It's not what I expected at all. Inside, the little house is decorated almost like a home. I look around, hoping to find something I can use as a weapon against him. In the main room, there is a daybed with a pretty yellow duvet on it. I see a coffee table, rocking chair, and a few crates that serve as side tables. On the crates and table are camping lanterns. To the left is a kitchenette with a mini fridge, and an old-fashioned combination sink and stove.

More plywood covers the windows from the inside, but there are pictures on this side of it. My mouth falls open as I look at them. They're all of Eva. I'm in some of them. Robert is, too. There are others that are of groups. Some have been altered so that Reid is beside Eva even though I know he wasn't really at her side there. He's cut and pasted them or in some cases altered them digitally before printing them.

"Do you think she'll like it?" His voice is still against my ear and neck because he has kept me in front of him. It's like an embrace, and it's adding to my steadily mounting fear.

I'm silent as he closes the door and puts the padlock on this side, locking us in together. Luckily, the increased darkness hides my expression. I don't want to anger him by telling him that Eva—or anyone else in their right mind—would be horrified, so I reply, "I can't imagine what she'll say."

"I don't think she'd mind you being here. You're special to her." He pulls me toward the daybed and spins me around, so I am facing him. "Sit."

Obeying him makes me want to scream, but being hip-to-hip with him seems awful, too. I sit. I sit on the daybed facing the killer who has kidnapped me and brought me God knows where. He hasn't stepped back, so I'm eye level with his crotch.

"I think I'm going to throw up," I half whisper.

"Don't!" He leans forward, reaching past me, and pulls a length of chain from beside the daybed. At the end of it is a leather dog collar. "Stay still."

I can't stop the tears that fall as he fastens it around my throat. He tucks a finger between the collar and my throat. "Is that too tight? Can you swallow?"

"Reid, you don't have to—"

"Stop." He holds up a smaller padlock so I can see it. "I'm going to put this through the rings. I bought this collar because it works with the lock."

"Please," I beg. "Just let me go."

"I can't. You're how I'm going to get Eva to come to me." Reid snaps the padlock onto the collar. I hear the click. Then he straightens and looks at me. "Now, if you need to puke, there's a bucket for that or bathroom needs." He motions to an old-fashioned wooden privacy screen that has cracks and a few small holes in it. "Your chain reaches. I planned this for Eva, so I thought of everything."

I don't move. I can't. I don't know what I'm to do here. I'm chained up in a cabin with a crazy person who is obsessed with my best friend. I look around the rest of the room. It's easier to make out a few other details when Reid lights some camping lanterns. A water heater with rust-covered pipes sits in the far corner where the privacy screen is. I see that the chain snakes toward it, and is attached to a thick pipe that extends into the ceiling. A doorway to at least one other room is to my right. I wonder what's in there.

After a moment, I ask, "What are you going to do to me?"

"Nothing, I hope . . . unless you mean you want to do something? I looked up some people you went to school with in Philadelphia and emailed them. I know your secrets, Grace. You're more like Amy than most people in Jessup know."

I remember him saying he "sacrificed" Amy, so I try to be careful in my words. "I don't . . . I can't do that sort of thing."

"Sex?"

I nod.

Reid looks upward at the ceiling. "This is part of the test, isn't it? I get it. I need to wait for Eva. Prove my worthiness. Fine." He looks at me again. "Maybe after Eva gets here you'll change your mind."

There is no answer here that seems safe, so I say nothing. I've never been as terrified as I am here in this place with him. I don't know how he expects to get Eva here, and I certainly don't want her imprisoned, too. What I *want* is someone to get me out of here.

"I don't want to die, Reid," I whisper.

He nods. "I understand. I hope you don't have to. It would upset Eva." He smiles and walks over to a bag in the rocking chair. He unzips it, digs around inside, and pulls out a black collar with a little rectangular box on it. Then he pulls out what looks like a remote control with an antenna on it. "If you're good, we can switch from the leash to a training collar. It's supposed to work on dogs up to large breeds, and I don't think you weigh as much as some of them."

I can't even speak right now. He's crazy, absolutely, completely, *dangerously* crazy.

Smiling, he walks over to me with the shock collar. "I can't use it when I'm out, but when I'm here, we could try it. It'll be tricky if you and Eva are both here and I need to leave. Maybe I'll pick up a second chain and collar while I'm out."

I close my eyes for a second. This cannot be happening—all because I opened my door. That was all I did. I opened my door to a boy I've known for a few years, a boy who drove me home yesterday, a boy who has hit on me at parties and joked with me at school. Now, I'm chained up listening to him explain the appeal of a shock collar instead of a chain.

This sort of thing is not supposed to happen, not anywhere, but especially not in Jessup, North Carolina.

Reid puts the collar and remote back in the bag and then he walks out of my line of sight through the unknown doorway, vanishing farther into the house. I hope he'll stay gone, but in a few minutes he comes back. He's no longer wearing trousers or a shirt. Instead, he's barefoot and wearing a pair of gym shorts. I've seen him and the rest of the guys in the same thing countless times. What draws my attention are the fingernail scratches on the base of his throat. Someone—presumably Madison—fought with him. I stare at him with mounting terror. Fighting him didn't help her. She's dead. I don't want to die, too.

Reid is silent as he opens a package of wet wipes. He moves the black bag to the floor, sits in the chair, and starts wiping his face, arms, and chest. I watch as he drops one of the wipes on the floor. It's not just mud he's wiping from his skin. There's blood, too. I realize with another wave of horror that it's probably Madison's.

After a few minutes, he walks over to the daybed and sits down beside me.

"Sit still, Grace. I don't want Eva to be upset when she sees you, and you look like you were rolling in the mud."

If I could stop staring at the blood on the wipes on the floor, maybe I would try to stop him from wiping my face and arms, but all I can think about is Madison's blood. He killed a girl this morning, and now he's cleaning mud from my skin.

"I've always liked you, Grace," he says, wiping my cheek. "You're a good friend to Eva."

"Thank you."

He tosses the wipe toward the others on the floor. "I'm tired."

I swallow and force myself to meet his eyes. "I'm sorry."

Reid nods. "It's been a difficult day." He walks back to the bag and pulls out a Jessup High T-shirt, a sports bottle, and a cup. He pours some into the cup and walks back toward me. The shirt is in his other hand. "I need you to drink this, so we can nap."

"Please," I whisper. "I can nap in the other room or the floor. Please?"

"Relax. It'll just make you sleepy." He holds it out to me.

When I don't speak or move, he adds, "I can *make* you drink it, but I don't want to upset Eva. I *explained* that already, didn't I?" He doesn't sound calm or gentle now. His words are sharp. I've heard him like this countless times, and it didn't scare me. That was before I realized he was a killer.

"Please don't hurt me," I beg. "You can nap without doing this. I promise."

He stares at me. "Eventually, I'll be able to, but not yet. My father kept *his* girlfriend here. He brought me to meet her when we were all in elementary school. Not you. You weren't here yet. Anyhow . . . He explained how long it takes to build trust. He brought me here to meet the *next* girlfriend, too. They changed and trusted him, but it takes time." He wiggles the cup a little. "Eva's the girl for me, but we'll talk about you once she comes to me. I thought she trusted me without this. I thought I could do it better than my father, but it didn't work."

"Maybe she didn't know that you felt—"

"No!" Reid yells. "I sent messages. I did everything she wanted . . ." He takes a breath, smiles at me, and sounds calm again when he continues, "Bouchet is the problem. Once he's gone, Eva will be better."

I try to stay still and calm. I'm not sure what to do around him. It's hard to believe that yesterday I laughed at his vulgarity, rolled my eyes at his attitude, and then rode home with him. I didn't know him at all. I thought I did, but the person in front of me is a stranger.

He lifts my hand and puts the cup in it. "Drink so I know I can try to trust you. Prove I don't have to force you to do this."

I'm shaking as I lift the cup and drink.

"Swallow it, Grace," he orders.

I'm crying again, but I do as he demands. I don't like how he keeps saying my name. Reid used to call me "Yeung"; he isn't doing that now. The person in front of me is calling me Grace.

"Good girl. In a few minutes, you'll be tired, too. We can nap. You should probably go use the bathroom first. Here. This is more comfortable." He hands me a T-shirt and points to the privacy screen where he said there were buckets. "Go on."

He watches me walk to the screen. The chain jangles and drags behind me. The sound and feel of it bring hot tears to my eyes. I hope he's not lying about wanting to sleep. I don't know what he gave me, but despite the myriad things that are horribly wrong, I am clinging to the hope that all that's about to happen is drugged sleep.

I change into his shirt like he orders me to, but keep on my bra and yoga pants.

When I return to the daybed, Reid is already there with his shoes kicked off. He doesn't comment on my clothes, and I'm relieved by that. I couldn't leave my legs bare, even though the shirt hangs past my hips. I know the thick layer of cotton won't protect me, but it eases my mind a tiny bit.

Reid pats the bed beside him. "I'll hold you until you fall asleep."

"I'm not tired."

"You will be." He pats the bed again, and I sit. Reid continues, "Then I can sleep, too. I do want to trust you, but we're not there yet and I don't want you to try to hurt me in my sleep. We won't always need the medicine."

"I thought you only wanted me so Eva would come." I try not to whimper as he wraps an arm around me and pulls me to him. He lies back on the bed, pulling me down so my head is on his shoulder, and wrapping an arm securely around me. It feels worse somehow that he's holding me like I'm his girl-friend.

He straightens the chain so it's behind me. "That was the plan, but everything happens for a reason. I don't always see the Lord's plans until I'm in them. It's hard to explain. We don't have to decide today."

I feel the drugs start to take hold of me, and I whisper a prayer in my mind, "Please don't do anything while I'm unconscious."

Obviously, I must have said it aloud not in my head, though, because he answers, "I wouldn't do that. I'm not a *monster*, Grace."

DAY 15: "THE GUN"

Eva

DETECTIVE GRANT ARRIVES QUICKLY. My mother had me forward that horrible picture to her before she even arrived.

"My husband's on his way home, but do you mind if I set the house alarm?" my mother asks.

"That's fine, Mrs. Tilling," Detective Grant says.

After my mother walks away, the detective sits in the chair across from me, and then she looks at me and turns on her recorder. "We're going to go through what happened step by step."

She says her name, the date, the time, where we are, and a case number. Then she says, "I need you to state your name, and then tell me about Reid Benson's arrival here today."

I summarize it as best I can, telling her that Reid was wet and muddy when he arrived, and that he seemed off and what he said as best I remember. I finish with ". . . and there was that picture. I can't believe this. I've known Reid my whole life. We're *friends*. He's friends with all of us."

"Including Amy Crowne?"

I nod.

"Michelle Adams?" the detective prompts.

"He knew Micki, but we all know the same people. Jamie, Grayson, Robert, Piper. We've *all* known each other our whole lives."

Nate comes to stand beside me, and I reach out and take his hand.

Detective Grant glances at Nate and then at my mother. "What was Mr. Reid's relationship with Madison Tremont?"

The tone in her voice lets me know more than I want. The detective sounds like she did when she asked about Amy; her voice has gone calm and emotionless.

"Madison was the one in the picture he sent," I say, hoping I'm wrong.

Detective Grant doesn't deny it.

Nate's grip on my hand tightens. There are tears falling down my cheeks, and I can't speak. I talked to Reid about her yesterday in this very room. I thought we were talking about him liking her. Then he showed up here today, mud covered and telling me he loved me. I think back to Amy's death, drowned at the lake, and the mud on Reid seems more damning than I can process. I take a breath, my chest shaking as I gulp air. I don't want these things to be true.

"He was here yesterday," Nate answers the detective. He sits down on the sofa next to me. "They both were. Eva thought he liked Madison."

I answer then, "Nate wasn't with me when Reid and I talked about Madison. Nate was with Madison, and Reid was watching her. I suggested . . ." I look at the detective, stare straight into her eyes as the unavoidable truth settles on me.

"I suggested he talk to Madison. I thought . . . I thought he meant to *date* her. . . . He killed her. Reid killed her."

"Miss Tremont is dead," Detective Grant confirms just as my mother returns.

Hearing it said aloud is somehow worse than just thinking it. I saw Madison yesterday. She was here in my house talking to Nate. I talked to Reid about her. He held my wrist, and I thought he was the victim. I wonder if I would've seen him kill Madison if she came near enough that I could see her death. I start shaking as I say, "He drove *Grace* home. Grace and CeCe Watkins. Oh my God! I need my phone." I try to get up, but Nate stops me.

"I'll grab it," he says.

"Grace needs to stay in her house." I look from the detective to my mother. My voice gets shriller and shriller as I tell them, "You need to find Mrs. Yeung and send her home, and CeCe, we need to text CeCe. What if he thinks I was telling him to talk to them, too. I sent them with him after I said I thought he should do something about his feelings for Madison."

My mother walks away to call Mrs. Yeung, and the detective offers me what looks like sympathy before she makes a quick call, too. Her sympathy makes me feel worse. Guilt twists through me. I think back to the messages in the flowers, the cicada, the card that said "yours," the words cut into Amy's skin, and the new words in Madison's skin. He did all of those things in some sick attempt to send me a message. I should've known. I should've figured it out somehow.

I'm still sitting there when Nate comes back and hands me my phone. I text Grace and CeCe. "Are you home and okay?"

The detective returns.

"I don't understand," I whisper. "He knows me. Why did he . . . do this? How can he think? . . . I don't understand how this happened. I should've seen something, a sign or whatever. I could've stopped him. If I'd seen it, I could've saved Maddy. . . ."

Detective Grant shakes her head. "Don't. You are *not* responsible for what he did. *He* is."

CeCe's text reply comes in: "Yes. What happened?"

"Can I tell CeCe?" I ask the detective.

She frowns. "Just tell her to stay home. Don't let anyone from school in, even people she knows."

I pass on the message with a note to tell all the girls and Robert, too. CeCe sends back a quick reply that she's "on it," and I look back at the marked lack of reply from Grace. I send her another text. I call.

"Grace isn't answering. She always answers." I look at Nate.

"I sent a car over," Detective Grant starts.

My mother returns and announces that Mrs. Yeung will be at their house in fifteen minutes. Mom shivers. "I'm going to be here, and my husband will be home shortly. We won't go anywhere."

The detective stands. "I need to take Grace's statement about her interaction with Reid Benson yesterday, as well as speak to Miss Watkins." She brushes her hands over her trousers like she has every other time. "I'll be back. If you think of anything else or hear from Reid, call me."

After she sees the detective out, my mother comes into the room and pulls me into a fierce hug. When she lets go, I see tears in her eyes. "He was in the house. I opened the door and let a killer into our house."

"He won't be here ever again," Nate says. "The door is locked, and Mr. Tilling is on the way. I'm here too, and I'm staying."

My mother nods.

"Why don't you relax there? I can get you . . . a drink or something?" Nate looks at me, and the expression on his face makes me smile briefly. He wants to help, but he doesn't know what to do.

My mother seems to collect herself at the thought of getting a drink. She stands, straightens her shoulders, and announces, "I'll fix a pot of tea."

Nate nods, and we watch her go.

I text Grace again, but there's still no answer. My mother is still in the kitchen when my father comes home. He looks in at me, sees Nate holding me while I cry, and asks, "Are you okay?"

"Nate is here," I answer.

"If you need me—"

"I know, Daddy."

He smiles in surprise at my words. It's been years since I called him that, but it's been years since I felt as close to them as I have the past couple days. He walks away to find my mother, who has been doing something or other in the kitchen that involves a lot of cupboards opening and closing.

Once I hear their muffled words in the kitchen, I turn to Nate. "I'm scared."

"You didn't see Grace's death happen," Nate reminds me.

"I *did* though. He put her in his trunk and took her. She was at the library, and then she was in his trunk." I smother a sob.

"Shhh. She didn't go to the library though. Right?"

He holds me, and I try to push past my fears. I know he's trying to help, but until I know that Grace is safe, nothing is going to be okay.

I need a plan. There has to be something I can do. I just have no idea what it could be.

Nate and I are still sitting in silence when my parents come into the room. I know by the look on my mother's face that it's bad. Gently, my father tells me, "Grace is missing." Before I can speak, he continues, "It's not like at Madison's house. There was no sign of a fight, nothing broken or anything at the Yeungs' house."

"Madison fought back," I say, not entirely surprised.

"She did." My father pauses, and I realize that he's debating hiding something.

"What? Tell me."

"Madison fought him in the foyer of the house," he says. "They think she was alive when she left the house. She was drowned, like Amy Crowne was."

"And Grace?"

"The police didn't find . . . Grace isn't at the lake. Eva, there's no reason to think Grace isn't going to be okay."

I realize that in some sick way, if Reid thinks this is about me, Grace is either safer than the others or she's in worse danger. She's my best friend. I think back to the vision of her death. I wish that I knew more so that I could try to help her. All that I remember that could be relevant is that she was leaving the library when it happened. I think back to it, letting the memory fill my mind.

Grace opens the trunk, drops a bag in, and reaches up for the lid to close it.

That's when it happens. He hits the back of her head, and she opens her mouth to scream, but a hand comes over it. Grace bites down, but the person holding her doesn't let go.

She tries dropping her weight like they tell you in street defense class, but a hand on her back shoves, and she falls into her own trunk. Her legs scrape against the car, and she feels like she can't breathe from the force of the fall.

Blinking against the pain and trying to push herself out,

Grace looks up and see someone standing there. Then the trunk closes, and it's all dark.

"He kidnapped her," I say aloud. "Then he took her somewhere. I'm not sure how he got her out of the house. Maybe because I trusted him, and so did she. If she's not home and not answering, he has her."

They all stare at me. Nate looks like he has questions, but he remains silent. I guess he figures that what I know is because of my death visions. It sort of is, but it's also the most logical answer. "Grace wouldn't ignore my texts. She was supposed to come see me today. Maybe Reid claimed he was sent to pick her up, like he drove her home yesterday. She doesn't know it's him, and she didn't know about Madison and—"

"Eva," my mother interrupts. "We aren't giving up. We don't know for certain that she's with Reid."

"Of course she is!" I look at them. "He's targeting my friends, Mom. Grace is my best friend. The only other one who's . . . Piper . . ."

It hits me. Piper was killed in her foyer; she was drugged, and then . . . she died. She was going to be the victim. Reid was going to kill her, and instead he killed Madison in her foyer. "He drugged her," I whisper.

"What?" my father asks.

I scramble to explain without admitting that I saw Piper die in the way that I now think Madison died. "If she fought but he still took her, he drugged her. Madison—did he drug her?"

"There's no way to know that," my mother says gently. "Eva, don't do this. Madison is with God now. What happened was awful, but she's gone. What you need to concentrate on is keeping faith that everything will be over soon."

My parents exchange a look, and then my father says, "We're going to wait and pray. The police are following every lead, Eva. They have everyone working on this. The detective is talking to CeCe, and I suspect they're going to talk to Robert, Jamie, and Grayson. They'll talk to Reid's grandmother, and they'll probably talk to Piper and the girls, too. Someone has to know where he would go."

"But he's already killed three people. What if—"

"Grace is a smart girl, and the police know who he is now," my mother interjects. She straightens her shoulders. "I'm going to call the courthouse and see if there are any properties that any of the Bensons own, and your father and I are going to talk to Sheila Benson's former coworkers. There are a lot of volunteers. We'll search door to door if we have to."

My father nods. "The police know what they're doing. Your grandfather is gathering the volunteers from the church to help, and we're asking the employees at the winery to help, too. Everyone is working together to find her."

"I want to help."

"No," they say in unison.

"You're on crutches," my father adds.

"And he's already hurt you once," my mother points out. "You are not going out searching for her."

I open my mouth to argue, but my father repeats, "No." He shakes his head at me. "I understand that you want to help, but the best thing you can do is stay here where it's safe. The police have asked that all of Reid's friends stay home. The last thing we need is to have to search for more than one missing girl."

"Daniel!" My mother snaps, but he waves her off.

"Reid won't come back to our house, and between the alarm and the police patrols, Eva is safe in the house." My father holds my gaze as he speaks. "She can agree to stay put, here with Nate, or we can stay here instead of helping with the search."

I sigh. "Fine. I won't join the search, but—"

"No 'buts,' Eva." My father sounds sterner than I've ever heard him sound. "You stay here with Nate, or we all stay."

"Go help them find Grace," I say. "Tell Grandfather Tilling thank you. Tell everyone thanks actually."

Both of my parents kiss me on top of my head, and after a few more reminders, they leave. I listen to the beep of the house alarm being reset, and then I turn to Nate. "In the death vision, he kidnapped Grace. She was at the library, and he hit her and pushed her into the car trunk. *Her* car. Remember how I told you the details of my vision of your death changes, but the big thing stays the same?"

Nate nods.

"He has her, and I have an idea."

"Eva . . ."

I hold up a hand and text a message to Grace's phone: "Reid, I'll never forgive you if you hurt Grace."

Nate looks at what I've texted and starts, "Are you sure that's—" His words stop as I tap send.

I wait. I stare at my phone, hoping that he'll reply. There is only silence. "Damn it!" I toss the phone on the floor. "He took her. It's all my fault. I sent her home with him yesterday, and now . . ." I start crying again. "I need to fix this. I *need* to."

Nate wipes my tears and tells me the same thing my parents and Detective Grant have said. "It's not your fault."

"What good is having visions, if I can't save her?" I let out a scream of frustration. I feel reckless in my desire to help Grace. I'd offer myself in her place if I could. I'd do anything Reid asked right now. I can't let him kill Grace.

"You saved *me*," Nate says. "You don't know if she's going to—"

"That's it!" I grab Nate's hand. "Reid is the killer, and you get attacked by him in every version of your death. I need my phone."

"I'm not following," Nate says.

"Will you trust me?"

"Of course, but—"

"I love you," I blurt.

Nate stares at me for a moment. "Eva, I—"

"Don't. I don't need you to say it; I just wanted you to know before I tell Reid." I offer him a tremulous smile. "Can I have my phone?"

He scoops it up off the floor where I flung it and hands it to me. "Are you going to fill me in?"

"I'm going to lure him out," I tell Nate. "He thinks he loves me, so he's not going to want me to be with you. You saw him earlier. That's what had him so upset. I need him to focus on me, on *us*, not on Grace."

For a moment, Nate is so motionless that I think he's going to object, but then he nods once. "Tell him."

Smiling, I type "I love Nate" and hit send. I wait. There's still no reply, so I type, "As soon as he gets back, I'm going to tell him. Then I'll do whatever you want if you set Grace free."

"I won't let you do that," Nate says, his voice grown taut with anger and something else. "I know you want to save her, but I won't let you—"

"I'm lying," I interrupt, which is a little bit true. "Reid doesn't know about my visions."

"Okaaay."

"He thinks you're out somewhere and that you'll come back to me, and we know that he's the one that attacks you on Old Salem." I grab Nate's hand. "We know where he'll be. We don't know when, but if I can lure him out, we can *make* the when be now."

Nate's eyes widen for a moment before he clarifies, "So you're going to send me to capture him?" Then he gets the same sort of look in his eyes that I've seen before he ends up in a fistfight. It's a mix of excitement and determination. "I can do it. Then he won't be able to ever hurt you again."

"I'm coming, too."

"Eva, he's obsessed with you. Taking you to him is—"

"The best plan we have. We know how he attacks you because I *saw it*. He'll force you off the road, and he'll think you don't expect an attack. You do though. So you'll be ready, and I'll be ready."

Nate watches me, but he doesn't raise any more objections. I can tell he's thinking about it.

"We know he's coming, and we know he's going to attack. We just need to be ready," I tell Nate.

"Let me go alone."

"No." I shake my head and give him my best I-don't-think-so glare. "In my visions, you were alone, and he killed you. You won't be alone this time. I'll be there, and that will make it end differently. Don't you see? We know things he doesn't, and we can use it to save Grace. Please?"

"You'll stay far away from the fight though? You'll let me handle that?"

"I'm not going to try to jump into a fight. I don't fight, and"—I motion to my crutches—"I'm not even standing on both feet right now."

Nate nods once.

"Thank you!" I reach out for his hand and say, "Help me upstairs, and then we'll go. I just need fifteen minutes."

Reluctantly, he agrees. I think he realizes I'm hiding something, but he isn't asking and I'm not volunteering any answers. I've seen other visions. Nate knows that. Maybe he isn't putting all the pieces together yet, but I am. The spot where Reid dies in my vision of him looks a lot like where he attacks Nate, too. I know how Reid dies now—and it's not the killer who shoots him. It's me.

As soon as Nate goes back downstairs, I go into my mother's room and hobble to the back of her walk-in closet. In the corner is a firebox. Awkwardly, I crouch down while balancing on my crutches, unlock it, and open it. The pistol is there where it's always been. Next to it is a faded blue-and-yellow cardboard box of bullets. I pick both items up and slip them into my purse. I've been going to the shooting range with my grandfather for years, so I feel as comfortable with a pistol as I do with a cell phone. It's a tool, one I'm hoping not to use. I want to change the vision I had of Reid's death, too. Despite everything he's done, I don't want anyone else to die, but if it's between Reid and Grace, she'll be the one who lives.

"Nate?" I call from the top of the stairs.

He comes around the corner, stops, and looks up at me. As he walks toward me, he says, "You know, I love you too."

I can't stop the smile that comes over me. "Yeah?"

In a blink, he's the rest of the way up the stairs and kissing me. When he pulls back, he says, "Yeah. I do." My crutches fall as he lifts me in his arms. "I wouldn't put my life in your hands if I didn't."

He carries me down to the ground floor and then runs up for my crutches. I watch him with a smile still on my lips. When he's back in front of me, I say, "The accident was never that bad in the death visions, but you'll need to be careful of the crowbar. He won't expect you to be prepared. You can use that. The Maglite helps, too. A baseball bat would be better, but I don't suppose you have one of those."

"No bats in the truck. Sorry," Nate says. "I'll be ready though. I can get the crowbar away from him and kick his ass. Then he'll tell us where Grace is, and *then* he'll get locked up so everyone is safe."

I nod as we leave the house. That's one possibility. The other possibility is in my purse. Killing isn't the first choice, but it's on the table. Reid put it there.

DAY 15: "THE FIGHT"

Judge

WHEN I WAKE, GRACE is still asleep. I check her pulse. She's
fine. I was careful with her dose. She'll probably wake while
I'm out. I check that her collar is secure, and then I kiss her. She
doesn't kiss me back, but that's just because of the medicine.
I slip out of bed and get her phone. I had turned it off when
Grace dropped it outside my car. I need to tell Eva that Grace
is safe. I can't tell her where we are, but I want her to know that
we're okay.

I glance at Grace and then turn on her phone. It blinks to
life, and over a dozen text messages flash across the screen. I
don't care about most of them, and I can't leave it on long just
in case it has a GPS chip. As soon as the messages stop, I go to
settings and set the phone to "airplane" mode so the Wi-Fi is
inactive. Then I return to the messages. They're not surprising.

Her mother, CeCe, and Eva all texted. I see messages asking where she is, saying that Madison is missing, but then I stop. Eva texted *me*. She knew I'd see these.

At first I'm elated, but then I see the lie. She says she "loves" Bouchet. I know it's either him sending a lie to anger me or another test. She couldn't love him—or anyone else.

I pull on my still-damp clothes, and in mere minutes, I'm outside and locking the door behind me. Grace will be safe in the house. Her leash stretches far enough that she can get to food and the buckets. There are cans of soda. She could stay here on her own for several days. It won't be that long though. Soon, I'll be back, and this time Eva will be with me.

It takes a while to get back to Jessup. The cabin is a little over forty minutes away, but I'm careful. I don't see any police officers, and even if I did, the tags on this car wouldn't come up under my name.

I'm on Old Salem Road when I see Bouchet's truck. I didn't expect to find him on the road. I thought I'd have to figure out how to get him out of his house, but he's here. The Lord simplified things to show he approves of my actions. I smile as I accept that the Lord put Bouchet in my path so he could be punished.

All of my earlier rage comes back. Bouchet touched Eva. *My* Eva. He had his lips on my soon-to-be-wife. After everything I've done, all of the sacrifices, he tried to steal her away. It won't work. I have Grace, and once I get rid of Bouchet, I'll find a way to let Eva know where to come looking for her.

Everything will be fine. I have faith in the Lord's plan.

I accelerate and swerve toward the truck, trying to force him to drive it into the trees.

The front of the truck clips a sapling.

I debate ramming it. I will if I have to, but then Bouchet swerves farther and smashes into a much larger tree.

The truck shudders to a stop at the tree, and he kills the engine. I wait to see what he'll do. I wonder if he'll call her. I can't use my phone. I shut it off so they can't track me. Maybe I can text her on his so she knows I'm safe. She's probably worried by now. She probably thinks I'll reject her.

Now that I've calmed down, I realize it was all his fault, not hers. She was weak without me to guide her, and he tricked her. There's no other explanation.

Bouchet pushes the driver's-side door open and steps out of his truck. He's limping slightly, probably from the accident. I smile as I watch him touch his head and then glance at his hand. He must be bleeding, too.

He looks back into the truck, and I realize that he's not alone. I see the outline of a passenger, and my heart feels like it's beating faster by the moment. I can't tell if it's her. I hope it is. I can't imagine who else it would be. It *has* to be Eva.

I know she's clever enough to see through his lies.

Maybe she brought him so we could kill him together.

I pull my car slowly toward them. I realize I'll have to be quick. There aren't a lot of people who drive along Old Salem Road, but there are a few houses and the reservoir. I don't want to be interrupted.

I grab the crowbar and think about what I'm about to do. I've practiced on pumpkins and a raccoon and a few possums I've trapped. I know Bouchet is bigger, but the basics are the same: I need to smash his skull or throat. Arms or legs are good to keep him from fighting back, and to hurt him, but the skull is the target. I know this, but I want him to feel pain like I did when he touched Eva. I didn't want the others—the messages—to be in pain, but I want Bouchet to bleed and scream and try to crawl away on broken legs.

I keep my arm straight down, motionless and tight against my body so I have the element of surprise, as I walk quickly toward the truck and my target. Unlike Madison, Bouchet is strong enough to fight back. I can do this though. I can show Eva that I'm strong enough to protect her.

I don't speak. I lift the crowbar and swing it as hard as I can. He dodges my first blow, making me stumble briefly, but I recover and catch his shoulder on the next swing. It's only a glancing hit, and he doesn't fall. The sound he makes is so different from the ones Amy and Madison made. It's a grunt like an animal. The girls made smaller noises, more ladylike.

I realize Bouchet has grabbed a Maglite from somewhere. It's not as long as a crowbar, but it's still more of a weapon than I want him to have. It makes me angry and my next swing misses him completely.

I slam my crowbar down into his already-injured leg. He falls to his left and swings at me with the Maglite, hitting my left knee and prompting a pained yell.

My next blow is unfocused, and the driver's-side window shatters as I hit it. As it breaks, I realize that I don't see anyone else in the truck. Maybe I imagined that Eva was here. That's happened before.

While I'm distracted Bouchet twists away and stands. I can see that his already-injured left leg is worse from my hit. He dives at me, his shoulder hitting my stomach, and while I'm down he punches me. We've both dropped our weapons, and for several minutes, we roll around on the ground exchanging punches and grappling like we're in a wrestling match.

Bouchet gets free of me and goes for his Maglite. I'm faster because my crowbar is closer. The Lord provides. I grab it and swing as I tell him, "You're not worthy. You aren't *worthy* to ever touch Eva."

Just as I'm about to hit his face, he rolls to the side and strikes my right wrist. The crowbar falls again, but he's crouched down, using the side of the truck to brace his back. It keeps him partially upright, but limits his movement. I hate to admit it, but I'm grateful that he's limited. I'm exhausted from the day I've had, and he's far more experienced at fighting than the girls were. I can't lose. I won't, but it's not easy.

I pull my knee up and slam it into his face. I follow quickly with a kick to the ribs.

Bouchet won't stay down though. He slams his fist into my knee, trying to knock me to the ground. I step back, searching for my weapon, and he kicks out with his injured leg.

I see the crowbar and grab it when I hear, "Stop!"

"Stop!" Eva repeats. "Reid! Stop it."

I turn to look at her, the girl who was made for me, and I'm torn between pride and fear. She *is* here, and she sees me. She's balanced on crutches, leaning against the front of Bouchet's truck; she's also holding a gleaming silver-and-black revolver in her hand. She's aiming it right at me, and her eyes are only on me.

I hear the click as she cocks the gun. It'll only take the touch of the trigger now. She's amazing.

My arm is raised, holding the crowbar up. I don't swing again, but I don't drop it to the ground either. She's here, and she's fierce. I am more in love with her than ever before.

"You came to me. The Lord sent you to me," I say.

She's shaking a little, even though she leans against the front of Bouchet's truck. Now that she's so close, I drop the crowbar. I know the look in her eyes. I've seen it once before when I was a lot younger. That was the night my mother permanently solved the problem of my father's infidelity. They always say boys pick girls like their mothers. I *knew* Eva was made for me.

DAY 15: "THE CONFESSION"

Eva

"I'LL SHOOT," I WARN Reid. "If you try to hit him again or try to leave, I'll shoot you."

I lean against Nate's truck because I'm not sure I can hold the gun and balance on crutches. It took far too long for me to get out of the truck and around to them as is. Seeing Reid try to kill Nate in front of me is even worse than feeling it when I've fallen into his death.

"I mean it, Reid." I hope I sound more confident than I feel. I *will* shoot if I have to, but I don't want to do it. I've seen this. I've felt Reid's emotions and pain when it happens. I don't want that—not even for him.

"I know you do." He steps away from Nate, but he doesn't look afraid at all. If anything, he looks happy. He's bleeding, and he's filthy, but he looks happy.

Nate doesn't. He walks toward me and holds out a hand. "Let me have that, Eva."

"If you do, I won't tell you where Yeung is," Reid blurts out. "She'll starve before anyone finds her."

My attention hasn't wavered from Reid. Even though Nate is walking toward me, I can't look away from Reid. I don't understand how we got here to this moment when I am aiming a gun at him. This is *Reid*. I've known him my whole life. I trusted him. I asked him to drive Grace home just yesterday. I don't even know where to start on my list of how fucked up this all is.

"You're more beautiful than ever right now," he says, adding to my mental list of things that are grievously wrong right now.

My hand doesn't tremble yet, but it will. There's only so long I can hold a gun without my muscles shaking. People in movies never seem to have that problem, but in the real world, guns are heavy.

"I want Grace," I tell him.

"I'll trade. Her for you," Reid offers.

"Not happening," Nate says, and I'm not sure if he's telling me or Reid, maybe both.

"What will you give me in exchange then?" Reid sits down on the ground, looking as calm as he has so many nights in our life.

In my vision, he was standing when he was shot. A car was coming. I remind myself that Reid doesn't know about my visions. He doesn't know that this is where he is supposed to die. I don't *want* to kill him. What I want is to rescue Grace, so I will try to negotiate.

"I'm not running, Eva. I've been waiting for you for years, wanting you to see me. You said you did. Yesterday, you said that to me. I did what you told me to do with Madison, but when I came to you—"

"No! You killed her."

"You said I should. I did what you wanted."

"I said you should *talk* to her." I hear the crack in my voice. Nate must too because he steps closer to me and starts to wrap an arm around my waist.

"Stop," Reid snaps. "If he touches you, I stop talking."

"I have a *gun*, Reid."

"And I have Yeung." He smiles self-assuredly, reminding me that he has the control; even now with a gun aimed at him, he has power over me. "Call the cops, and I won't tell you. Cuddle up with him, and I won't tell you. Shoot me, and you'll never know where to find her."

Maybe he's lying. Maybe the police can get an answer out of him, but I can't be sure.

"What do you want?" I ask.

"You."

This time Nate and I both answer, "No."

"I'll take you to her. You can keep your gun, and even your cell phone *and* his. He"—Reid motions to Nate—"can follow us in his truck."

"Eva, don—"

"What's the catch?" I cut off Nate.

"I just want you to hear me. I want you to understand." Reid stares at me with such a hopeful expression that it makes me feel like running. He's obsessed and a killer—and he thinks he loves me. The last place I want to be is alone with him.

"I did all of this for you, so we could be together," he adds.

I swallow to ease my suddenly dry mouth before I ask, "If I ride in your car, you'll drive me to where Grace is? You promise?"

"Eva, you can't trust him," Nate starts.

Reid's attention snaps to Nate. "I've *never* lied to Eva. Not even once. Can you say that? Can Robert? Amy? Micki? Madison? No." He looks back at me. "*Never once,* Eva. I'm not lying now either."

Maybe I'm the world's biggest idiot, but I believe him. More importantly, I don't see any other choice. If Nate wasn't here, I would've already traded myself for Grace. She's my best friend, the closest thing I have to a sister; I have to try. "Nate will give me his phone, and he'll follow us, and you'll drive me to Grace."

"And not wreck the car," Nate adds.

Reid doesn't reply, so I repeat, "And you won't wreck. Those are my terms."

"Deal." Reid stands and brushes off his trousers despite the fact that they're filthy, ripped, and stained with both blood and dirt. "And you'll listen to me. I'll tell you everything, and then you'll see why you should stay with me. You just have to listen, and you'll understand."

"I'll listen," I agree. It makes me sick to think about the things he might say. It's been hard enough hearing the news and seeing the photographs, but I'll listen. I'll listen to anything he says if it means he'll take me to Grace.

Reid walks over to his car as if I'm not pointing a gun at him. I lower it briefly, making do with one crutch, as I follow Reid to his car. It's awkward and slow, but I don't want to hand the gun to Nate. I don't want his prints on it. If I shoot Reid, there will be no confusion as to who's responsible.

"You brought a *gun*, Eva?" Nate asks as we walk. "You should've told me."

"I said he wasn't going to kill you. I said that I'd be here, and that would change everything. It did." I try to sound like I have a valid argument, but I know I really don't and truthfully, this isn't the time to play word games. I think I'm going to survive this, but I can't swear it. I whisper, "I should've told you. I'm sorry. I was trying to protect you. I saw how he dies though, Nate. Remember? Someone shoots him."

Nate stops mid-step. "Eva . . ."

"It's *fine*." I keep my voice low as I try to explain, "You're alive, and Reid is taking me to Grace."

"You're getting into a car with a crazy killer. That wasn't part of the plan . . . as far as I knew." He stares at me intently.

"I'm improvising a little," I murmur. "But it'll be okay. He's taking me to Grace. You're following us. It'll be okay."

Nate opens the back door of the car, and I slide inside.

"Don't try to run," Nate orders. "I'll be right behind you."

Reid scoffs, "Eva is getting into my car, leaving *you* to come with *me*, why would I run?" He flashes a smile at us and opens the door. "Give her your phone, Bouchet. I trust her not to call the cops, but I don't trust you."

Nate opens his mouth to retort, but I stop him. "Please, Nate?"

"I don't like this," he mutters, but he still pulls his phone out of his pocket and drops it into my lap. He puts my crutches at my feet, too.

When Reid opens the driver's door, Nate leans into the car and whispers in my ear, "I love you."

"Me too," I mouth.

Then Nate straightens and closes the door, and I'm alone in the car with the boy who almost killed me—who *did* kill my friends. I stare at the back of his head for a moment, the gun aimed at him, and wonder how many ways this could go wrong. Would he kill us both? What if Nate can't keep up or runs out of gas or . . . something happens that means we're separated? What if the police come and think I'm an accomplice? I shove the thoughts away and say, as steadily as I can, "I don't want to have to shoot you, but I will."

Reid looks over his shoulder and smiles before saying, "I know."

He doesn't look afraid. That alone would be enough for me to suspect he was crazy. The other things I now know make "crazy" seem like too mild of a word.

"Your phones won't work, by the way," Reid says. "I have a machine to block them."

"I said I wouldn't call the police," I remind him.

"I know, and I *want* to trust you, but . . . you were with someone else, Eva. That hurt me." He watches me expectantly, like he thinks I should apologize.

The lights from Nate's truck shine into the car, and I hear his truck engine. I take a steadying breath and say, "Just take me to Grace, Reid."

"I am. You can trust me, Eva." Reid turns the key in the ignition and pulls onto the road. "We have about an hour to talk."

For the next forty minutes, I listen as he tells me about his father, about his mother killing his father, about how he's had to hide that his whole life, about how his grandmother made him lie about them, about how he's prayed to know the right choices. He tells me about having sex with Amy in some strange attempt to get closer to me, about how he remembers "locking gazes" with me and knowing that I meant for him to speak to me through flowers. He tells me about parties where he watched me and how he was "faithful" to me aside from Amy the past year—and how he knows that I know she doesn't "count" because she was really Amy-Eva, a girl who adopted my "impure" needs so I could stay untainted.

As he talks, I try to record all of it. I might not be able to call the police, but I can get at least some of his confession on record. I'm not sure if my phone can record conversations this long. I think the app claims to be unlimited, but I've never recorded more than quick memos to myself. I'm not looking away from Reid to check if it's still recording either. I can't. I watch him with my gun aimed at him. I realize as he talks that he's far less stable than I thought. He still sounds like the boy I've always known, but the things he's telling me are horribly wrong.

The more he speaks, the more I'm grateful that he doesn't really want a conversation. What he apparently wants is to tell me everything. He even explains that we can "keep" Grace at our home after this. He has a plan for this, too. "I'll let you shoot Bouchet, and then you and I can get married," Reid explains. "Grace is like a sister to you, so she can be your sister-wife. The way my father did it was wrong. He tried to hide things from my mother. That's why it all went wrong."

We pull off the road onto a dirt path, and the bumps shake me enough that it's hard to keep the gun trained on Reid. "She's unhurt though, right?"

"Of course!" He meets my eyes in the rearview mirror. "I was careful because I knew you'd want that. That's what no one else understands: I've only done things you'd want or that would *teach* you. Everything has been for you, for us. They just don't understand us. They never will."

I feel like throwing up, and I'm certain I may never sleep without nightmares after this is all over. Right now, though, I need to get to the point when it *is* over. I need to get to Grace. Then, I can deal with coping with the *after*.

DAY 15: "THE PIPE"

Grace

I WAKE ALONE. AT first, I think he's in the other room, but when I get out of the bed and walk around to see if I can find some sort of weapon, I notice that the padlock is no longer on the hinge inside the door. I'd love to believe that means he decided to leave the door unlocked and leave, but I suspect it simply means that the lock is outside, where it was when we arrived here. I start to walk over to check, but I can't reach. My *leash* isn't long enough to reach the door.

Tears fill my eyes at the reality of where I am now and what will happen if I can't get free, but crying isn't going to help me. I need a weapon or a way to escape, preferably both.

This could be a trap of some sort, a test to prove I'm not trustworthy. He seems a little obsessed with building trust. How he expects to do that after kidnapping, chaining, and drugging me, I'm not sure, but I don't want to know how his mind works. He killed three girls. I'm not going to become number four.

"Reid?" I call out. I stay still and listen. No sounds of any sort greet me. That's about the best I can do right now. If he's here and watching, I guess I'll deal with it when he reveals himself.

"Right, then," I mutter. Somehow talking to myself seems to help keep back the weight of the silence.

I start by feeling the collar around my throat. It takes only moments to determine that it is, in fact, padlocked onto me. I won't be getting that off easily. I follow the chain to the water heater. The end of the chain is looped around a thick pipe that stretches into the ceiling.

"Don't suppose you left a saw anywhere, Reid?" I force myself to snort at the ridiculousness of that possibility. I won't cry again. Sarcasm is better.

I push on the pipe, examine the chain—which is looped around the pipe and padlocked—and don't see any solution there either. The chain slides up and down the pipe, but I don't think that's helpful.

I sit, grab the chain with both hands, brace my feet on the water heater, and tug. It feels like it bends a bit, but bending it doesn't help. Bending isn't the same as breaking.

"Next?" I study it. There are no rings I could try to twist open, no rusted spots that look prone to breaking. I kick it at the base. Nothing happens. I do it again kicking as hard as I can. All that happens is that dust falls on me from the ceiling. *Rust*, not dust, I realize. I stare up and kick again. It's not a lot, but there is some give where the pipe connects to the ceiling.

Maybe there was another level or a loft or something up there at one point. Whatever it is, the connection seems to be weak or broken on the other side of the ceiling. That's where the weakest part is.

I jump up and get the rocking chair so I can stand on it to reach higher. Then I slide the chain up as high as I can, grab it, and hop off the chair, using the force of my jump to add to the pull of the chain. I keep it held taut, so the chain doesn't slide back down, and wrap it around my whole body so it's my whole weight pulling against the pipe.

It creaks. The pipe creaks. It's a nails-on-chalkboards noise, but it sounds utterly and completely beautiful to me.

I keep working on the pipe—frantically because I have no idea how long Reid will be gone. Rust is raining all over the floor, and sweat drips down my neck. The pipe is working loose of the ceiling. After about twenty minutes, a loud clank sounds as the pipe comes free of whatever it was attached to above or in the ceiling.

"Yes, yes, yes!" I climb back onto the rocking chair, stretch my hands up, and grab the pipe. I pull as I jump down and it gives until there is a gap between the pipe and the ceiling.

Again, I stand on the chair, and this time I slip the chain through the gap. It works, and the heavy loop falls to the floor with a clatter. I smile and mutter, "Screw you, Reid."

I drape the chain over my arm. The last thing I want is for it to snag on something. I have no idea how long I have until he returns. It could be minutes, or hours, or days.

I rush to the door and try to open it. I hear the clank of the lock straining against the hinge.

I try the plywood on every window, but without a crowbar, there's no way I'm getting out of those. My heart sinks. I'm free of the chain, but that doesn't mean I'm free of the cabin.

"Weapons," I announce. "Or cell phone."

The first thing I check is the black bag. There are a few clothing items, some snacks, and a bottle of water. I'm dry mouthed, but I don't know if the water is drugged. Luckily, a can of soda is in the bag too, so I pop the top and drink. Whatever Reid used to drug me has left my mouth feeling worse than a hangover does, and my head throbs. I chug about half the can while I search the bag. There's nothing useful in it though.

I search the cabin, opening the fridge, the crates, and going into the second room—which is a bedroom, complete with a bed and dresser. I stop and stare at it. He didn't have to force me to sleep next to him like he did. He didn't need to drug me. I hate him more in that moment. I thought I was full up on hate, but seeing this adds to it.

By the time I'm done searching, my inventory of possible weapons includes a lightweight pot, a pan, the chain itself, a lantern, and the burners from the stove. None of them are great weapons, but it's better than nothing. My phone was nowhere to be found.

I gather my weapons beside the door and sit there to wait for his return. I'll hear him, and then I'll stand and attack. I can do this. I *will* do this. If I don't, he'll chain me up again, or simply kill me. I'm not letting any of that happen.

I sit, and I wait. After what feels like at least an hour, I hear him pull up. I grab the lantern. It's the heaviest of my options. If I bash him in the head, maybe that'll knock him out.

My body feels tense and ready like it does before a race. Then I hear a voice. *Eva.* She found me. It's not Reid outside. It's Eva.

Another car pulls up.

I can't see anything, but I know that a second car could be Reid. I'm trapped inside, and Eva is out there with a madman. There's nothing I can do but wait. If he drags her in here, I'll just have to be sure I hit him hard.

DAY 15: "THE KILLER"

Eva

WHEN REID PULLS UP outside a small shack, I can't decide if I'm more afraid or relieved. Nate's truck is coming up behind us as I steady myself for what comes next. I don't think Reid understands that no amount of explanation will change my acceptance. He's a killer. I'm not going to ride off into the sunset with him. The best-case scenario here is that he survives the next half hour.

"We can't stay here. I hoped we could for a little while, but that won't work . . . unless we kill Bouchet." Reid twists his body so he's face-to-face with me. "I can do it."

"No. *Neither* of us will kill Nate." My hand tightens on the pistol, fearing that he'll try to take it.

Instead, Reid sighs. "Fine. We can get Grace and then shoot him in the knees or something."

My mouth drops open, but I don't even know how to formulate a reply. After almost an hour of listening to Reid describe killing and the things he did when he was alone in his room with pictures of me, I feel like no amount of bathing will ever get the disgust off of my skin.

"Grace is in there?" I ask.

"Locked in safely," Reid answers. "Do you want me to go get her?"

"Please."

"As you wish." Reid gets out of the car with his keys in hand, and without a look behind him, he walks to the little cabin. I hear the keys on his ring jangle as he sorts through them.

Nate is beside my door, opening it. "Are you okay?"

"I will be." I turn and climb out of Reid's car.

"Don't touch Eva, Bouchet," Reid calls back to us. "She's *mine*. I explained everything. We're going to get Grace and go."

Nate looks at me and raises both brows, but he says nothing. He doesn't need to: we both know that I'm not going anywhere else with Reid. He brought me to Grace. That was what I needed. Now that we're here, I'm staying with her and Nate.

"Maybe we can lock him in there," I whisper. I want a solution that doesn't include another death. "We get Grace, lock him in, and wait for the police."

"It's worth a try," Nate agrees.

I still think we might be okay—until Reid opens the door. That's when everything falls apart. He lets out a howl of pain. Grace is there. I can see her swinging a lantern at Reid.

"Run, Eva!" she yells.

Nate runs toward the door to help Grace.

Reid ducks and grabs a chain that is hanging from around her throat. He yanks, and she stumbles. She's trying to dig her heels in to stop him from dragging her to him.

I stare in shock. For a moment, I'm too stunned to react. Grace was *chained up.*

"Asshole," Grace yells at him. She grabs the chain—which Reid is still using to jerk her toward him—and yanks back, but even in her anger, she's not stronger than him.

Nate leaps on Reid, knocking him to his knees, and Reid releases the end of the chain that's attached to some sort of collar around Grace's throat. She crab-crawls backward and struggles to her feet.

I'm trying to reach her, but I'm on one crutch and holding a gun in my hand. I move far too slowly, and even if I *can* reach her, my only way to help is to shoot Reid. I don't want to do that. I keep thinking of my vision of his death. It's almost like it's superimposed on the world around me.

Just as Grace is passing Reid, he shoves away from Nate and grabs her again.

Nate takes another swing, knocking Reid into Grace accidentally, and they all tumble together on the ground in a mess of legs, arms, and chain.

Both Grace and Nate are hitting Reid now.

Everything feels like it's happening at once. Grace is screaming; Reid is punching Nate—who is returning his blows.

"Stop it!" I yell. "Stop!"

No one listens. Reid has the loose end of the chain and is pulling it around Nate's throat. This is it: Reid's death.

I thought I'd stopped it. I *want* to stop it.

This isn't what I want.

I *have* to stop it.

"Just shove him in the cabin!" I yell.

Reid is staring at me. "What?"

His calm vanishes, and he grabs Grace and throws her to the ground. There's a sickening *thunk* as her head hits some-thing, a rock or tree root, I can't tell. It doesn't matter though. What matters is that she's not moving.

"Grace!"

At my scream, Nate sees that Grace is motionless. He's distracted and in that moment Reid takes advantage of his inattention to slam his elbow into Nate's throat.

Nate lets out a gurgling noise, as Reid follows the throat-blow with a kick to the groin.

Nate goes down. He and Grace are on the ground. I'm not sure how badly she's hurt, but Nate, at least, is conscious. He's trying to get to his feet, but he's clearly in too much pain.

Reid pushes to his feet. "Get in the car, Eva."

He raises his foot to stomp on Nate's throat.

"No!" I take aim and squeeze the trigger.

The sound Reid makes is more of a scream than a yell.

He falls to the ground.

He clutches his wound. The blood is thick and instant.

It's not exactly the same as my vision. In the *real* moment, I made a different choice: I had aimed for his upper leg, and that's what I hit.

I hear a car coming, but I move closer to them instead of turning to see who's arrived.

Grace isn't moving, but her eyes flutter open. She starts to pull herself toward me, farther away from Reid, who is sprawled on the ground, hands clutching his bleeding leg.

I lift the gun again, aim it at Reid, and ask, "Did he . . . what did he do to you, Grace?"

"Nothing. I'm okay, Eva," Grace says in a raspy voice. "I swear it."

Nate crawls toward Grace and pulls her into his arms. "Her head is bleeding," he says. His hand is wet with her blood, and his face is filled with scrapes and the yellow beginnings of bruises.

I hear car doors closing now. I turn to see who's arrived.

My gun arm is partway up again when I hear Detective Grant order, "Lower it, Eva."

I swallow a sob and realize that I started crying at some point.

Then the detective is beside me. She takes the gun from my hand carefully and hands it to another officer.

Several more officers arrive. One of them is restraining

Reid; another is checking on Grace. In a matter of minutes, an ambulance arrives, as do my parents and the Yeungs and Nate's mother.

EMTs take over care for Grace, Nate, and Reid. They've taken Grace and Reid away from where we all were, but Nate is still on the ground near me. I hear him say, "I can stand."

Officers go into the cabin. I watch it all in a stunned silence. It's all so fast. I feel like they're on fast-forward, and I'm moving on slow.

"Is he going to die?" I finally ask. I look at Detective Grant and say, "I'm the one who shot him. It was only me. No one else knew about the gun."

My parents are hugging me, and I see that my mother is crying. I don't look away from the detective though. "I can make a full statement. I texted him on Grace's phone, set a trap, and then I brought my mother's gun. I held him at gun-point while he drove me to—"

"Nate called us, Eva," she interrupts gently. "We know."

I nod. I'm not sure how Nate called after he gave me his phone. I glance at him.

"Backup cell because of . . . the things you told me before," he says in a still-hoarse voice.

My visions of Nate and my decision to *trust* Nate enough to tell him about the vision, those are what changed everything. He had a second phone; he called for help.

"Thank you," I whisper.

I want to be in his arms right now, but my mother is

clutching me to her. My father gives Nate a wide smile, and then he reaches down and squeezes Nate's shoulder. Then his arms are around my mother—who is still hugging me.

When they release me, I turn so I can see Grace. The EMTs are still with her, and her parents are hovering at Grace's side. When Mrs. Yeung sees me looking at them, she murmurs something to Grace and comes toward me.

"You're utterly irresponsible, and I can't believe you put yourself in this kind of danger, and"—she wraps both arms around me—"you saved my Gracie. Thank you. I'm furious at the risks you took, but right now, *thank* you."

I nod again. I swallow, and try to say something, but I'm not sure what it would be so I close my mouth again.

"Are you charging her?" my dad asks, and I realize that Detective Grant has joined us.

"Charging her? With what?" Mrs. Yeung asks with a frown.

"Eva shot Reid." My mother sniffles as she says it, and then she turns to the detective. "It was self-defense."

Detective Grant shakes her head at us. "We'll sort it all out. Right now, Miss Tilling should see the EMTs. She's in shock. Then we'll deal with the rest."

"Shock," I echo. That makes sense. I just shot a boy I've known my whole life. I'm in shock. I nod again, and then my parents and I sit down while a very nice man examines me.

Afterward, my parents take me in their car to the hospital. Nate is with his mother, following us. The police need to take possession of his truck temporarily to collect evidence.

He couldn't have driven it anyhow. He wasn't injured enough to go in the ambulance, but he wasn't in any shape to drive either.

I know that there are things that have to happen, but I need to be there for Grace, as she was for me, and I need Nate with me. I try to explain this to my parents several times, but they aren't able to help me. Grace, Nate, and I all need to be checked out by the doctors and talk to the police. We're all in separate vehicles—Grace in the ambulance, Nate with his mother, and me with my parents. After the past few hours, that seems wrong. We should be together.

Thoughts of the things Reid *did*, the awful events I heard about and the ones I saw, threaten to overwhelm me. I don't want to think about any of it. Mixed in with all of those horrible details is one more truth that repeats like a refrain: I shot a boy tonight.

I shot him.

In that last moment, I wanted to kill him.

I shot him.

For a moment, I came near to shooting him again.

"Eva?" My mother's voice pulls me out of my thoughts and closer to the world around me.

"I shot him," I whisper to her.

"I know," she says.

I reach up and take her hand in mine. I try not to think about sitting in another car earlier tonight. My mother's hand in mine is an anchor, one I am afraid to release. "He would've killed Grace. She wasn't moving. I wasn't sure . . . I thought she might have died for a minute, and then Reid was going to kill Nate. He told me to get in his car, and he wanted to kill them, and I didn't know what else to do."

"Shhh," my mother says. She holds my hand tighter. "It's okay. They're safe. You're safe."

"Everything is going to be all right," my father adds. He has both hands on the steering wheel, and I can see how tightly he holds it. "Everyone is safe now, and your grandfather's attorney is already at the police station. You'll be *fine*, Eva."

DAY 136: "THE AFTERMATH"

Eva

4 months later

LATE THE NIGHT WE were released to my parents' custody, I copied the recording of Reid's confession onto my laptop. I also gave the police a copy the next day, along with my statement. They took my phone into evidence, but I'd have given them pretty much anything they asked without hesitation anyhow.

I'm glad I kept my own copy of Reid's confession though. It's not right to let the true story be controlled by lawyers and journalists. Micki wasn't *their* friend. Amy wasn't in *their* school. Madison didn't spend her last day in *their* homes. It's my story. These were things that happened to me, in my life, to my friends.

Over the last month, I've transcribed it. I've typed out every sick thing Reid said to me when he drove me to see Grace.

Once I started doing it, Grace and I both started writing down our own memories of what happened. Last week, we told our therapist.

He says it'll help. I don't know if he's right or not. All I have figured out is that having our part of the story typed up on my laptop seems like a good idea. It makes me feel better knowing that Reid's version of reality isn't the only one on record.

I'm not sure if anyone will read it, but I'm keeping it all the same. I reread what I just wrote:

> He's made the national news because of their deaths. We all have. For the first time since I can recall, I don't want to watch the news. My father has started sending me texts of news articles unrelated to this so I can keep up on the news but don't have to wade through discussions of the "Code Killer," as the media has dubbed him. Papers and magazines are filled with speculation on the girl the media says was "made for" a killer, the girls he murdered, and, of course, the Code Killer himself. I'm grateful the media didn't explode with stories about all of us while Reid was on the loose and unidentified, but they're plenty attentive during his trial and incarceration. The media has latched on to Reid, and his lawyers are letting it happen—maybe they're trying for sympathy or maybe he's overruling their decisions. I don't know.

What I do know is that I've researched far more about killers than I want to. It's not that knowing more helps, but I keep thinking it will. There aren't a lot of serial killers as young as Reid. I know now that there were some: American killer Jesse Pomeroy was only fourteen, and so was the British murderer Graham Young. There are others, and whether or not Reid is a serial killer is not something I can debate now.

Maybe it's because of Reid or maybe it's my death visions—which aren't going away—but I finally know what I want to do next. I might not have the specifics all figured out, but I'm looking at a future in law or criminology. If I'm going to be seeing deaths anyhow, I want to find a way to stop some of them. I want

A voice interrupts my typing: "Eva?"

I look up to find Nate standing in my doorway. He's been at my side through every awkward day in the aftermath of Reid's arrest. The first week back at school was hard, but it's getting easier. People stare. They whisper. The rumors are worse because of the news coverage, but I walk through the halls of Jessup High with either Grace, Nate, Piper, Robert, or CeCe at my side. I'm never alone even though I no longer need help navigating crutches and books. After a little over four months on crutches, I'm finally walking well.

"Your parents are watching a movie with Aaron," Nate says. "We can join them or go out."

"I swear they think he's their nephew these days." I shake my head at how things have changed. My parents and Grace's parents have all grown closer to Nate, and by extension, closer to Aaron and to a lesser degree Nate's mom *and* Aaron's mom. The downside, of course, is that getting any alone time with Nate is harder than I could've expected. When everyone watches your every move, stealing away is a challenge.

I click save and turn my attention to Nate. "So they're downstairs with the television on?"

He grins and steps farther into the room. "They are."

"And we're up here alone for a few minutes?" I pull him closer.

"True."

"Why aren't you kissing me already?" I wrap my arms around him as he lowers his mouth to mine.

We're safe, and we're together. That thought has carried me through a lot the past few months. It carries me through early morning nightmares. Things get better every day, and I know I'll be okay. *We'll* be okay.

Acknowledgments

THE MEDICAL ADVISORS: KATHY Lamb and Lauren Remley for prescription help and TBI info; the entire amazing team at EMMC Pediatrics for being the inspiration for my pediatrics ward in a fictional hospital; Kimberly and Kaitlyn Vargas for talking to me about living with cystic fibrosis; Dr. Jennifer Lynn Barnes for articles on prosopagnosia.

The criminal advisors: Diana Williams for insight on forensics and crime scene investigation; Laura Bickle for patients' rights and legal procedure; Bryan Jeter (chief of police in Puyallap, Washington), Michael Prince (Apex, North Carolina, police department), and Detective Suzie Ivy for information on police procedure and criminal investigation. All the things that are right are theirs; the ones that are *wrong* are mine.

The support system: Kimberly Derting, John Kwiatkowski,

Jeanette Battista, Jeaniene Frost, Sera Lewis, Nikki Marckel, and John Dixon for critical reading and moral support; Laura Kalnajs for copious copyediting and general life organization; Alison Donalty for cover magic, gluten-free snacks, and ongoing fabulousness; and Anne Hoppe, Molly O'Neill, Kristen Pettit, Kate Jackson, Sally Wilcox, and Merrilee Heifetz for shepherding a book on obsession, murder, and romance over this long, long window of time.

The essential: Asia for reading a dozen drafts of this and offering me wise notes every single time; Dylan for *not* reading this one; both of you for helping with your baby brother and a gajillion little things that you do that enable me to write; and Loch for giving me the idea that became a book (and being an amazing father to all three of our babies during such a difficult year).

Read on for a sneak peek at
Melissa Marr's new world of faeries

CHAPTER 2

Lily

"YOU NEED TO STOP hiding and go downstairs." Shayla stood in the doorway to Lily's bedroom. Her long graying hair fell neatly over her shoulders instead of being bound into some kind of twist or held captive under one of her innumerable scarves. An elegant dress, no doubt by a runway designer, made her look like the lady of the house rather than Lily's caretaker, assistant, governess, whatever-her-title-was-now.

"I know. I just don't *want* to. Daidí knows I don't like parties."

Shayla's entire attitude switched from sweet to stern. "You're being *honored*. Act like it."

Lily couldn't meet Shayla's eyes.

"You will put a smile on that pretty little face of yours and march yourself down there," Shayla continued. "You'll go thank your father for the party, and you'll smile at the guests, and make a point to say hello to that Morris boy that's going to sing."

Despite herself, Lily smiled. Creed Morrison was in every tabloid, toured worldwide, and was even in a movie. As if being a rock star wasn't enough, he had to add acting. He had been her fantasy since she'd seen her first photo of him—and now he was here in her home.

"Morrison," she said. "His name is *Creed Morrison*, Shayla."

Shayla waved her hand dismissively. "Whatever. Creed. Morris. Unless he is in one of those musicals your father gets me tickets to see, I don't care." She came over to stand in front of Lily and fussed with her hair, pulling at the curls, unpinning and re-pinning it in several places as she spoke. "What matters, Lilywhite, is that Nicolas brought the boy here to sing for *you*. So go be charming."

"Yes, ma'am." Lily leaned in and kissed Shayla's cheek before heading toward the door. Once she was sure she was out of reach, she teased, "Maybe you ought to come down too and check on Daidí. Make sure he's not under siege from one of the fripperies."

"Your father can handle himself just fine with those girls," Shayla said.

"Come on. For me?"

"Hmph." Shayla didn't bother arguing further. She went on in front of Lily, effectively buying her a few minutes of peace.

Shayla was the closest thing to a mother that Lily had. Shayla and Daidí both swore that there was nothing romantic between them, but Lily kept hoping. Her mother had been gone for twelve years, and Shayla had filled her vacant place. They certainly functioned like a family. Shayla raised Lily when Daidí was off on business trips, and she looked after both of them when he was home.

Slowly, Lily walked through the hall, hating that she had to wear shoes, even though the tiny sandals were nothing more than a few strips of leather. She'd learned to tolerate shoes, but heels still made her feel wrong. Feet were meant to touch the earth, the floor, the sea. They weren't to be locked away in prisons of leather or fabric. Sandals were the closest to normal that Lily had found, and tonight—surrounded by people—she needed the comfort of nearly bare feet.

At the top of the great staircase, just out of sight, Lily paused to smooth down the skirt of the dress she'd been given to wear. It wasn't as fancy as Shayla would like, but the pale-green dress made especially for her was as flattering as any dress could be. An asymmetrical neckline and fitted bodice topped a skirt made up of layers of some sort of delicate material. Tiny stones sewn into the layers caught the light and shimmered as she moved. Lily didn't have the heart to ask if they were real gems or not. It was easier to avoid an argument if she didn't know. She'd already lost the fights about her bracelets. Obscenely expensive diamonds and emeralds dangled from her wrists and ears.

The short blade that Lily had sheathed in a hand-sewn leather holster under her ephemeral dress was real too, though. Its weight made her feel secure despite the glittering facade. Lilywhite's blade was a double-edged dagger that had been handcrafted for her. She wasn't eager to use it, preferring the tidiness of her longer blades, but she could never be truly unarmed.

For all of her father's protections, he'd also taught her that she was ultimately responsible for her own safety. The party was at her home, and the guests had all entered through a metal detector *and* been patted down, but she was the daughter of the head of one of the most successful criminal organizations in the world. That meant that, even here, she was armed.

Lily rounded the corner and started down the stairs. Her father looked up at her, and the pride in his face made her feel guilty for delaying. He smiled at her, and she knew that she'd been wrong to stall. Mingling at the over-the-top birthday party that Daidí insisted on this year was a little bit beyond terrifying, but he wanted to celebrate her birthday, so celebrate they would. These events layered civility and elegance onto their often violent world, and Lily knew well that the layer of softness was important—not just for how others saw the underworld, but for how the demimonde saw itself.

As she walked down the stairs, she could hear soft music in the ballroom. Soon, Creed Morrison would sing, but right now, a chamber orchestra played classical music that wove around the spaces between conversations. Servers circulated with finger foods and drinks. Usually, Lily stayed at her father's side when she had to attend these sorts of things. Tonight, though, Daidí insisted that she talk to people her own age— other than just her friend, Erik.

Erik was there, of course, but for Lily's seventeenth birthday celebration, Daidí had invited all of his associates' children, and he'd hired her favorite singer. It was perfect on paper, but Lily didn't mingle with people her own age. She could escort Daidí to parties, play hostess of the manor as needed, make small talk with the leaders of the underworld, but around other teenagers—even those groomed in the odd etiquette of their society—she felt awkward.

And Creed Morrison? How, or even *why*, her father hired him for her birthday party was a mystery. He was only a year older than her, but he was already an international phenomenon. If he wanted to, Creed could have dropped out of school entirely. He'd never need the things that were taught in the classroom—any more than she would. Her curriculum consisted of drug routes, interrogation methods, and old family hierarchies.

Those lessons left her ill equipped for casual conversations, but they would be essential if she took over the family business. The social part didn't come naturally to her. It never had, but she'd never be much of an asset to Daidí if she couldn't handle her peers.

Smile firmly affixed, she descended the stairs until she reached the landing. Daidí stayed where he was, talking to one of the growers from the South Continent. As she walked through the black-tie crowd, Daidí's associates smiled and wished her a happy birthday. Their children were a little less practiced in their false magnanimity, but they were far more polished than they'd been the last time Daidí had to insist on their socializing. Being Nicolas Abernathy's heir apparent *and a daughter* meant that people her own age weren't sure what to do with her.

Several boys nodded at her. The girls, however, kept their eyes carefully averted. Lily wasn't like them. She wasn't a bartering chip that would be used to strengthen ties to other organizations, nor was she sheltered from the ugliness of her father's job. The boys acknowledged her, even though they weren't sure if they should approach her as a potential date or as a future colleague. The one exception was her friend, Erik. They'd shared a few kisses now and again, but under threat of retribution if any word of it was spoken.

Daidí knew, of course, as did Shayla, but they also under-stood that Erik didn't occupy her heart. Instead, she fantasized about Creed Morrison and Zephyr Waters—celebrity darlings she suspected of sharing her same hidden, and illegal, heritage. She'd studied them in the magazines, but she'd had no intention of ever meeting them. That was part of their appeal. Having one of *them* here was not something she knew how to address.

Daidí didn't mean to upset me. As she did with every-thing confusing in life, Lily thought through the Abernathy

Commandments until she found her answer: *Commandment #9: Be kind to those who deserve it.* Her father deserved her kindness.

As she walked toward her father, her step was measured, and her smile was convincing. She might be filled with anxiety, but no one would know.

The crowd was manageable. Everything was okay. She could succeed at this if she thought of it like a regular business gathering.

She straightened her shoulders and sailed through the crowd—until Creed Morrison stepped into her path, stopping her advance, leaving her uneasy in a way no one ever had.

Creed had the beautiful dark complexion of the Seelie fae. The fae long thought to be both *kinder* and *better* were those whose skin was sun-burnished. Creed's skin had the telltale signs of fae heritage, but Creed's human father was African American, so Creed had an explanation for his Seelie-dark skin. Lily shared his heritage, but she had less chance of exposure for her heritage because she'd inherited her father's pale skin instead of her mother's dark skin. Not all of the fae-blood were able to pass as human, not like Lily was.

"Lilywhite," he said. She'd heard his speaking voice, listened to interviews for hours actually, but hearing her name from his lips made her unable to reply.

She nodded. *Abernathy Commandment #2: Be yourself.*

"I looked for you before the crowd arrived," he said, as if they were friends.

In the tuxedo- and gown-filled room, Creed's jeans, T-shirt, and boots were very out of place. The art etched on his skin stood out, more because it was visible than because it existed. He was far from the only person in the room with tattoos, but his weren't hidden under sleeves or jackets. Creed Morrison demanded attention. It was a well-documented—and oft-photographed—fact. She'd read every article on him, clipped pictures from magazines and filed them away. It wasn't an obsession; actually *speaking* to him was the last thing she wanted. What she wanted was to understand how other fae-bloods lived. Now seeing him in person for the first time, she *knew.* Now, he was here, and he was *exactly* what she suspected—and she wanted to flee.

She fidgeted with one of her bracelets, twisting it around her wrist, staring at the glittering green stones. "Had you needed something, Mr. Morrison?"

"Creed," he stressed.

"Creed," she repeated quietly.

He smiled and said, "I wanted to wish you happy birthday before I sing."

Again, she nodded. This time, though, she looked up—and wished she hadn't.

Creed was watching her with an utterly inappropriate intensity. If her father saw, he'd toss Creed out the door, despite the obscene sum he'd probably paid for his presence. Lily felt like her skin was electrified everywhere his gaze fell. She'd felt a tingle of recognition a few times when she'd seen other fae-bloods, but not like this. *Nothing* had ever felt like this.

"I didn't know you did these sort of things," she finally managed to say.

"Talk to beautiful girls at parties?"

"No. Sing for hire at parties," she corrected him.

"I don't." He smiled, and she wondered how anyone ever thought he was anything other than fae-blood. He radiated energy. Maybe it was harder for people without fae ancestry to see it, but she'd glimpsed it even in photographs.

Lily resisted the urge to match his smile with one of her own and added, "Incidentally, flattering me is pointless. The sons of Daidí's associates all try it to curry favor with him. I'm immune to praise." She met his eyes, reminding herself who she was, reminding them both that she was not the shy creature she felt like in that moment when she'd first seen him. "The no-one-else-matters gaze is a nice touch, but Daidí hired you to perform. Tonight will be the beginning and the end of your contact with the notorious Mr. Abernathy, no matter what you do or say."

"What if I want *your* favor?" Creed asked as he took a drink from a tray that a waiter held out to both of them.

Lily gave him a derisive smile, but said nothing.

Once the waiter was gone, and they were again alone in the crowd, Creed continued in a low voice, "You're a hard girl to get to meet, Lilywhite. I took this job specifically to meet you. No publicity. No one outside of the guests here right now even knows I'm doing this."

"Fantasies of the crime lord's daughter on your arm to add to your image?"

Creed laughed. "Not quite."

"I might not believe everything I read, but I've seen enough photos of you with different girls to know that you have two types: ones who add to your reputation and ones who are simply . . . unusual. I'm guessing your interest in Nick Abernathy's daughter is about a fifty-fifty split between intrigue and business."

Creed shook his head. "What if it isn't Nicolas Abernathy's daughter I wanted to meet, but *Iana*'s?"

Lily stilled. No one talked about her mother. It simply wasn't done. Daidí's considerable reputation for cold vengeance prevented it. "Those are dangerous words."

"For people of *our* heritage, there are a lot of dangerous words," Creed murmured as he leaned close and brushed a kiss on her cheek.

The feel of his skin on hers resonated through her body like she was a vessel for nature itself. If Creed Morrison's words hadn't confirmed that he was a fae-blood, his touch would have.

When he leaned back, he paused as if the contact had jolted him like it had her, but then a heartbeat later he was kissing her other cheek and saying, "If you want to talk privately later, I'd like that."

Lily realized that he was pressing a small card into her hand. She curled her fingers around it so it wasn't visible to anyone when he stepped back.

Whatever angle Creed Morrison had, Lily couldn't risk honesty with him. The world was divided: humans made up most of the population, fae-bloods—those with any degree of fae ancestry—existed in secret among them, and true fae lived in the Hidden Lands. Any drop of fae blood was enough to result in imprisonment, but the alternative was to find a way to seek out the entrance to the Hidden Lands, to turn away from humanity. For many fae-bloods, it was safest to simply pass as human. The war carried out by the Queen of Blood and Rage meant that *any* of her subjects were considered war criminals by the human courts, even those who had not sworn fealty to the faery queen.

"My only heritage is as Nick Abernathy's heir," Lily said levelly, suppressing the wince from the physical pain of the lie.

She was, in fact, more fae than human. She'd known that for years. Being so fae meant that the words *hurt* to utter, but admitting her ancestry to the wrong person could mean the kind of imprisonment that would try even the considerable limits of Daidí's power. Lily wasn't foolish enough to risk that with someone she'd just met.

"Liar," Creed whispered.

"Fae-blood can't be liars," she said, twisting the truth just enough to ease the pain of a *complete* falsehood.

Creed's expression went carefully blank and he said, "I'm not fae-blood either. Not a drop." He paused, watching her study him, and then added, "You can learn to hide the physical pain of lying, Lilywhite; surely you know that as well as I do. I know what you are, what *we* are."

There was nothing she could say to that, no retort that would disprove his blatant truth.

Creed glanced briefly at her hand, which was curled around his card so tightly that the edges of it were pressed into her skin. Casually, he reached out and trailed his fingers over the knuckles of her closed fist.

She concentrated on not reacting.

"Tonight," he said. "Later. *Anytime*. I want to talk to you."

"I don't . . ." She looked down at her hand. "I don't know why you think I'm . . . what you say I am."

He stared so intently that she could swear she felt his gaze like a physical thing, but she refused to look at him as he said, "Impure water burns your throat. The wrong soap makes your skin blister . . . and alcohol, cigarettes, drugs, they all affect you so much more than they do other people, non-fae people."

Lily kept her lips firmly closed. She still wasn't admitting a thing, but she obviously didn't need to. Creed wasn't guessing. He *knew*. He'd known before he'd met her—as she had about him.

"You don't need much sleep at all unless you have their toxic food," he continued. "When you *do*, you feel weak and need to sleep for hours."

She looked up finally.

"And I'd bet that you have a bit of yard that is meticulously kept up, no pesticides, no gardener allowed in it. You feel it there without needing to hide. Soil or air, water trickling under the earth, or stone humming secrets. You know what you are when you are connected to nature. You know what *we* are." His voice grew soft, lulling her into a peace that she only ever felt outside. Suddenly, all Lily wanted was to sit and listen to him forever. There was magic in the way words slid from his lips, magic in the truth of them and in the boy speaking them.

She took a step closer to him.

"You like to stand on the bare ground, burrow your toes into the soil when you're tired, feel the earth and its pulse beating to match your own. Nature calls to us, Lilywhite."

Lily reached out and touched his wrist. She wanted to deny everything, but she couldn't lie again. Not to him, not right now. Creed reached out and covered her hand with his.

She wasn't sure how long they stood like that—or how long they would've stayed that way, but Daidí walked over and held out his hand to her. "Lilywhite."

She moved to him obediently, grateful for the familiarity of being at his side at a party, grateful to have a routine to fall into instead of whatever was happening with Creed.

Daidí extended a hand to the boy, who accepted it easily.

"Mr. Abernathy," he greeted, shaking Daidí's hand briefly. "I'm glad I made an exception to my manager's rules to be here to sing for Lilywhite."

Daidí's stiff expression flickered briefly to amusement at the reminder that Creed was there as a favor and a very expensive one no doubt. "My daughter likes your music, and there is nothing in this world I wouldn't do for her happiness—or for her safety."

Creed nodded, acknowledging the warning implicit in Daidí's voice, and glanced at her again. "Any particular songs you want to hear, Miss Abernathy?"

The titles of Creed's songs, some of which she'd listened to until she could pick them out after only a few notes, all fled her mind. "Surprise me."

"Haven't I already?"

Her eyes widened just enough that Lily was glad Daidí was frowning at Creed instead of scrutinizing her.

Creed smiled, a genuine soul-searing smile that she'd rarely glimpsed in the hundreds of photos she'd seen in magazines, and then with a nod to them both he walked toward the stage that had been set up for him.

At her side, Daidí was silent as they walked to the table at the front of the ballroom where she was to sit like a regent holding court. For all of her father's suggestions that she mingle with those her own age, he still set her apart. Soon, his colleagues would come and give her gifts. Shayla would arrive and catalogue them, and Daidí would nod approvingly. Everyone would pretend that the people her own age who did approach her did so by their own choice. All the while, she would watch Creed sing for her as if private concerts from global celebrities were her due.

"He's like you," Daidí whispered as he seated her at the birthday table. It was a question as much as a statement.

Lily nodded.

On stage, Creed inserted a little earpiece into his ear and nodded at the man who was stationed to the side at a complex-looking control board. Creed felt more familiar now, like the unapproachable rock star in her fantasies. He was safer now that he was at a distance.

"I thought as much from the way you studied him in those journals," Daidí said with a satisfied tone that made her glance his way.

She caught her father's hand as he started to turn away. When she tugged him down beside her, he didn't resist. She kissed his cheek as an excited daughter should and assured him, "I admitted nothing. I *never* have to anyone."

"You can with him," he said.

When Daidí straightened again, she knew that her father had his people thoroughly investigate Creed. No one was admitted to Abernathy Estates without thorough background searches.

As Creed started the opening chords to "Deadly Girl," his eyes were fixed steadfastly on her and her father. She could feel his words like a lure.

Air. Creed Morrison's affinity was air.

The articles she'd read all explained that fae-blood were typically associated with one element. Those of purer fae lines had a second. True fae had two or sometimes three. *Nothing* explained why she had four, and she'd never met another fae-blood she could ask.

Here, though, was one in her home.

The music covered Daidí's words as he told her, "I want you to talk to him. If he doesn't give you his contact information, I'll have Shayla get it for you. You need to know more of your people. That's why I brought him here."

Lily glanced from her father to Creed and back again.

"Happy birthday, Lilywhite," Daidí said.

The real present wasn't the party, or the jewelry, or even the concert. Her father had delivered Creed Morrison to her like a gift. All he needed was a bow.